Plays by Shakespeare in this series

AS YOU LIKE IT

CORIOLANUS

HAMLET

HENRY IV—PART I

HENRY IV—PART II

HENRY V

HENRY VIII

JULIUS CÆSAR

KING JOHN

KING LEAR

MACBETH

MERCHANT OF VENICE

MIDSUMMER NIGHT'S DREAM

MUCH ADO ABOUT NOTHING

OTHELLO

RICHARD II

RICHARD III

ROMEO AND JULIET

THE TEMPEST

TWELFTH NIGHT

ii

The Teaching of English Series

OTHELLO
THE MOOR OF VENICE

No. 230

OTHELLO
THE MOOR OF VENICE

by
WILLIAM SHAKESPEARE

Edited by
NORA RATCLIFF, M.A.

THOMAS NELSON AND SONS LTD
LONDON AND EDINBURGH

First published in this series
November 1941

CONTENTS

INTRODUCTION

    How to read the Play vii
    The Play and its Background . . . x

OTHELLO, THE MOOR OF VENICE . 15

AFTER A FIRST READING

    About the Characters 149
    Shakespeare's Stage and Actors . . . 170
    The Man who wrote *Othello* . . . 175

AFTER A SECOND READING

    The Text of the Play 182
    Shakespeare's Workshop . . . 188
    Modern Presentation of the Play . . 208

QUESTIONS AFTER A SECOND READING . 213

QUESTIONS ON LATER READINGS . . 222

CHIEF EVENTS OF SHAKESPEARE'S LIFE . 231

▼

INTRODUCTION

How to Read the Play

It would be hypocrisy to pretend that a play by Shakespeare makes as easy reading as, say, a novel by J. B. Priestley or a play by Bernard Shaw. Nor is it easy to play golf or the fiddle at the first attempt. Few intelligent relaxations can be fully enjoyed without a certain amount of practice and mental concentration. Similarly, the enjoyment of Shakespeare calls for the taking of a little trouble. On the other hand, it may be of some encouragement to the student who has to " do " a play for examination purposes to discover that even so arbitrary a task can be undertaken with a delight which physics pain.

The main difficulty is that Shakespeare's plays were written more than three hundred years ago (so, for that matter, was the Authorized Version of the Bible), and they contain not only obsolete words, words of topical significance that have little force to-day, but also words that have so changed their meaning that the danger of misunderstanding is even greater than that of not understanding at all. This difficulty is finally overcome by such constant reading of the plays that we begin automatically to *think* in Shakespeare's own idiom and period. To read a French novel whilst still under the necessity of word-for-word translation is a fairly dull business ; but the keen student (including the amateur) soon finds that he is understanding without conscious translation : that he is thinking in French as he reads. Similarly, the constant reader of Shakespeare will find that he begins to apprehend the meaning of a speech or line without having to " straighten it out " or mentally paraphrase it into modern speech. This full enjoyment will come to the novice on a third or fourth reading of the same text if on the second reading he has taken the pains to look up obscure words and references, to translate difficult passages into modern English, and to assemble in his mind what is often called the " sub-text " * of the dialogue. On the second reading ? Why not the first ?

Because the play should first be read, however stumblingly, as quickly as possible, pausing only for a brief glance at the footnotes when the reader encounters an unknown word or obscure line whose meaning is essential to an understanding of the story. The strength of Shakespeare's passion and the music of his poetry can be sensed at a first reading, even though the passion may echo like distant thunder only and the music haunt and evade us like snatches of a symphony concert heard on a spasmodically fading wireless set.

The second great difficulty is one that is inherent in all true poetry, namely, the fact that what is implied is far more important than what is said. Here, on a first reading, no notes can help, or they can help but little. Some effort has been made, by explanation of obscurities, to help the reader to sense the poetic texture of a word or phrase. Poetic value lies not only in the sound of a word, or in the skilful stringing of words as in a necklace of precisely graded and matched pearls, but to a very great extent in the halo of associations round each word used. Nickel or tin can be shaped and stamped to look like a half-crown piece, but the fraud is obvious when the supposed silver is rung upon the counter. The false coin is betrayed by its lack of a quality not

---

* Sub-text : the inner meaning of apparently superficial lines and the unexpressed thoughts in the minds of the characters.

visible to the eye. And so with words. Face value, efficiency for the mere conveying of an isolated fact, is not enough for poetry.

> Not poppy nor mandragora
> Nor all the drowsy syrups of the world
> Shall ever medicine thee to that sweet sleep
> Which thou ow'dst yesterday.

This is true currency of poetry when weighed against : "No drug on the world's market can ever restore to you the undisturbed rest you have hitherto enjoyed." And yet, as far as plain sense goes, the second is the clearer. The text is crowded with similes and metaphors. A reference to page 82 will show that it needs a note of some length to explain the hawking metaphor in :

> If I do prove her haggard,
> Though that her jesses were my dear heart strings
> I'd whistle her off and let her down the wind
> To prey at fortune.

Not until these references are understood can the deep poignancy of Othello's sorrow be gauged. But even before we have trained ourselves to catch all the overtones, the sound and rhythm of the lines can give us their emotional import. It is possible to enjoy Italian opera without any knowledge of the language or of musical technicalities.

For practical purposes the text, on a first reading (particularly for reading aloud by a group of enthusiasts), can be shortened down to the following significant scenes and extracts : *

ACT I. Scene i. to line 151
         Scene iii., line 48 to end
ACT II. Scene i., line 182 to end
         Scene iii., lines 49–335

---

* A word of thanks is due here to Mr. Geoffrey H. Crump and his excellent little book, *A Guide to the Study of Shakespeare's Plays* (Harrap, 1925).

INTRODUCTION

Act III. Scene iii.   Scene iv., lines 33–106 ; 169 to end
Act IV. Scene i., line 71 to end
          Scene ii., line 97 to end
Act V. Scene ii.

Such a short first reading will give the story, the passion, and something of the poetry. Nor should the notes be allowed to clog enjoyment. " Let him read on, through brightness and obscurity, through integrity and corruption ; let him preserve his comprehension of the dialogue and interest in the fable. And when the pleasures and novelty have ceased, let him attempt exactness and read the commentators." * And then let him read, read, and read again. For who, looking through his friend's collection of gramophone records, lays aside a favourite symphony with the comment, " Oh, yes ; I've heard that one."

THE PLAY AND ITS BACKGROUND

In *Othello* Shakespeare tells the story of how Iago, a man with the cunning and heartlessness of a fiend, brings about the destruction of his patron, Othello, a gallant soldier, a doting husband, and a man of such crystal honesty that it is not within his power to suspect the professed good offices of Iago.

The story is played out against a background of disturbance and military activity : *e.g.* in Act I. we move from a first scene when Iago persuades Brabantio to seek Othello at the point of the sword, through a threatened street fight, to an emergency sitting of the Senate called to discuss the urgent dispatches arriving from the fleet. Othello's long speech in this scene is a thumbnail sketch of a soldier's troubled life.

It is from this scene that we are able to place the

* Dr. Johnson.

date of the events shown in the play as during 1570, the year when the Turkish fleet made a determined attack on Cyprus. But it is impossible not to realize the close analogy with later Elizabethan days. Many such disturbed nights must there have been for the Queen's ministers when Spain's armada threatened the country. Shakespeare's first audiences would well remember those days of feverish preparation against the threat of invasion. The constantly recurring military terms and army slang would be as familiar to them as words like blitz, quisling, fifth column, etc., became to us in 1940. This topical background is made part of the texture of the play itself : Cassio's drunken brawl is all the more reprehensible because the town is in constant fear of a surprise attack by the Turks ; Iago uses the sudden recall of Othello to spur on Roderigo's attempt on Cassio's life. All this lends to the action of the play an urgency and actuality that could easily have been overlooked by an unskilled dramatist, preoccupied with the tremendous task of exploring the psychology of Iago and Othello.

The costumes, of course, would be those of the Elizabethan court and army. Cassio and Iago are obviously both wearing the soldier's leather jerkin, which saves the first from the sword of Roderigo, and Iago from Othello's attack. Othello, by tradition, wears the flowing robes of the Easterner. Such clothing serves the additional dramatic purpose of giving him extra height and distinction. Of the three women, Desdemona is the most simply dressed, Bianca the most extravagantly. A richness of colour in Emilia's dress will not only help to underline her full-blooded character but serve as a foil to the paler, more girlish clothes of Desdemona.

To discuss the setting is to raise the vexed question of the " delocalized " stage (i.e. like Shakespeare's own, where there is no attempt at a realistic background) versus eighteenth- and nineteenth-century efforts to place each scene in " a garden," " a room in the palace," etc. The *reductio ad absurdum* of this school of staging can best be illustrated by a story of Mr. John Gielgud's about Sir Beerbohm Tree : " At the first rehearsal of his *Othello* he is supposed to have said to Roderigo—Ernest Thesiger—' We enter at the back in a gondola, and I thought it would be effective if you were hauling down the sail.' " *

Some people, when they read a play, see the story as if played upon a stage ; interpret moves and actions as if watching them from the auditorium. The reader well versed in Shakespeare or trained to modern architectural permanent settings asks only for a neutral background in mood with the theme and the actors. To such readers, it is easy to say, as Professor Granville-Barker does, " Erase from your book all the localization of the editors." Readers who need realistic settings have, in the theatre of their imagination, command of the ideal revolving stage where life-like set can follow set without delay or difficulty. For such readers the " localization of the editors " has been retained in the script, but with this warning : that they are watching Irving or Tree and not Shakespeare's players or a modern production. The " localization " has been retained also for the use of those who cannot read a play except in the terms of a novel ; who see the action as it were from the ceiling or the heavens and are themselves present in the way one often is in dreams.

Let this last group of readers see the tragedy played out in sixteenth-century Venice and inside the white walls of a Mediterranean garrison. Let them conjure up the mediæval streets, the buildings lit with the flare of torches ; the sun-baked courtyard of a

* *John Gielgud's Hamlet*, by Rosamund Gilder (*Methuen*, 1937).

INTRODUCTION

Cyprus castle ; the cool, half-darkened interiors ; and finally the candle-lit bedchamber of the doomed Desdemona. What any reader may *see* in his imagination as he reads is of little importance beside what he will hear and feel ; for, to quote Bernard Shaw, " *Othello* remains magnificent by the volume of its passion and the splendour of its word music." Let each, then, choose the stage for himself ; and now, on to the scene, whether it be bare boards and trestles or the mechanical miracles of Broadway, or along the dark and cobbled streets of Venice itself— enter Iago and his poor dupe, Roderigo.

DRAMATIS PERSONÆ

DUKE OF VENICE
BRABANTIO, *a senator* (father of Desdemona)
GRATIANO, *brother to Brabantio*
LODOVICO, *kinsman to Brabantio*
OTHELLO, *a noble Moor in the service of the Venetian State*
CASSIO, *his lieutenant*
IAGO, *Othello's ensign* was accepted ideals for wrong motives
RODERIGO, *a Venetian gentleman*
MONTANO, *Governor of Cyprus before Othello's arrival*
CLOWN, *servant to Othello*
DESDEMONA, *daughter of Brabantio, Othello's wife*
EMILIA, *wife of Iago*
BIANCA, *mistress of Cassio*

Sailor, Messenger, Herald, Officers, Senators,
    Gentlemen, Musicians, and Attendants

SCENE—Act I., Venice
        Acts II.–V., a seaport in Cyprus

PERIOD—About 1570

OTHELLO

THE MOOR OF VENICE

ACT I

SCENE I. *Venice. A street at night.*

(Enter Roderigo *and* Iago.*)*

RODERIGO. Tush, never tell me ; I take it much
 unkindly
That thou, Iago, who hast had my purse
As if the strings were thine, shouldst know of this.

 IAGO. 'Sblood, but you will not hear me :
If ever I did dream of such a matter,
Abhor me.

 RODERIGO. Thou told'st me thou didst hold him in
 thy hate.

 IAGO. Despise me, if I do not. Three great ones
 of the city,
In personal suit to make me his lieutenant,
10 Off-capp'd to him : and, by the faith of man,
I know my price, I am worth no worse a place.
But he, as loving his own pride and purposes,
Evades them, with a bombast circumstance
Horribly stuff'd with epithets of war ;
And, in conclusion,
Nonsuits my mediators ; for, " Certes," says he,
" I have already chose my officer."
And what was he ?

---

13 *bombast circumstance,* exaggerated self-importance.

Forsooth, a great arithmetician,
20 One Michael Cassio, a Florentine,
A fellow almost damn'd in a fair wife ;
That never set a squadron in the field,
Nor the division of a battle knows
More than a spinster ; unless the bookish theoric,
Wherein the toged consuls can propose
As masterly as he : mere prattle, without practice
Is all his soldiership. But he, sir, had the election ;
And I, of whom his eyes had seen the proof
At Rhodes, at Cyprus and on other grounds
30 Christian and heathen, must be be-lee'd and calm'd
By debitor and creditor : this counter-caster,
He, in good time, must his lieutenant be,
And I—God bless the mark !—his Moorship's ancient.

RODERIGO. By heaven, I rather would have been
    his hangman.

IAGO. Why, there's no remedy ; 'tis the curse of
    service,
Preferment goes by letter and affection,
And not by old gradation, where each second
Stood heir to the first. Now, sir, be judge yourself,
Whether I in any just term am affin'd
40 To love the Moor.

RODERIGO.   I would not follow him then.

IAGO. O sir, content you ;
I follow him to serve my turn upon him :

21 *A fellow almost damn'd . . . wife.* Possibly referring to Cassio's
    entanglement with Bianca and an Italian proverb, " You
    have married a fair wife ? You are damned."
25 *toged* (hard g), toga-wearing, of senatorial rank. Folio gives
    tongued, wordy, speech-making.
    consuls. There was no such office in Venice. Here it means
    senators.
    propose, expound.
31 *counter-caster,* an adder-up, *i.e.* by counters on an abacus.
33 *ancient,* ensign, the lowest commissioned rank in the army.
37 *old gradation . . . heir to the first,* promotion by seniority, when
    the next in rank automatically filled the vacant post.

We cannot all be masters, nor all masters
Cannot be truly follow'd.   You shall mark
Many a duteous and knee-crooking knave,
That, doting on his own obsequious bondage,
Wears out his time, much like his master's ass,
For nought but provender and, when he's old,
   cashier'd :
Whip me such honest knaves.   Others there are
Who, trimm'd in forms and visages of duty,
Keep yet their hearts attending on themselves,
And throwing but shows of service on their lords
Do well thrive by them ; and when they have lin'd
   their coats
Do themselves homage :   these fellows have some
   soul,
And such a one do I profess myself.   For, sir,
It is as sure as you are Roderigo,
Were I the Moor, I would not be Iago :
In following him, I follow but myself ;
Heaven is my judge, not I for love and duty,
But seeming so, for my peculiar end :
For when my outward action doth demonstrate
The native act and figure of my heart
In complement extern, 'tis not long after
But I will wear my heart upon my sleeve
For daws to peck at : I am not what I am.
   RODERIGO. What a full fortune does the thick-lips
      owe,
If he can carry't thus !
   IAGO.   Call up her father,

---

57 *Were I the Moor . . . Iago*, had I Othello's authority, I
   should have no need to ape servility.   Note the implication
   that Roderigo is what he is—a dupe.
61 *For when my outward action . . . extern*, when my outward behaviour reveals what is actually in my heart.
64 *wear my heart upon my sleeve*, like a lady's favour or badge of
   service.
65 *daws*, crows, jackdaws. Possibly a pun. *Cf.* dow, a simpleton.

Rouse him : make after him, poison his delight,
Proclaim him in the streets ; incense her kinsmen,
70 And, though he in a fertile climate dwell,
Plague him with flies : though that his joy be joy,
Yet throw such changes of vexation on't,
As it may lose some colour.

    RODERIGO. Here is her father's house ; I'll call
      aloud.

    IAGO. Do, with like timorous accent and dire yell
As when, by night and negligence, the fire
Is spied in populous cities.

    RODERIGO. What, ho, Brabantio ! Signior Bra-
      bantio, ho !

    IAGO. Awake ! what, ho, Brabantio ! thieves !
      thieves ! thieves !
80 Look to your house, your daughter and your bags !
Thieves ! thieves !

               (BRABANTIO *appears above, at a window.*)

    BRABANTIO. What is the reason of this terrible
      summons ?
What is the matter there ?

    RODERIGO. Signior, is all your family within ?

    IAGO. Are all doors lock'd ?

    BRABANTIO.   Why, wherefore ask you this ?

    IAGO. 'Zounds, sir, you're robb'd ; for shame,
      put on your gown ;
Your heart is burst, you have lost half your soul ;
Awake the snorting citizens with the bell
Or else the devil will make a grandsire of you.
90 Arise, I say.

    BRABANTIO. What, have you lost your wits ?

    RODERIGO. Most reverend signior, do you know
      my voice ?

    BRABANTIO. Not I : what are you ?

---

71 *flies.* The one drawback to hot weather is that it breeds flies.
75 *timorous,* causing fear (*not* " frightened ").
76 *As when, by night and negligence, i.e.* caused by darkness and
    the carelessness of the guards.

RODERIGO. My name is Roderigo.

BRABANTIO.   The worser welcome :
I have charged thee not to haunt about my doors.
In honest plainness thou hast heard me say
My daughter is not for thee ; and now, in madness,
Being full of supper and distempering draughts,
Upon malicious knavery, dost thou come
To start my quiet.

RODERIGO. Sir, sir, sir,—

BRABANTIO.   But thou must needs be sure
My spirit and my place have in them power
To make this bitter to thee.

RODERIGO.   Patience, good sir.

BRABANTIO. What tell'st thou me of robbing ?
    This is Venice ;
My house is not a grange.

RODERIGO.   Most grave Brabantio,
In simple and pure soul I come to you.

IAGO. 'Zounds, sir, you are one of those that will
    not serve God, if the devil bid you.   Because we
    are come to do you service, you think we are
    ruffians.

BRABANTIO. Thou art a villain.

IAGO.   You are—a senator.

BRABANTIO. This thou shalt answer ; I know thee,
    Roderigo.

RODERIGO. Sir, I will answer any thing.   But, I
    beseech you,
If't be your pleasure and most wise consent,
As partly I find it is, that your fair daughter,
At this odd-even and dull watch o' the night,

98 *knavery.*   Folio gives " bravery," *i.e.* **bravado.**
99 *start,* disturb.
104 *grange,* a lonely country house.
113 *If't be your pleasure . . . straight satisfy yourself,* omitted in
    First Quarto.
115 *odd-even.*   Cf. *Macbeth,* " Almost at odds with morning,
    which is which."

Transported, with no worse nor better guard
But with a knave of common hire, a gondolier,
To the gross clasps of a lascivious Moor,—
If this be known to you and your allowance,
120 We then have done you bold and saucy wrongs ;
But if you know not this, my manners tell me
We have your wrong rebuke.   Do not believe
That, from the sense of all civility,
I thus would play and trifle with your reverence :
Your daughter, if you have not given her leave,
I say again, hath made a gross revolt,
Tying her duty, beauty, wit and fortunes
In an extravagant and wheeling stranger
Of here and every where.   Straight satisfy yourself :
130 If she be in her chamber or your house,
Let loose on me the justice of the state
For thus deluding you.

BRABANTIO.   Strike on the tinder, ho !
Give me a taper !   Call up all my people !
This accident is not unlike my dream :
Belief of it oppresses me already.
Light, I say ! light !   (*Exit above.*)

IAGO.   Farewell, for I must leave you :
It seems not meet, nor wholesome to my place,
To be produced—as if I stay I shall—
Against the Moor.   For I do know the state,
140 However this may gall him with some check,
Cannot with safety cast him ; for he's embark'd
With such loud 'reason to the Cyprus wars,
Which even now stand in act, that, for their souls,
Another of his fathom they have none,
To lead their business.   In which regard,

119 *your allowance*, (with) your permission.
123 *from the sense of*, away from, having lost all sense of.
128 *In an extravagant and wheeling*, in a wandering and vacillat-
     ing.   *Cf. Hamlet*, I. i. : " The extravagant and erring
     spirit."
141 *cast*, period term for cashier ; dismiss.

Though I do hate him as I do hell-pains,
Yet, for necessity of present life,
I must show out a flag and sign of love,
Which is indeed but sign. That you shall surely find
   him,
150 Lead to the Sagittary the raised search ;
And there will I be with him. So, farewell.

                            (Exit IAGO.)

(Enter, below, BRABANTIO, in night attire, and Servants
                with torches.)

   BRABANTIO. It is too true an evil : gone she is,
And what's to come of my despised time
Is nought but bitterness. Now, Roderigo,
Where didst thou see her ? O unhappy girl !
With the Moor, say'st thou ? Who would be a
   father !
How didst thou know 'twas she ? O, she deceives me
Past thought ! What said she to you ? Get more
   tapers,
Raise all my kindred. Are they married, think you ?
160   RODERIGO. Truly, I think they are.
   BRABANTIO. O heaven ! How got she out ? O
   treason of the blood !
Fathers, from hence trust not your daughters' minds
By what you see them act. Is there not charms
By which the property of youth and maidhood
May be abused ? Have you not read, Roderigo,
Of some such things ?
   RODERIGO.   I have, sir.
   BRABANTIO. Call up my brother. O, would you
   had had her !
Some one way, some another. Do you know

---

150 *Sagittary.* No such building can be traced in Venice. Three
    different explanations are offered—(i) the State Armoury.
    Though the place would be known to all (*cf.* the Tower
    of London), a guide would be needed to find Othello's
    lodging (see I. iii. 121) ; (ii) an inn ; or (iii) the street of
    the arrow-makers, the Frezzaria.

Where we may apprehend her and the Moor ?
170 Roderigo. I think I can discover him, if you
        please
To get good guard and go along with me.
    Brabantio. Pray you, lead on. At every house I'll
        call ;
I may command at most.   Get weapons, ho !
And raise some special officers of night.
On, good Roderigo : I'll deserve your pains.

(Exeunt.)

SCENE II.   *Another street.*

(*Enter* Othello, Iago, *and* Attendants *with torches.*)
    Iago. Though in the trade of war I have slain
        men,
Yet do I hold it very stuff o' the conscience
To do no contriv'd murder : I lack iniquity
Sometimes to do me service : nine or ten times
I had thought 'to have yerk'd him here under the ribs.
    Othello. 'Tis better as it is.
    Iago.   Nay, but he prated
And spoke such scurvy and provoking terms
Against your honour
That, with the little godliness I have,
10 I did full hard forbear him.   But, I pray you sir,
Are you fast married ?   For be sure of this,
That the magnifico is much belov'd,
And hath in his effect a voice potential
As double as the duke's : he will divorce you ;
Or put upon you what restraint and grievance

---

175 *officers of night.* According to a book on Venice, published
        1599, six " officers of night " were responsible for the
        city's safety.
  5 *yerk'd,* dealt a quick blow.
 14 *As double as the duke's,* referring to the chairman's double
        vote ; or simply meaning " strong."

The law, with all his might to enforce it on,
Will give him cable.
    OTHELLO.   Let him do his spite ;
My services which I have done the signiory
Shall out-tongue his complaints. 'Tis yet to know—
20 Which, when I know that boasting is an honour,
I shall promulgate—I fetch my life and being
From men of royal siege, and my demerits
May speak unbonneted to as proud a fortune
As this that I have reach'd.   For know, Iago,
But that I love the gentle Desdemona,
I would not my unhoused free condition
Put into circumscription and confine
For the sea's worth.   But, look ! what lights come
    yonder ?
    IAGO. Those are the raised father and his friends :
30 You were best go in.
    OTHELLO.   Not I ; I must be found :
My parts, my title and my perfect soul
Shall manifest me rightly.   Is it they ?
    IAGO. By Janus, I think no.
    (*Enter* CASSIO, *and certain* Officers *with torches.*)
    OTHELLO. The servants of the duke, and my lieu-
    tenant.
The goodness of the night upon you, friends !
What is the news ?
    CASSIO.   The duke does greet you, general,
And he requires your haste-post-haste appearance,
Even on the instant.
    OTHELLO.   What is the matter, think you ?
    CASSIO. Something from Cyprus, as I may divine ;
40 It is a business of some heat.   The galleys

---

17 *give him cable*, give him freedom to act, give him "rope."
19 *'Tis yet to know . . . promulgate*, It is not yet known—nor shall
    I publicly proclaim it until I believe it honourable to
    boast.
22 *siege*, rank ; literally, seat of precedence.

Have sent a dozen sequent messengers
This very night at one another's heels,
And many of the consuls, rais'd and met,
Are at the duke's already. You have been hotly
    call'd for ;
When, being not at your lodgings to be found,
The senate hath sent about three several quests
To search you out.
    OTHELLO.   'Tis well I am found by you.
I will but spend a word here in the house,
And go with you.   (*Exit* OTHELLO.)
    CASSIO.   Ancient, what makes he here ?
50 IAGO. 'Faith, he to-night hath boarded a land
    carack :
If it prove lawful prize, he's made for ever.
    CASSIO. I do not understand.
    IAGO.   He's married.
    CASSIO.   To who ?
        (*Re-enter* OTHELLO.)
    IAGO. Marry, to—(*to* OTHELLO) Come, captain, will
    you go ?
    OTHELLO.   Have with you.
    CASSIO. Here comes another troop to seek for
    you.
    IAGO. It is Brabantio. General, be advis'd,
He comes to bad intent.
    (*Enter* BRABANTIO, RODERIGO, *and* Officers *with
    torches and weapons.*)
    OTHELLO.   Holla ! stand there !
    RODERIGO. Signior, it is the Moor.

41 *sequent*, one following another.
49 *what makes he here ? Cf.* III. iii. 94-6. But Cassio may well have
    known of the wooing and not of the elopement, or possibly
    may have been doubtful how far Iago was in Othello's
    confidence.
50 *carack*, Spanish merchant vessel which carried the richest
    cargoes. Refers, of course, to Desdemona's wealth.
55 *advis'd*, discreet.

OTHELLO

BRABANTIO. Down with him, thief!
(They draw on both sides.)

IAGO. You, Roderigo! come, sir, I am for you.

OTHELLO. Keep up your bright swords, for the dew
will rust them.

60 Good signior, you shall more command with years
Than with your weapons.

BRABANTIO. O thou foul thief, where has thou
stow'd my daughter?
Damn'd as thou art, thou hast enchanted her;
For I'll refer me to all things of sense,
If she in chains of magic were not bound,
Whether a maid so tender, fair, and happy,
So opposite to marriage that she shunn'd
The wealthy curled darlings of our nation,
Would ever have (to incur a general mock)
70 Run from her guardage to the sooty bosom
Of such a thing as thou? to fear, not to delight.
Judge me the world, if 'tis not gross in sense
That thou hast practis'd on her with foul charms,
Abus'd her delicate youth with drugs or minerals
That weaken motion: I'll have't disputed on;
'Tis probable and palpable to thinking.
I therefore apprehend and do attach thee
For an abuser of the world, a practiser
Of arts inhibited and out of warrant.
80 Lay hold upon him. If he do resist,
Subdue him at his peril.
*(BRABANTIO's Officers move forward; OTHELLO's
men draw in his defence.)*

OTHELLO. Hold your hands,

---

68 *curled*, fashionable. *Cf.* the carefully arranged love-lock.
See *Antony and Cleopatra*, " If she first meet the curled
Antony . . ."

72 *gross in sense*, obvious to the eye.

75 *motion*, sound reasoning.

76 *probable*, provable, certain. Does not imply doubt as in
modern use.

Both you of my inclining, and the rest.
Were it my cue to fight, I should have known it
Without a prompter.   Where will you that I go
To answer this your charge ?
   BRABANTIO.   To prison, till fit time
Of law and course of direct session
Call thee to answer.
   OTHELLO.   What if I do obey ?
How may the duke be therewith satisfied,
Whose messengers are here about my side,
90 Upon some present business of the state
To bring me to him.
   FIRST OFFICER.   'Tis true, most worthy signior ;
The duke's in council, and your noble self,
I am sure, is sent for.
   BRABANTIO.   How ! the duke in council !
In this time of the night !   Bring him away.
Mine's not an idle cause : the duke himself,
Or any of my brothers of the state,
Cannot but feel this wrong as 'twere their own ;
For if such actions may have passage free,
Bond-slaves and pagans shall our statesmen be.
                        (*Exeunt.*)

SCENE III.   *A council-chamber.*

(*The* DUKE *and* Senators *sitting at a table with lights ;*
          Officers *attending.*)
   DUKE. There is no composition in these news
That gives them credit.
   FIRST SENATOR. Indeed, they are disproportion'd ;
My letters say a hundred and seven galleys.
   DUKE. And mine, a hundred and forty.
   SECOND SENATOR.   And mine, two hundred

---

    1 *composition,* consistency.

But though they jump not on a just account—
As in these cases, where they aim reports,
'Tis oft with difference—yet do they all confirm
A Turkish fleet, and bearing up to Cyprus.

DUKE. Nay, it is possible enough to judgement :
10 I do not so secure me in the error,
But the main article I do approve
In fearful sense.

SAILOR (*within*). What, ho ! what, ho ! what, ho !

FIRST OFFICER. A messenger from the galleys.

> (*Enter a* Sailor.)

DUKE.   Now, what's the business ?

SAILOR. The Turkish preparation makes for
    Rhodes ;
So was I bid report here to the state
By Signior Angelo.

DUKE. How say you by this change ?

FIRST SENATOR.   This cannot be,
By no assay of reason : 'tis a pageant,
To keep us in false gaze, when we consider
20 The importancy of Cyprus to the Turk ;
And let ourselves again but understand,
That as it more concerns the Turk than Rhodes,
So may he with more facile question bear it,
For that it stands not in such warlike brace,
But altogether lacks the abilities
That Rhodes is dress'd in. If we make thought of
    this,

---

5 *jump*, agree. Still occasionally used for the fitting of wood
    joints, cloth, etc.
6 *they aim reports*, they make a rough guess.
10 *I do not . . . sense*, I do not allow the non-agreement as to
    number to deceive me into disbelieving danger in the main
    fact.
18 *pageant . . . gaze*, a demonstration or feint to distract our
    attention.
23 *with more facile question bear it*, capture it (Cyprus) more easily
    than Rhodes.
24 *brace*, defence, protection.

27

We must not think the Turk is so unskilful
To leave that latest which concerns him first,
Neglecting an attempt of ease and gain,
30 To wake and wage a danger profitless.

    Duke. Nay, in all confidence, he's not for Rhodes
    First Officer. Here is more news.

               (*Enter a* Messenger.)

    Messenger. The Ottomites, reverend and gracious.
Steering with due course towards the isle of Rhodes,
Have there injointed them with an after fleet.

    First Senator. Ay, so I thought. How many, as
      you guess ?

    Messenger. Of thirty sail : and now they do re-
      stem
Their backward course, bearing with frank appear-
      ance
Their purposes toward Cyprus. Signior Montano,
40 Your trusty and most valiant servitor,
With his free duty recommends you thus,
And prays you to believe him.

    Duke. 'Tis certain, then, for Cyprus.
Marcus Luccicos, is not he in town ?

    First Senator. He's now in Florence.

    Duke. Write from us to him ; post-post-haste
      dispatch.

    First Senator. Here comes Brabantio and the
      valiant Moor.

    (*Enter* Brabantio, Othello, Iago, Roderigo,
             and Officers.)

    Duke. Valiant Othello, we must straight employ
      you
Against the general enemy Ottoman.
50 (*To* Brabantio) I did not see you ; welcome, gentle
      signior ;
We lack'd your counsel and your help to-night.

        35 *injointed . . . fleet*, united with a second fleet.
        41 *recommends*, informs.

BRABANTIO. So did I yours. Good your grace,
pardon me ;
Neither my place nor aught I heard of business
Hath rais'd me from my bed, nor doth the general
care
Take hold on me ; for my particular grief
Is of so flood-gate and o'erbearing nature
That it engluts and swallows other sorrows
And it is still itself.

DUKE. Why, what's the matter ?

BRABANTIO. My daughter ! O my daughter !

DUKE and SENATORS. Dead ?

BRABANTIO. Ay, to me ;
60 She is abus'd, stol'n from me, and corrupted
By spells and medicines bought of mountebanks ;
For nature so preposterously to err,
Being not deficient, blind, or lame of sense,
Sans witchcraft could not.

DUKE. Whoe'er he be that in this foul proceeding
Hath thus beguil'd your daughter of herself
And you of her, the bloody book of law
You shall yourself read in the bitter letter
After your own sense, yea, though our proper son
70 Stood in your action.

BRABANTIO. Humbly I thank your grace.
Here is the man, this Moor, whom now, it seems,
Your special mandate for the state-affairs
Hath hither brought.

DUKE and SENATORS. We are very sorry for't.

DUKE (to OTHELLO). What, in your own part, can
you say to this ?

BRABANTIO. Nothing, but this is so.

---

57 *engluts*, swallows. *Cf.* French *engloutir*. For repetition of
   same meaning in two words see Prayer Book, " to acknow-
   ledge and confess," " assemble and meet together."
68 *read in the bitter letter*, interpret (the law) as severely as you
   please.
69 *proper*, own (*cf.* property).

OTHELLO. Most potent, grave, and reverend
    signiors,
My very noble and approv'd good masters,
That I have ta'en away this old man's daughter,
It is most true ; true, I have married her ;
80 The very head and front of my offending
Hath this extent, no more. Rude am I in my speech,
And little bless'd with the set phrase of peace ;
For since these arms of mine had seven years' pith,
Till now, some nine moons wasted, they have us'd
Their dearest action in the tented field,
And little of this great world can I speak,
More than pertains to feats of broil and battle,
And therefore little shall I grace my cause
In speaking for myself. Yet, by your gracious
    patience,
90 I will a round unvarnish'd tale deliver
Of my whole course of love ; what drugs, what
    charms,
What conjuration and what mighty magic,
For such proceeding I am charged withal,
I won his daughter.

BRABANTIO.   A maiden never bold ;
Of spirit so still and quiet that her motion
Blush'd at herself ; and she, in spite of nature,
Of years, of country, credit, every thing,
To fall in love with what she fear'd to look on !
It is a judgement maim'd and most imperfect
100 That will confess perfection so could err
Against all rules of nature, and must be driven
To find out practices of cunning hell,

82 *set phrase of peace.* Folio reads "soft."
84 *Till now . . . wasted,* until nine months ago.
90 *round,* plain, sincere. (*Cf.* " Sir Toby, I must be round
    with you.")
95 *motion . . . herself,* she blushed even at her own thoughts
    and impulses.
101 *and must be driven, i.e.* judgement must be driven to find out,
    etc.

Why this should be.   I therefore vouch again
That with some mixtures powerful o'er the blood,
Or with some dram conjur'd to this effect,
He wrought upon her.

DUKE.   To vouch this, is no proof,
Without more wider and more overt test
Than these thin habits and poor likelihoods
Of modern seeming do prefer against him.

110 FIRST SENATOR. But, Othello, speak :
Did you by indirect and forced courses
Subdue and poison this young maid's affections ?
Or came it by request and such fair question
As soul to soul affordeth ?

OTHELLO.   I do beseech you,
Send for the lady to the Sagittary,
And let her speak of me before her father.
If you do find me foul in her report,
The trust, the office I do hold of you,
Not only take away, but let your sentence
120 Even fall upon my life.

DUKE.   Fetch Desdemona hither.

OTHELLO. Ancient, conduct them ; you best know
        the place.   (*Exeunt* IAGO *and* Attendants.)
And, till she come, as truly as to heaven
I do confess the vices of my blood,
So justly to your grave ears I'll present
How I did thrive in this fair lady's love,
And she in mine.

DUKE. Say it, Othello.

OTHELLO. Her father lov'd me, oft invited me,
Still question'd me the story of my life,
130 From year to year : the battles, sieges, fortunes,
That I have pass'd.
I ran it through, even from my boyish days,
To the very moment that he bade me tell it :

108 *thin habits*, flimsy clothing, *i.e.* superficial appearances.   We
        still talk of "threadbare excuses."
109 *modern*, commonplace, ordinary.   *Cf.* new-fangled.

31

Wherein I spake of most disastrous chances,
Of moving accidents by flood and field,
Of hair-breadth scapes i' the imminent deadly
    breach,
Of being taken by the insolent foe
And sold to slavery, of my redemption thence
And portance in my travels' history :
140 Wherein of antres vast and deserts idle,
Rough quarries, rocks and hills whose heads touch
    heaven,
It was my hint to speak.   Such was the process ;
And of the Cannibals that each other eat,
The Anthropophagi and men whose heads
Do grow beneath their shoulders.   This to hear
Would Desdemona seriously incline ;
But still the house-affairs would draw her thence :
Which ever as she could with haste dispatch,
She'ld come again, and with a greedy ear
150 Devour up my discourse.   Which I observing,
Took once a pliant hour, and found good means
To draw from her a prayer of earnest heart
That I would all my pilgrimage dilate,
Whereof by parcels she had something heard,
But not intentively : I did consent,
And often did beguile her of her tears,
When I did speak of some distressful stroke,
That my youth suffer'd.   My story being done,
She gave me for my pains a world of sighs :
160 She swore, i' faith, 'twas strange, 'twas passing
    strange,
'Twas pitiful, 'twas wondrous pitiful ;
She wish'd she had not heard it, yet she wish'd

---

139 *portance*, deportment, carriage, *i.e.* behaviour.
140 *antres*, caves ; *idle*, uncultivated.
143 *Cannibals, Anthropophagi.* For extended comment on this
    speech of Othello's, see " Shakespeare's Workshop,"
    p. 194.
154 *by parcels*, piecemeal.

That heaven had made her such a man : she thank'd
    me,
And bade me, if I had a friend that lov'd her,
I should but teach him how to tell my story,
And that would woo her. Upon this hint I spake :
She lov'd me for the dangers I had pass'd,
And I lov'd her that she did pity them.
This only is the witchcraft I have us'd.
Here comes the lady ; let her witness it.
    (*Enter* DESDEMONA, IAGO, *and* Attendants.)

DUKE. I think this tale would win my daughter
    too.
Good Brabantio,
Take up this mangled matter at the best :
Men do their broken weapons rather use
Than their bare hands.

BRABANTIO.   I pray you, hear her speak :
If she confess that she was half the wooer,
Destruction on my head, if my bad blame
Light on the man ! Come hither, gentle mistress :
Do you perceive in all this noble company
Where most you owe obedience ?

DESDEMONA.   My noble father,
I do perceive here a divided duty :
To you I am bound for life and education ;
My life and education both do learn me
How to respect you. You're lord of all my duty,
I am hitherto your daughter ; but here's my husband,
And so much duty as my mother show'd
To you, preferring you before her father,
So much I challenge that I may profess
Due to the Moor my lord.

BRABANTIO.   God be wi' you ! I ha' done.
Please it your grace, on to the state-affairs :
I had rather to adopt a child than get it.
Come hither, Moor :

---

173 *Take up this mangled matter*, make the best of a bad job.

I here do give thee that with all my heart
Which, but thou hast already, with all my heart
I would keep from thee.   For your sake, jewel,
I am glad at soul I have no other child,
For thy escape would teach me tyranny,
To hang clogs on them.   I have done, my lord.
   DUKE. Let me speak like yourself, and lay a sen-
      tence,
200 Which, as a grise or step, may help these lovers
Into your favour.
When remedies are past, the griefs are ended,
By seeing the worst, which late on hopes depended.
To mourn a mischief that is past and gone
Is the next way to draw new mischief on.
What cannot be preserv'd when fortune takes,
Patience her injury a mockery makes.
The robb'd that smiles steals something from the
    thief ;
He robs himself that spends a bootless grief.
210   BRABANTIO. So let the Turk of Cyprus us beguile ;
We lose it not, so long as we can smile.
He bears the sentence well that nothing bears
But the free comfort which from thence he hears,
But he bears both the sentence and the sorrow,
That, to pay grief, must of poor patience borrow.
These sentences, to sugar, or to gall,
Being strong on both sides, are equivocal :
But words are words ; I never yet did hear
That the bruis'd heart was pierced through the
    ear.
220 Beseech you now,—to the affairs of state.

---

194 *which . . . heart.* This line is not found in First Quarto.
    Its omission certainly makes the sentence more direct.
199 *like yourself*, as if in your place.
   lay a sentence, quote a proverb (*cf.* sententious).
200 *grise*, step.
210 *So let the Turk, etc.* Compare this speech with that of Leonato
    in *Much Ado*, V. i., 3–32.

DUKE. The Turk with a most mighty preparation makes for Cyprus. Othello, the fortitude of the place is best known to you ; and though we have there a substitute of most allowed sufficiency, yet opinion, a sovereign mistress of effects, throws a more safer voice on you. You must therefore be content to slubber the gloss of your new fortunes with this more stubborn and boisterous expedition.

OTHELLO. The tyrant custom, most grave senators,
30 Hath made the flinty and steel couch of war
My thrice-driven bed of down : I do agnize
A natural and prompt alacrity
I find in hardness, and do undertake
These present wars against the Ottomites.
Most humbly therefore bending to your state,
I crave fit disposition for my wife,
Due reverence of place and exhibition,
With such accommodation and besort
As levels with her breeding.

DUKE.   If you please,
40 Be't at her father's.

BRABANTIO.   I'll not have it so.

OTHELLO. Nor I.

DESDEMONA.   Nor I ; I would not there reside,

221 *The Turk, etc.* Note the finality of the rhymed exchange between the Duke and Brabantio, and the opening of a new sequence in prose.
222 *fortitude,* military strength.   Contrast modern use.
224 *yet opinion . . . effects,* yet public opinion, where lies the final control of affairs.
226 *slubber,* tarnish or obscure, therefore neglect.   (*Cf. Merchant of Venice,* " Slubber not business for my sake.")
228 *boisterous,* violent.   Note that the meaning of the word has weakened.   (*Cf.* Milton, " the brute and boisterous force of violent men.")
231 *thrice-driven bed,* " thrice-driven " actually refers to the down of which the bed is made.   Down for the best beds was winnowed (driven) three times.
agnize, admit (*cf.* recognize).
237 *exhibition,* allowance.   Still used for university and other scholarships.

To put my father in impatient thoughts
By being in his eye.   Most gracious duke,
To my unfolding lend your prosperous ear ;
And let me find a charter in your voice,
To assist my simpleness.
    DUKE. What would you, Desdemona ?
    DESDEMONA. That I did love the Moor to live with
      him,
My downright violence and scorn of fortunes
250 May trumpet to the world : my heart's subdued
Even to the very quality of my lord :
I saw Othello's visage in his mind,
And to his honours and his valiant parts
Did I my soul and fortunes consecrate.
So that, dear lords, if I be left behind,
A moth of peace, and he go to the war,
The rites for which I love him are bereft me,
And I a heavy interim shall support
By his dear absence.   Let me go with him.
260   OTHELLO. Let her have your voices.
Vouch with me, heaven, I therefore beg it not,
To please the palate of my appetite,
Nor to comply with heat—the young affects
In me defunct—and proper satisfaction,
But to be free and bounteous to her mind.
And heaven defend your good souls, that you think
I will your serious and great business scant
For she is with me : no, when light-wing'd toys

---

244 *prosperous*, propitious.
249 *scorn of fortunes*, defiance of worldly interest. Folio gives
    "storm."   The meaning is the same in either case.
251 *quality of my lord*, his profession, *i.e.* a soldier's life.
256 *A moth of peace*, useless and self-indulgent.
257 *The rites for which I love him*, *i.e.* sharing his soldier's life.
259 *dear*, grievously bought.   The word is used of any extremes,
    joy or sorrow, love or hate.   *Cf. Richard II.* " The dateless
    limit of thy dear exile."
263 *the young affects*, the appetites of youth.
264 *proper satisfaction*, self-indulgence.

Of feather'd Cupid foils with wanton dullness
70 My speculative and active instruments,
That my disports corrupt and taint my business,
Let housewives make a skillet of my helm,
And all indign and base adversities
Make head against my estimation !

DUKE. Be it as you shall privately determine,
Either for her stay or going : the affair cries haste,
And speed must answer it.

FIRST SENATOR. You must away to-night.

OTHELLO.   With all my heart.

DUKE. At nine i' the morning here we'll meet again.
80 Othello, leave some officer behind,
And he shall our commission bring to you ;
With such things else of quality and respect
As doth import you.

OTHELLO.   So please your grace, my ancient ;
A man he is of honesty and trust ;
To his conveyance I assign my wife,
With what else needful your good grace shall think
To be sent after me.

DUKE.   Let it be so.
Good night to every one.   (*To* BRABANTIO) And,
          noble signior,
If virtue no delighted beauty lack,
290 Your son-in-law is far more fair than black.

FIRST SENATOR. Adieu, brave Moor ; use Desde-
          mona well.

BRABANTIO. Look to her, Moor, have a quick eye
          to see :
She has deceiv'd her father, and may thee.

                    (*Exeunt* DUKE, SENATORS, Officers, *etc.*)

---

269 *feather'd Cupid . . . instruments*. Folio gives "seel with
     wanton dullness. My speculative and offic'd instrument."
270 *speculative and active*, speculative instruments=the eyes, *i.e.*
     intelligent appraisal of affairs ; active (or offic'd) instru-
     ments=the limbs, *i.e.* efficient performance of duty.
272 *skillet*, saucepan.

OTHELLO. My life upon her faith ! Honest Iago,
My Desdemona must I leave to thee :
I prithee, let thy wife attend on her,
And bring them after in the best advantage.
Come, Desdemona ; I have but an hour
Of love, of worldly matters and direction,
300 To spend with thee. We must obey the time.

               (*Exeunt* OTHELLO *and* DESDEMONA.)

RODERIGO. Iago !—
IAGO. What say'st thou, noble heart ?
RODERIGO. What will I do, thinkest thou ?
IAGO. Why, go to bed, and sleep.
RODERIGO. I will incontinently drown myself.
IAGO. If thou dost, I shall never love thee after.
Why, thou silly gentleman ?
RODERIGO. It is silliness to live when to live is
torment ; and then have we a prescription to die
310 when death is our physician.
IAGO. O villanous ! I have looked upon the world
for four times seven years ; and since I could distinguish betwixt a benefit and an injury, I never found
man that knew how to love himself. Ere I would say
I would drown myself for the love of a guinea-hen, I
would change my humanity with a baboon.
RODERIGO. What should I do ? I confess it is my
shame to be so fond ; but it is not in my virtue to
amend it.
320 IAGO. Virtue ! a fig ! 'tis in ourselves that we are
thus or thus. Our bodies are our gardens, to the
which our wills are gardeners ; so that if we will plant
nettles, or sow lettuce, set hyssop and weed up thyme,
supply it with one gender of herbs, or distract it with

---

305 *incontinently*, immediately.   318 *fond*, foolish.
318 *not in my virtue*, not in my power. *Cf.* Machiavellian *Virtù*,
    strength. Its modern meaning of moral excellence is
    secondary. Virtue, a man's ability, is essentially an
    inborn quality. Iago disputes the assumption, and in
    doing so offers a useful clue to his own character.

many, either to have it sterile with idleness, or manured
with industry, why, the power and corrigible authority
of this lies in our wills. If the balance of our lives had
not one scale of reason to poise another of sensuality,
the blood and baseness of our natures would conduct
330 us to most preposterous conclusions : but we have
reason to cool our raging motions, our carnal stings,
our unbitted lusts, whereof I take this that you call
love to be a sect or scion.

RODERIGO. It cannot be.

IAGO. It is merely a lust of the blood and a permission of the will. Come, be a man. Drown thyself?
drown cats and blind puppies. I have professed me
thy friend and I confess me knit to thy deserving with
cables of perdurable toughness ; I could never better
340 stead thee than now. Put money in thy purse ;
follow thou the wars ; defeat thy favour with an
usurped beard ; I say, put money in thy purse. It
cannot be that Desdemona should long continue
her love to the Moor—put money in thy purse—nor
he to her. It was a violent commencement, and
thou shalt see an answerable sequestration :—put
but money in thy purse. These Moors are changeable
in their wills,—fill thy purse with money. The
food that to him now is as luscious as locusts, shall be
350 to him shortly as bitter as coloquintida. She must
change for youth : when she is sated with his body,
she will find the error of her choice. She must have
change, she must : therefore put money in thy purse.
If thou wilt needs damn thyself, do it a more delicate
way than drowning, make all the money thou canst.

326 *corrigible*, controlling, in the sense of correcting.
332 *unbitted*, uncontrolled.
333 *sect or scion* (continuation of gardening metaphor), a cutting
  or off-shoot.
341 *defeat thy favour*, disguise your appearance.
346 *answerable sequestration*, a similar withdrawal or separation.
350 *coloquintida*, colocynth. A bitter purgative drug made from
  the pulp of the wild gourd.

If sanctimony and a frail vow betwixt an erring
barbarian and a super-subtle Venetian be not too
hard for my wits and all the tribe of hell, thou
shalt enjoy her ; therefore make money. A pox of
360 drowning thyself ! it is clean out of the way. Seek
thou rather to be hanged in compassing thy joy than
to be drowned and go without her.

RODERIGO. Wilt thou be fast to my hopes, if I
depend on the issue ?

IAGO. Thou art sure of me : go, make money. I
have told thee often, and I re-tell thee again and
again, I hate the Moor ; my cause is hearted, thine
hath no less reason. Let us be conjunctive in our
revenge against him. There are many events in the
370 womb of time which will be delivered. Traverse !
go, provide thy money. We will have more of this
to-morrow. Adieu.

RODERIGO. Where shall we meet i' the morning ?

IAGO. At my lodging.

RODERIGO. I'll be with thee betimes.

IAGO. Go to : farewell. (*Calling him back.*) Do
you hear, Roderigo ?

RODERIGO. What say you ?

IAGO. No more of drowning, do you hear ?

380 RODERIGO. I am changed : I'll go sell all my land.
(*Exit.*)

IAGO. Thus do I ever make my fool my purse ;
For I mine own gain'd knowledge should profane,
If I would time expend with such a snipe,
But for my sport and profit. I hate the Moor.
He holds me well ;
The better shall my purpose work on him.

356 *sanctimony*, holiness.
356 *erring*, wandering (its original meaning).
368 *hearted*, deep-set ; *conjunctive*, united.
370 *Traverse !* Military term of the period. " Forward march ! "
       (*Cf.* American slang, " Scram ! ")
384 *I hate the Moor*. Notice that Iago repeats this when he is
       alone.

40

Cassio's a proper man : let me see now :
To get his place and to plume up my will
In double knavery—How, how ?—Let's see.
After some time, to abuse Othello's ear
That he is too familiar with his wife.
He hath a person and a smooth dispose
To be suspected, fram'd to make women false.
The Moor is of a free and open nature,
That thinks men honest that but seem to be so,
And will as tenderly be led by the nose
As asses are.
I have't.   It is engender'd.   Hell and night
Must bring this monstrous birth to the world's light.
                                          (*Exit.*)

388 *plume up my will* . . . *knavery*, encourage myself, as a bird
    ruffles up his feathers, by a twofold purpose.
392 *dispose*, bearing (*cf.* disposition).

ACT II

SCENE I.   *A Sea-port in Cyprus.   An open place near
the quay.*
(*Enter* Montano *and two* Gentlemen.)

> Montano. What from the cape can you discern
> at sea ?
> First Gentleman. Nothing at all : it is a high-
> wrought flood ;
> I cannot, 'twixt the heaven and the main,
> Descry a sail.
> Montano. Methinks the wind hath spoke aloud
> at land ;
> A fuller blast ne'er shook our battlements.
> If it hath ruffian'd so upon the sea,
> What ribs of oak, when mountains melt on them,
> Can hold the mortise ?   What shall we hear of this ?
> 10   Second Gentleman. A segregation of the Turkish
> fleet :
> For do but stand upon the foaming shore,
> The chidden billow seems to pelt the clouds ;
> The wind-shaked surge, with high and monstrous
> mane,
> Seems to cast water on the burning bear,
> And quench the guards of the ever-fixed pole :
> I never did like molestation view
> On the enchafed flood.

5 *at land.*   Nowadays we say *on* land, but " ashore," " at sea."
8 *mountains*, of waves.   9 *mortise*, joints.
10 *segregation*, breaking up, scattering.
15 *the guards*, the Pointers of the Pole Star.

42

MONTANO.   If that the Turkish fleet,
Be not enshelter'd and embay'd, they are drown'd ;
It is impossible they bear it out.
              (*Enter a* Third Gentleman.)
o THIRD GENTLEMAN. News, lads ! our wars are
        done.
The desperate tempest hath so bang'd the Turks,
That their designment halts. A noble ship of Venice
Hath seen a grievous wreck and sufferance
On most part of their fleet.
    MONTANO. How ! is this true ?
    THIRD GENTLEMAN.   The ship is here put in,
A Veronesa ; Michael Cassio,
Lieutenant to the warlike Moor Othello,
Is come on shore : the Moor himself at sea,
And is in full commission here for Cyprus.
30 MONTANO. I am glad on't ; 'tis a worthy governor.
    THIRD GENTLEMAN. But this same Cassio, though
        he speak of comfort
Touching the Turkish loss, yet he looks sadly,
And prays the Moor be safe ; for they were parted
With foul and violent tempest.
    MONTANO.   Pray heaven he be ;
For I have serv'd him, and the man commands
Like a full soldier.   Let's to the seaside, ho !
As well to see the vessel that's come in
As to throw out our eyes for brave Othello,
Even till we make the main and the aerial blue

---

21 *bang'd*, battered. Shakespeare's first audiences would well
      remember how a similar storm had destroyed Spain's
      Armada.
22 *designment*, enterprise.
23 *sufferance*, disaster, persecution. *Cf.* Our expression "punish-
      ment" in warfare and boxing.
26 *A Veronesa*, Verona was one of the cities under Venetian control.
      According to the Folio Veronesa applies to Cassio, but he
      is described elsewhere as a Florentine.
39 *till we make . . . an indistinct regard*, until we can no longer
      distinguish sea from sky.

40 An indistinct regard.

THIRD GENTLEMAN. Come, let's do so :
For every minute is expectancy
Of more arrivance.

                    (*Enter* CASSIO.)

CASSIO. Thanks, you the valiant of this warlike
    isle,
That so approve the Moor !   O, let the heavens
Give him defence against the elements,
For I have lost him on a dangerous sea.

MONTANO. Is he well shipp'd ?

CASSIO. His bark is stoutly timber'd, and his pilot
Of very expert and approv'd allowance ;
50 Therefore my hopes, not surfeited to death,
Stand in bold cure.

            (*A cry within* " A sail, a sail, a sail ! ")
            (*Enter a* Fourth Gentleman.)

CASSIO. What noise ?

FOURTH GENTLEMAN. The town is empty ; on the
    brow o' the sea
Stand ranks of people, and they cry " A sail ! "

CASSIO. My hopes do shape him for the governor.

                    (*Guns heard.*)

SECOND GENTLEMAN. They do discharge their shot
    of courtesy ;
Our friends at least.

CASSIO.   I pray you, sir, go forth,
And give us truth who 'tis that is arrived.

SECOND GENTLEMAN. I shall.   (*Exit.*)

60   MONTANO. But, good lieutenant, is your general
    wiv'd ?

CASSIO. Most fortunately :   he hath achiev'd a
    maid
That paragons description and wild fame ;
One that excels the quirks of blazoning pens,

49 *Of very expert . . . allowance*, generally acknowledged to be
    efficient.
51 *Stand in bold cure*, stand a good chance of fulfilment.

And in the essential vesture of creation
Does tire the ingener.
(Re-enter Second Gentleman.)
How now ! who has put in ?
SECOND GENTLEMAN. 'Tis one Iago, ancient to the
general.

CASSIO. He has had most favourable and happy
speed :
Tempests themselves, high seas and howling winds,
The gutter'd rocks and congregated sands,
70 Traitors ensteep'd to clog the guiltless keel,
As having sense of beauty, do omit
Their mortal natures, letting go safely by
The divine Desdemona.

MONTANO. What is she ?

CASSIO. She that I spake of, our great captain's
captain,
Left in the conduct of the bold Iago,
Whose footing here anticipates our thoughts
A se'nnight's speed. Great Jove, Othello guard,
And swell his sail with thine own powerful breath,
That he may bless this bay with his tall ship,
80 And swiftly come to Desdemona's arms,
Give renew'd fire to our extinct spirits,
And bring all Cyprus comfort !

(<i>Enter</i> DESDEMONA, EMILIA, IAGO, RODERIGO, <i>and</i>
Attendants.)

O behold,
The riches of the ship is come on shore !

64 *essential*, actual, *i.e.* the beauty of the woman herself defeats
the poet.
65 *ingener*, craftsman. " Poet " means, literally, a maker.
69 *gutter'd*, furrowed, fluted.
71 *omit their mortal natures*, lay aside their fatal character.
76 *footing*, landing.
anticipates . . . A se'nnight's speed, a week earlier than expected.
79 *tall*, well built, fine to look at.
80 *And swiftly come to*. Folio gives " Make love's quick pants
in—"

45

Ye men of Cyprus, let her have your knees.
Hail to thee, lady ! and the grace of heaven,
Before, behind thee, and on every hand,
Enwheel thee round !

DESDEMONA.   I thank you, valiant Cassio.
What tidings can you tell me of my lord ?

CASSIO. He is not yet arriv'd : nor know I aught
90 But that he's well and will be shortly here.

DESDEMONA. O, but I fear—How lost you com-
pany ?   (*Within* " A sail, a sail ! "   *Guns heard*.)

CASSIO. The great contention of the sea and skies
Parted our fellowship—But, hark ! a sail.

SECOND GENTLEMAN. They give their greeting to
the citadel :
This likewise is a friend.

CASSIO.   See for the news.   (*Exit* Gentleman.)
Good ancient, you are welcome.
          (*To* EMILIA.) Welcome, mistress. (*He kisses her*.)
Let it not gall your patience, good Iago,
That I extend my manners ; 'tis my breeding
That gives me this bold show of courtesy.

100 IAGO. Sir, would she give you so much of her lips
As of her tongue she oft bestows on me,
You'ld have enough.

DESDEMONA.   Alas, she has no speech.

IAGO. In faith, too much ;
I find it still, when I have list to sleep.
Marry, before your ladyship, I grant,
She puts her tongue a little in her heart,
And chides with thinking.

EMILIA. You have little cause to say so.

IAGO. Come on, come on ; you are pictures out of
doors,

84 *let her have your knees*, kneel to her.
97 (*He kisses her*.) This was, as Cassio explains, a form of
courtesy of the period. Cassio's apology possibly suggests
that Iago is reputed a jealous husband.
102 *she has no speech*. An interesting comment in view of
Emilia's later volubility.   105 *still*, always.

110 Bells in your parlours, wild-cats in your kitchens,
Saints in your injuries, devils being offended.
Players in your housewifery; and housewives in your
    beds.

    DESDEMONA. O fie upon thee, slanderer !

    IAGO. Nay, it is true or I am a Turk ;
You rise to play, and go to bed to work.

    EMILIA. You shall not write my praise.

    IAGO.   No, let me not.

    DESDEMONA. What wouldst thou write of me, if
    thou shouldst praise me ?

    IAGO. O gentle lady, do not put me to't ;
For I am nothing if not critical.

120   DESDEMONA. Come on, assay. . . . There's one gone
    to the harbour ?

    IAGO. Ay, madam.

    DESDEMONA. I am not merry ; but I do beguile
The thing I am, by seeming otherwise.
Come, how wouldst thou praise me ?

    IAGO. I am about it ; but indeed my invention
comes from my pate as birdlime does from frize ;
it plucks out brains and all : but my Muse labours,
and thus she is deliver'd.
    If she be fair and wise, fairness and wit,
130   *The one's for use, the other useth it.*

    DESDEMONA. Well prais'd ! How if she be black
    and witty ?

    IAGO. *If she be black, and thereto have a wit,*
    She'll find a white that shall her blackness fit.

---

110 *Bells in your parlours . . . being offended.* Sweet-voiced to
    visitors ; wild-cats to your servants ; self-righteous when
    you do wrong ; devils when others wrong you.

112 *housewives,* pronounced "hussifs." Here it has the same
    meaning as modern word "hussy."   121 *assay,* try.

126 *frize,* cloth with a coarse nap, made in Ireland (now "frieze").

129 *If she be fair . . . useth it,* the good-looking woman with
    brains uses her wit to exploit her beauty.

133 *She'll find a white,* she'll get what she wants. The "white"
    was the bull's-eye of the archery target. Possibly also a
    pun on white and "wight" (creature).

DESDEMONA. Worse and worse.

EMILIA. How if fair and foolish?

IAGO. *She never yet was foolish that was fair ;*
For even her folly help'd her to an heir.

DESDEMONA. These are old fond paradoxes to make
fools laugh 'i the alehouse.   What miserable praise
140 hast thou for her that's foul and foolish?

IAGO. *There's none so foul and foolish thereunto,*
But does foul pranks which fair and wise ones do.

DESDEMONA. O heavy ignorance !   thou praisest
the worst best.   But what praise couldst thou bestow
on a deserving woman indeed, one that, in the
authority of her merit, did justly put on the vouch
of very malice itself?

IAGO. *She that was ever fair and never proud,*
Had tongue at will and yet was never loud,
150   *Never lack'd gold and yet went never gay,*
Fled from her wish and yet said " Now I may,"
She that being anger'd, her revenge being nigh,
Bade her wrong stay and her displeasure fly,
She that in wisdom never was so frail
To change the cod's head for the salmon's tail,
She that could think and ne'er disclose her mind,
See suitors following and not look behind,
She was a wight, if ever such wight were—

DESDEMONA. To do what?

160 IAGO. *To suckle fools and chronicle small beer.*

DESDEMONA. O most lame and impotent conclusion !
Do not learn of him, Emilia, though he be thy

---

141 *There's none so foul . . . wise ones do.*   Even an ugly woman
will find an opportunity for wantonness.

146 *put on the vouch of very malice*, incite even malice to praise
her virtue.

155 *To change . . . salmon's tail*, give away a valuable thing (the
salmon's tail) in exchange for the worthless (the cod's
head).   *Cod's head* also means a fool.

160 *To suckle fools . . . beer*, fit for nothing better than child-
bearing and the recording of petty household affairs.
Cynical anticlimax.

husband. How say you, Cassio? is he not a most
profane and liberal counsellor?

CASSIO. He speaks home, madam: you may relish
him more in the soldier than in the scholar.

(CASSIO *chats quietly with* DESDEMONA, *with the
gestures and courtesies of a trained courtier.*)

IAGO (*aside*). He takes her by the palm: ay, well
said, whisper: with as little a web as this will I
ensnare as great a fly as Cassio. Ay, smile upon
70 her, do; I will gyve thee in thine own courtship.
(*Mimicking* CASSIO.) "You say true; 'tis so, indeed,"—if such tricks as these strip you out of your
lieutenantry, it had been better you had not kissed
your three fingers so oft, which now again you are
most apt to play the sir in. Very good; well kissed!
an excellent courtesy! "'Tis so, indeed." Yet
again your fingers to your lips? (*Trumpet within.*)
The Moor! I know his trumpet.

CASSIO. 'Tis truly so.

80 DESDEMONA. Let's meet him and receive him.

CASSIO. Lo, where he comes!

(*Enter* OTHELLO *and* Attendants.)

OTHELLO. O my fair warrior!

DESDEMONA. My dear Othello!

OTHELLO. It gives me wonder great as my content
To see you here before me. O my soul's joy!
If after every tempest come such calms,
May the winds blow till they have waken'd death,
And let the labouring bark climb hills of seas
Olympus-high and duck again as low
As hell's from heaven! If it were now to die,
190 'Twere now to be most happy; for I fear
My soul hath her content so absolute
That not another comfort like to this

165 *you may relish him more*, you will appreciate him better.
189 *If it were now to die*, if it were now (the time) to die. Note
the dramatic irony; Othello has now arrived upon the
scene of his coming agony.

Succeeds in unknown fate.

DESDEMONA.   The heavens forbid
But that our loves and comforts should increase,
Even as our days do grow !

OTHELLO.   Amen to that, sweet powers !
I cannot speak enough of this content ;
It stops me here ; it is too much of joy :
And this, and this, the greatest discords be.

                                         (*Kissing her.*)

That e'er our hearts shall make !

IAGO (*aside*).   O, you are well tun'd now !
200 But I'll set down the pegs that make this music,
As honest as I am.

OTHELLO.   Come, let us to the castle.
News, friends ; our wars are done, the Turks are
    drown'd.
How does my old acquaintance of this isle ?
Honey, you shall be well desir'd in Cyprus ;
I have found great love amongst them.   O my
    sweet,
I prattle out of fashion, and I dote
In mine own comforts.   I prithee, good Iago,
Go to the bay and disembark my coffers :
Bring thou the master to the citadel ;
210 He is a good one, and his worthiness
Does challenge much respect.   Come, Desdemona,
Once more, well met at Cyprus.

                    (*Exeunt* ALL *but* IAGO *and* RODERIGO.)

IAGO. Do you meet me presently at the harbour.
Come hither.   If thou be'st valiant (as, they say,

---

197 *It stops me here, i.e.* at the throat.   The beginning of a musical
    metaphor carried on in the next line and by Iago, " I'll
    set down the pegs," *i.e.* throw the instrument out of tune.
204 *Honey. Cf. Henry V.* II. iii. 1, " Prithee, honey-sweet hus-
    band . . ."   Not the only instance of Shakespeare's antici-
    pating American usage.
    well-desir'd, welcome.
206 *I prattle out of fashion . . . comforts*, I'm chattering nonsense
    because I'm so happy.

base men being in love have then a nobility in their
natures more than is native to them), list me. The
lieutenant to-night watches on the court of guard.
First, I must tell thee this—Desdemona is directly in
love with him.

20 RODERIGO. With him? why, 'tis not possible.

IAGO. Lay thy finger thus, and let thy soul be in-
structed. Mark me with what violence she first loved
the Moor, but for bragging and telling her fantastical
lies: and will she love him still for prating? let
not thy discreet heart think so. Her eye must be fed;
and what delight shall she have to look on the devil?
When the blood is made dull there should be, again
to inflame it and to give satiety a fresh appetite,
loveliness in favour, sympathy in years, manners
230 and beauties; all which the Moor is defective in.
Now, for want of these required conveniences, her
delicate tenderness will find itself abused, begin to
heave the gorge, disrelish and abhor the Moor;
very nature will instruct her to it and compel her
to some second choice. Now, sir, this granted—as
it is a most pregnant and unforced position—who
stands so eminent in the degree of this fortune as
Cassio does? a knave very voluble, no further conscionable than in putting on the mere form of civil
240 and humane seeming, for the better compassing of his
salt and most hidden loose affection? Why, none;
why, none: a slipper and subtle knave, a finder of

218 *Desdemona is directly in love.* Note the twist from what Iago
    himself " well believes " (see below). He knows it to be
    more effective to tell Roderigo that it is Desdemona who
    desires Cassio.
221 *Lay thy finger thus, i.e.* on your lips. Be quiet and listen.
224 *love him still for prating?* Will she go on loving him for the
    sake of his talk?
236 *most pregnant and unforced,* inherent in the situation itself
    without any help from us. 239 *voluble,* fickle, wanton.
238 *conscionable,* scrupulous. 242 *salt,* adj., rank, lecherous.
242 *slipper,* slippery.

occasions, that has an eye can stamp and counterfeit advantages, though true advantage never present itself ; a devilish knave. Besides, the knave is handsome, young, and hath all those requisites in him that folly and green minds look after ; a pestilent complete knave ; and the woman hath found him already.

RODERIGO. I cannot believe that in her ; she's full
250 of most blessed condition.

IAGO. Blessed fig's-end ! The wine she drinks is made of grapes : if she had been blessed, she would never have loved the Moor. Blessed pudding ! Didst thou not see her paddle with the palm of his hand ? didst not mark that ?

RODERIGO. Yes, that I did ; but that was but courtesy.

IAGO. Lechery, by this hand ; an index and obscure prologue to the history of lust and foul
260 thoughts. They met so near with their lips that their breaths embraced together. Villanous thoughts, Roderigo ! when these mutualities so marshal the way, hard at hand comes the master and main exercise, the incorporate conclusion : pish ! But, sir, be you ruled by me : I have brought you from Venice. Watch you to-night ; for the command, I'll lay't upon you. Cassio knows you not. I'll not be far from you : do you find some occasion to anger

243 *can stamp and counterfeit advantages*, can " coin occasions " ;
can turn the most innocent opportunities to his use.
251 *The wine . . . grapes*, she has the same appetites as any
ordinary woman.
254 *paddle*, toy with. *Cf. Winter's Tale*, I. iii. 115, " Paddling
palms and pinching fingers."
262 *when these mutualities . . . incorporate conclusion*. Military
metaphor. The context makes the meaning obvious
enough.
266 *for the command . . . upon you*. Iago would set the guard
and see that Roderigo was conveniently placed. See
II. iii. 4 and 55.
267 *Cassio knows you not*. Possibly because of the " usurped
beard."

Cassio, either by speaking too loud, or tainting his
270 discipline ; or from what other course you please,
which the time shall more favourably minister.

RODERIGO. Well.

IAGO. Sir, he is rash and very sudden in choler, and
haply may strike at you : provoke him, that he may ;
for even out of that will I cause these of Cyprus to
mutiny, whose qualification shall come into no true
taste again but by the displanting of Cassio. So
shall you have a shorter journey to your desires by
the means I shall then have to prefer them ; and the
280 impediment most profitably removed, without the
which there were no expectation of our prosperity.

RODERIGO. I will do this, if I can bring it to any
opportunity.

IAGO. I warrant thee. Meet me by and by at the
citadel. I must fetch his necessaries ashore. Farewell.

RODERIGO. Adieu.   (*Exit* RODERIGO.)

IAGO. That Cassio loves her, I do well believe it ;
That she loves him, 'tis apt and of great credit.
The Moor, howbeit that I endure him not,
290 Is of a constant, loving, noble nature,
And I dare think he'll prove to Desdemona
A most dear husband. Now, I do love her too ;
Not out of absolute lust, though peradventure
I stand accountant for as great a sin,
But partly led to diet my revenge,
For that I do suspect the lusty Moor
Hath leap'd into my seat ; the thought whereof
Doth, like a poisonous mineral, gnaw my inwards ;
And nothing can or shall content my soul
300 Till I am even'd with him, wife for wife,

273 *rash . . . choler.* A downright lie. See V. i. 19, and Cassio's
general behaviour, except when drunk.
276 *whose qualification . . . Cassio,* who will only be appeased (*i.e.*
their anger qualified to satisfaction) by dismissing Cassio.
288 *apt and of great credit,* quite possibly true. An off-hand justification for the lie he told Roderigo.   296 *diet,* to feed.

Or failing so, yet that I put the Moor
At least into a jealousy so strong
That judgement cannot cure.   Which thing to do,
If this poor trash of Venice, whom I trash
For his quick hunting, stand the putting on,
I'll have our Michael Cassio on the hip,
Abuse him to the Moor in the rank garb—
For I fear Cassio with my night-cap too—
310 Make the Moor thank me, love me and reward me,
For making him egregiously an ass,
And practising upon his peace and quiet
Even to madness.   'Tis here, but yet confus'd :
Knavery's plain face is never seen till us'd.   (*Exit.*)

SCENE II.   *A street.*

(*Enter a* Herald *with a proclamation ;* People *following.*)
    HERALD. It is Othello's pleasure, our noble and
valiant general, that, upon certain tidings now
arrived, importing the mere perdition of the Turkish
fleet, every man put himself into triumph ; some to
dance, some to make bonfires, each man to what
sport and revels his addiction leads him ; for, besides
these beneficial news, it is the celebration of his
nuptial.   So much was his pleasure should be pro-

---

304 *trash . . . trash.* A pun, using hunting terms.   Trash, *noun,*
        was a worthless creature.   To trash a hound was to hang
        a clog upon him to keep back his speed.   For Iago's
        success in " trashing " Roderigo, see IV. ii. 172.
307 *in the rank garb,* in frank terms.
308 *I fear Cassio with my night-cap,* I suspect him of familiarity
        with my own wife.
313 *Knavery's plain face . . . us'd.* Iago keeps his schemes elastic,
        prepared to act on opportunity.
Scenes ii. and iii. With reference to these rapid scene changes
        see p. 210.   The First Folio has only two scenes in this act.
    3 *mere,* complete.   6 *addiction,* inclination.

claimed. All offices are open, and there is full
10 liberty of feasting from this present hour of five till
the bell have told eleven. Heaven bless the isle of
Cyprus and our noble general Othello !　　(*Exeunt.*)

SCENE III.　*A hall in the castle.*

(*Enter* OTHELLO, DESDEMONA, CASSIO, *and*
Attendants.)

OTHELLO. Good Michael, look you to the guard
　　to-night :
Let's teach ourselves that honourable stop,
Not to outsport discretion.

CASSIO. Iago hath direction what to do ;
But, notwithstanding, with my personal eye
Will I look to't.

OTHELLO.　　　Iago is most honest.
Michael, good night : to-morrow with your earliest
Let me have speech with you. (*To* DESDEMONA)
　　Come, my dear love,
The purchase made, the fruits are to ensue,
10 The profit's yet to come 'twixt me and you.
　　　　　　　　　　　　　(*To* CASSIO.)
Good night.
　　(*Exeunt* OTHELLO, DESDEMONA, *and* Attendants.)
　　　　　　　　(*Enter* IAGO.)

CASSIO. Welcome, Iago ; we must to the watch.

IAGO. Not this hour, lieutenant ; 'tis not yet ten o'
the clock. Our general cast us thus early for the love
of his Desdemona ; who let us not therefore blame.
He hath not yet made wanton the night with her, and
she is sport for Jove.

CASSIO. She's a most exquisite lady.

IAGO. And, I'll warrant her, full of game.

---

9 *offices are open*, kitchens, buffets open, *i.e.* free refresh-
　　ments.
14 *cast us*, dismissed us.

20 Cassio. Indeed, she's a most fresh and delicate creature.

Iago. What an eye she has ! methinks it sounds a parley of provocation.

Cassio. An inviting eye ; and yet methinks right modest.

Iago. And when she speaks, is it not an alarum to love ?

Cassio. She is indeed perfection.

Iago. Well, happiness to their sheets. . . . Come, 30 lieutenant, I have a stoup of wine ; and here without are a brace of Cyprus gallants that would fain have a measure to the health of black Othello.

Cassio. Not to-night, good Iago : I have very poor and unhappy brains for drinking. I could well wish courtesy would invent some other custom of entertainment.

Iago. O, they are our friends ; but one cup. I'll drink for you.

Cassio. I have drunk but one cup to-night, and 40 that was craftily qualified too, and, behold, what innovation it makes here. I am unfortunate in the infirmity, and dare not task my weakness with any more.

Iago. What, man ! 'tis a night of revels, the gallants desire it.

Cassio. Where are they ?

Iago. Here at the door ; I pray you, call them in.

Cassio. I'll do't ; but it dislikes me.   (*Exit.*)

Iago. If I can fasten but one cup upon him,
50 With that which he hath drunk to-night already,
He'll be as full of quarrel and offence

14–28. Iago tries to draw Cassio into an indiscreet comment. Cassio's replies are guarded.

37 *I'll drink for you*, I'll keep the ball rolling after the first round and drink your share.

40 *craftily qualified*, watered down on the sly.

41 *innovation*, change ; probably pointing to his flushed face.

As my young mistress' dog. Now my sick fool
    Roderigo,
Whom love hath turn'd almost the wrong side out,
To Desdemona hath to-night carous'd
Potations pottle-deep ; and he's to watch.
Three lads of Cyprus, noble swelling spirits,
That hold their honours in a wary distance,
The very elements of this warlike isle,
Have I to-night fluster'd with flowing cups,
And they watch too. Now, 'mongst this flock of
    drunkards,
Am I to put our Cassio in some action
That may offend the isle.—But here they come :
If consequence do but approve my dream,
My boat sails freely, both with wind and stream.
    (*Re-enter* CASSIO ; *with him* MONTANO *and* Gentlemen ;
      Servants *following with wine.*)

    CASSIO. 'Fore God, they have given me a rouse
    already.

    MONTANO. Good faith, a little one ; not past a
pint, as I am a soldier.

    IAGO. Some wine, ho !
(*Sings*)   *And let me the canakin clink, clink ;*
        And let me the canakin clink :
          A soldier's a man ;
          A life's but a span ;
        Why, then, let a soldier drink.
Some wine, boys !

    CASSIO. 'Fore God, an excellent song.

    IAGO. I learned it in England, where, indeed, they
are most potent in potting : your Dane, your German,

---

55 *pottle-deep*, no heel-taps. A pottle was two quarts.
63 *If consequence . . . dream.* If events fit in with my plans.
65 *rouse*, a large glass in which healths were drunk.
70 *Iago sings.* It is very much to Iago's purpose to play the lively
    boon companion, and, artist as he is, he does the job well.
    "A man may smile and smile and be a villain" (*Hamlet*).
77 *England . . . potting.* A deserved reputation at the time,
    referred to by many contemporary writers.

and your swag-bellied Hollander—Drink, ho !—are 80 nothing to your English.

CASSIO. Is your Englishman so expert in his drinking ?

IAGO. Why, he drinks you with facility your Dane dead drunk ; he sweats not to overthrow your Almain ; he gives your Hollander a vomit, ere the next pottle can be filled.

CASSIO. To the health of our general !

MONTANO. I am for it, lieutenant ; and I'll do you justice.

90 IAGO. O sweet England !

> *King Stephen was a worthy peer,*
>   *His breeches cost him but a crown ;*
> *He held them sixpence all too dear,*
>   *With that he call'd the tailor lown.*
> *He was a wight of high renown,*
>   *And thou art but of low degree :*
> *'Tis pride that pulls the country down ;*
>   *Then take thine auld cloak about thee.*

Some wine, ho !

100 CASSIO. 'Fore God, this is a more exquisite song than the other.

IAGO. Will you hear't again ?

CASSIO. No ; for I hold him to be unworthy of his place that does those things. Well, God's above all ; and there be souls must be saved, and there be souls must not be saved.

IAGO. It's true, good lieutenant.

CASSIO. For mine own part,—no offence to the general, nor any man of quality—I hope to be saved.

---

79 *swag-bellied*, over-hanging, swinging (*cf.* swagger, and thieves' slang " swag," a swinging sack).

83 *your Dane. Cf. Hamlet*, I. iv. 19.

91 *King Stephen*, the ballad is in Percy's *Reliques*.

100 *'Fore God*. Cassio is now definitely drunk.

105 *there be souls . . . not be saved*. A dig at the doctrines of the Puritans (Calvinists), constant enemies of the playhouses.

10   IAGO. And so do I too, lieutenant.

     CASSIO. Ay, but, by your leave, not before me; the lieutenant is to be saved before the ancient. Let's have no more of this; let's to our affairs.—God forgive us our sins!—Gentlemen, let's look to our business. Do not think, gentlemen, I am drunk: this is my ancient; this is my right hand, and this is my left hand. I am not drunk now; I can stand well enough, and speak well enough.

     ALL. Excellent well.

20   CASSIO. Why, very well then; you must not think then that I am drunk.   (*Exit.*)

     MONTANO. To the platform, masters; come, let's set the watch.

     IAGO. You see this fellow that is gone before;
He is a soldier fit to stand by Cæsar
And give direction: and do but see his vice;
'Tis to his virtue a just equinox,
The one as long as the other: 'tis pity of him.
I fear the trust Othello puts him in,
On some odd time of his infirmity,
130 Will shake this island.

     MONTANO.   But is he often thus?

     IAGO. 'Tis evermore the prologue to his sleep ﹕
He'll watch the horologe a double set,
If drink rock not his cradle.

     MONTANO.   It were well
The general were put in mind of it.
Perhaps he sees it not; or his good nature
Prizes the virtue that appears in Cassio,
And looks not on his evils: is not this true?

           (*Enter* RODERIGO.)

     IAGO (*aside to him*). How now, Roderigo!

---

122 *platform*, terrace where the guns were set.
126 *his vice . . . a just equinox*, his vice is exactly equal to his virtue, as night equals day at the equinox.
133 *watch . . . a double set*, stay awake the whole twenty-four hours. (*Horologe*=clock or watch.)

I pray you, after the lieutenant ; go.

                      (Exit Roderigo.)

140 Montano. And 'tis great pity that the noble Moor
Should hazard such a place as his own second
With one of an ingraft infirmity :
It were an honest action to say
So to the Moor.

    Iago.   Not I, for this fair island :

                 (Cry within : " Help ! help ! ")

I do love Cassio well ; and would do much
To cure him of this evil—But, hark ! what noise ?

          (Re-enter Cassio, *driving in* Roderigo.)

    Cassio. 'Zounds, you rogue ! You rascal !

    Montano. What's the matter, lieutenant ?

    Cassio. A knave teach me my duty !
150 I'll beat the knave into a twiggen bottle.

    Roderigo. Beat me !

    Cassio.   Dost thou prate, rogue ?

                 (Striking Roderigo.)

    Montano.   Nay, good lieutenant !

                   (Staying him.)

I pray you, sir, hold your hand.

    Cassio.   Let me go, sir,
Or I'll knock you o'er the mazzard.

    Montano.   Come, come, you're drunk.

    Cassio. Drunk !   *(They fight.)*

    Iago *(aside to* Roderigo). Away, I say ; go out,
    and cry a mutiny.   *(Exit* Roderigo.)

Nay, good lieutenant,—God's will, gentlemen ;—
Help ho !—Lieutenant,—sir,—Montano,—sir ;—
Help, masters !—Here's a goodly watch indeed !

                   (Bell rings.)

Who's that which rings the bell ?—Diablo, ho !
160 The town will rise : God's will, lieutenant, hold !

---

142 *ingraft,* deep-rooted.
150 *twiggen bottle,* a bottle encased in criss-cross straw or twigs of
     wicker. *Cf.* a Chianti flask.
153 *mazzard,* head. Literally, a round cup or bowl.

You will be sham'd for ever.
> (*Re-enter* OTHELLO *and* Attendants.)

OTHELLO.   What is the matter here?

MONTANO. 'Zounds, I bleed still; I am hurt to the
death.   (*Faints.*)

OTHELLO. Hold, for your lives!

IAGO. Hold, hold! Lieutenant,—sir,—Montano,—
gentlemen,—

Have you forgot all sense of place and duty?

Hold! the general speaks to you; hold, hold, for
shame!

OTHELLO. Why, how now, ho! from whence ariseth
this?

Are we turn'd Turks, and to ourselves do that

Which heaven hath forbid the Ottomites?

170 For Christian shame, put by this barbarous brawl:

He that stirs next to carve for his own rage

Holds his soul light; he dies upon his motion.

Silence that dreadful bell, it frights the isle

From her propriety. What is the matter, masters?

Honest Iago, that look'st dead with grieving,

Speak, who began this? on thy love, I charge thee.

IAGO. I do not know: friends all but now, even
now,

In quarter, and in terms like bride and groom;

And then, but now—

180 As if some planet had unwitted men—

Swords out, and tilting one at other's breast,

In opposition bloody. I cannot speak

Any beginning to this peevish odds;

And would in action glorious I had lost

These legs that brought me to a part of it!

OTHELLO. How comes it, Michael, you are thus
forgot?

172 *upon his motion*, the moment he moves.
174 *From her propriety*, from orderliness and self-control.
178 *In quarter*, the guardroom, officers' quarters.
186 *are thus forgot*, have so far forgotten yourself.

    Cassio. I pray you, pardon me ; I cannot speak.

    Othello. Worthy Montano, you were wont be civil ;

The gravity and stillness of your youth
190 The world hath noted, and your name is great
In mouths of wisest censure : what's the matter,
That you unlace your reputation thus
And spend your rich opinion for the name
Of a night-brawler ? give me answer to it.

    Montano. Worthy Othello, I am hurt to danger :
Your officer, Iago, can inform you—
While I spare speech, which something now offends me—
Of all that I do know : nor know I aught
By me that's said or done amiss this night,
200 Unless self-charity be sometimes a vice,
And to defend ourselves it be a sin
When violence assails us.

    Othello.   Now, by heaven,
My blood begins my safer guides to rule ;
And passion, having my best judgement collied,
Assays to lead the way : 'zounds, if I stir,
Or do but lift this arm, the best of you
Shall sink in my rebuke.   Give me to know
How this foul rout began, who set it on,
And he that is approv'd in this offence,
210 Though he had twinn'd with me, both at a birth,
Shall lose me.   What ? in a town of war,
Yet wild, the people's hearts brimful of fear,
To manage private and domestic quarrel,
In night, and on the court and guard of safety !
'Tis monstrous.   Iago, who began't ?

---

192 *unlace*, loosen, as if preparing to throw off a garment.
193 *spend your rich opinion*, barter the good opinion men have of you.
197 *now offends me*, causes me pain (because of his wound).
204 *collied*, blackened, obscured.   *Cf.* " collier."
213 *manage*, make occasion for.

MONTANO. If partially affin'd, or leagu'd in office,
Thou dost deliver more or less than truth,
Thou art no soldier.

IAGO.   Touch me not so near :
I had rather have this tongue cut from my mouth
220 Than it should do offence to Michael Cassio ;
Yet, I persuade myself, to speak the truth
Shall nothing wrong him.   Thus it is, general.
Montano and myself being in speech,
There comes a fellow crying out for help,
And Cassio following him with determin'd sword,
To execute upon him.   Sir, this gentleman
Steps in to Cassio, and entreats his pause :
Myself the crying fellow did pursue,
Lest by his clamour—as it so fell out—
230 The town might fall in fright : he, swift of foot,
Outran my purpose ; and I return'd the rather
For that I heard the clink and fall of swords,
And Cassio high in oath ; which till to-night
I ne'er might say before.   When I came back—
For this was brief—I found them close together,
At blow and thrust, even as again they were
When you yourself did part them.
More of this matter can I not report :
But men are men ; the best sometimes forget ;
240 Though Cassio did some little wrong to him,
As men in rage strike those that wish them best,
Yet surely Cassio, I believe, receiv'd
From him that fled some strange indignity,
Which patience could not pass.

OTHELLO.   I know, Iago,
Thy honesty and love doth mince this matter,
Making it light to Cassio.   Cassio, I love thee,
But never more be officer of mine.

216 *If partially affin'd . . . office,* if through partiality or loyalty to
    a fellow-officer.
246 *Cassio.* Note the change from the familiar "Michael"
    which Othello has previously used.

(*Re-enter* DESDEMONA, *attended.*)

Look, if my gentle love be not rais'd up !
I'll make thee an example.

    DESDEMONA.   What's the matter ?

250   OTHELLO. All's well now, sweeting ; come away to
        bed.

Sir, for your hurts, myself will be your surgeon :
Lead him off.   (*To* MONTANO, *who is led off.*)
Iago, look with care about the town,
And silence those whom this vile brawl distracted.
Come, Desdemona : 'tis the soldiers' life
To have their balmy slumbers wak'd with strife.

                (*Exeunt* ALL *but* IAGO *and* CASSIO.)

    IAGO. What, are you hurt, lieutenant ?

    CASSIO. Ay, past all surgery.

    IAGO. Marry, God forbid !

260   CASSIO. Reputation, reputation, reputation ! O, I
have lost my reputation ! I have lost the immortal
part of myself, and what remains is bestial. My
reputation, Iago, my reputation !

    IAGO. As I am an honest man, I thought you had
received some bodily wound ; there is more sense in
that than in reputation. Reputation is an idle and
most false imposition, oft got without merit, and lost
without deserving. You have lost no reputation at all,
unless you repute yourself such a loser. What, man !
270 there are ways to recover the general again : you are
but now cast in his mood, a punishment more in policy
than in malice ; even so as one would beat his offence-
less dog to affright an imperious lion : sue to him
again, and he's yours.

    CASSIO. I will rather sue to be despised than to

---

265 *sense*, sensibility, feeling.
267 *imposition*, something imposed on one by others.
271 *cast in his mood*, dismissed in anger.
272 *even so as one . . . lion*, as one punishes a harmless fellow in
      order to teach others a lesson; *i.e.* Othello had to show his
      authority before the men of Cyprus.

deceive so good a commander with so slight, so drunken, and so indiscreet an officer. Drunk? and speak parrot? and squabble? swagger? swear? and discourse fustian with one's own shadow? O thou invisible spirit of wine, if thou hast no name to be known by, let us call thee devil!

IAGO. What was he that you followed with your sword? What had he done to you?

CASSIO. I know not.

IAGO. Is't possible?

CASSIO. I remember a mass of things, but nothing distinctly; a quarrel, but nothing wherefore. O God, that men should put an enemy in their mouths to steal away their brains! that we should, with joy, pleasance, revel and applause, transform ourselves into beasts!

IAGO. Why, but you are now well enough: how came you thus recovered?

CASSIO. It hath pleased the devil drunkenness to give place to the devil wrath: one unperfectness shows me another, to make me frankly despise myself.

IAGO. Come, you are too severe a moraler: as the time, the place, and the condition of this country stands, I could heartily wish this had not befallen; but, since it is as it is, mend it for your own good.

CASSIO. I will ask him for my place again; he shall tell me I am a drunkard! Had I as many mouths as Hydra, such an answer would stop them all. To be now a sensible man, by and by a fool, and presently a beast! O strange! Every inordinate cup is unblessed and the ingredient is a devil.

IAGO. Come, come, good wine is a good familiar

---

277 *Drunk . . . shadow,* omitted in First Quarto.
279 *Discourse fustian,* talk in high-flown language meaning nothing.
304 *Hydra,* mythical monster with nine heads. The slaying of it was one of the labours of Hercules.

creature, if it be well used : exclaim no more against
310 it. And, good lieutenant, I think you think I love
you.

CASSIO. I have well approved it, sir. . . . I drunk !

IAGO. You or any man living may be drunk at
some time. I'll tell you what you shall do. Our
general's wife is now the general : I may say so in this
respect, for that he hath devoted and given up himself
to the contemplation, mark, and denotement of her
parts and graces. Confess yourself freely to her ; importune her help to put you in your place again. She
320 is of so free, so kind, so apt, so blessed a disposition,
she holds it a vice in her goodness not to do more than
she is requested. This broken joint between you and
her husband entreat her to splinter ; and, my fortunes against any lay worth naming, this crack of your
love shall grow stronger than it was before.

CASSIO. You advise me well.

IAGO. I protest, in the sincerity of love and honest
kindness.

CASSIO. I think it freely, and betimes in the morn-
330 ing I will beseech the virtuous Desdemona to undertake for me : I am desperate of my fortunes if they
check me here.

IAGO. You are in the right. Good night, lieutenant
I must to the watch.

CASSIO. Good night, honest Iago.   (*Exit.*)

IAGO. And what's he then that says I play the
villain,
When this advice is free I give and honest,
Probal to thinking and indeed the course
To win the Moor again ?   For 'tis most easy

---

312 *I have well approved it,* I have reason to believe so.
323 *splinter,* put in splints, metaphor from surgery. *Cf. Henry IV.
       Part II.,* IV. i. 222.
329 *I think it freely,* I sincerely think so.
338 *Probal to thinking,* logical. Iago takes an artistic delight in
       using details of truth to build up a horrible fiction.

The inclining Desdemona to subdue
In any honest suit : she's fram'd as fruitful
As the free elements.   And then for her
To win the Moor—were't to renounce his baptism,
All seals and symbols of redeemed sin—
His soul is so enfetter'd to her love,
That she may make, unmake, do what she list,
Even as her appetite shall play the god
With his weak function.   How am I then a villain
To counsel Cassio to this parallel course,
Directly to his good ?   Divinity of hell !
When devils will the blackest sins put on,
They do suggest at first with heavenly shows,
As I do now : for whiles this honest fool
Plies Desdemona to repair his fortunes,
And she for him pleads strongly to the Moor,
I'll pour this pestilence into his ear,
That she repeals him for her body's lust ;
And by how much she strives to do him good,
She shall undo her credit with the Moor.
So will I turn her virtue into pitch,
And out of her own goodness make the net
That shall enmesh them all.
                    (*Re-enter* RODERIGO.)
                                    How now, Roderigo ?
RODERIGO. I do follow here in the chase, not like

341 *fruitful*, bountiful.
347 *Even as her appetite . . . function*, whatever her caprice may
        dictate, it is tyrant over his will.
350 *Divinity of hell*, devil's theology, *i.e.* policy.
352 *They do suggest . . . heavenly shows*, first temptations are
        hidden under a guise of goodness. "The devil can cite
        Scripture for his purpose."
357 *repeals him*, reinstates Cassio. Iago now prepares to build
        the big lie.
360 *pitch*, double meaning : (i) black, defiling substance ;
        (ii) net cast or set for catching fish. (Murray's *New
        English Dictionary*.)
361 *her own goodness*, her kindness which will make her plead for
        Cassio.

a hound that hunts, but one that fills up the cry.
My money is almost spent ; I have been to-night
exceedingly well cudgelled ; and I think the issue will
be, I shall have so much experience for my pains,
and so, with no money at all and a little more wit,
return again to Venice.

370   Iago. How poor are they that have not patience !
What wound did ever heal but by degrees ?
Thou know'st we work by wit, and not by witchcraft ;
And wit depends on dilatory time.
Does't not go well ?   Cassio hath beaten thee,
And thou, by that small hurt, hast cashier'd Cassio :
Though other things grow fair against the sun,
Yet fruits that blossom first will first be ripe :
Content thyself awhile.   By the mass, 'tis morning ;
Pleasure and action make the hours seem short.
380 Retire thee ; go where thou are billeted :
Away, I say ; thou shalt know more hereafter :
Nay, get thee gone.   (*Exit* Roderigo.)   Two things
    are to be done :
My wife must move for Cassio to her mistress ;
I'll set her on.
Myself the while to draw the Moor apart,
And bring him jump when he may Cassio find
Soliciting his wife : ay, that's the way :
Dull not device by coldness and delay.   (*Exit.*)

364 *one that fills up the cry.* Certain hounds were kept only for
    the quality of their cry ; they were not in at the kill.
376 *Though other things . . . ripe,* though all our schemes prosper
    well enough, those which are first helped by opportunity
    will be the first to show results.
387 *bring him jump,* bring him at the exact time. See footnote on
    page 27.

ACT III

SCENE I.   *Before the castle.*

(*Enter* CASSIO *and some* Musicians.)

CASSIO. Masters, play here ; I will content your
   pains ;
Something that's brief ; and bid " Good morrow,
   general."   (*Music.*)

(*Enter* Clown.)

CLOWN. Why, masters, have your instruments been
in Naples, that they speak i' the nose thus ?

FIRST MUSICIAN. How, sir, how ?

CLOWN. Are these, I pray you, wind-instruments ?

FIRST MUSICIAN. Ay, marry, are they, sir.

CLOWN. O, thereby hangs a tale. But, masters,
here's money for you : and the general so likes your
music, that he desires you, for love's sake, to make
no more noise with it.

FIRST MUSICIAN. Well, sir, we will not.

CLOWN. If you have any music that may not be
heard, to't again : but, as they say, to hear music
the general does not greatly care.

FIRST MUSICIAN. We have none such, sir.

Before the castle, i.e. before Othello's *quarters in* the castle.
   Imagine a band of musicians serenading an officer " outside the Tower of London " ! See note to Scene ii. on
   page 71.

2 *Good morrow, general,* the aubade (dawn-song) was as cus-
   tomary as the serenade (evening song).

4 *speak i' the nose,* possibly alluding to the Neapolitan nasal
   accent. The instruments would be pipes, etc.

69

CLOWN. Then put up your pipes in your bag, for I'll away : go ; vanish into air ; away !

(Exeunt Musicians.)

CASSIO. Dost thou hear my honest friend ?

20 CLOWN. No, I hear not your honest friend ; I hear you.

CASSIO. Prithee, keep up thy quillets. There's a poor piece of gold for thee : if the gentlewoman that attends the general's wife be stirring, tell her there's one Cassio entreats her a little favour of speech : wilt thou do this ?

CLOWN. She is stirring, sir : if she will stir hither, I shall seem to notify unto her.

CASSIO. Do, good my friend.   (Exit Clown.)

(Enter IAGO.)

In happy time, Iago.

IAGO. You have not been a-bed, then ?

30 CASSIO. Why, no ; the day had broke
Before we parted.   I have made bold, Iago,
To send in to your wife : my suit to her
Is, that she will to virtuous Desdemona
Procure me some access.

IAGO.   I'll send her to you presently ;
And I'll devise a mean to draw the Moor
Out of the way, that your converse and business
May be more free.

CASSIO. I humbly thank you for't.   (Exit IAGO.)   I never knew
A Florentine more kind and honest.

(Enter EMILIA.)

40 EMILIA. Good morrow, good lieutenant : I am sorry

---

21 *keep up*, put away.
   quillets, quips and play on words, from Latin *quid libet*.
22 *poor*, modest.
34 *presently*, at once.
39 *Florentine*, see I. i. 20. Not even one of my own town could be kinder.

For your displeasure, but all will sure be well.
The general and his wife are talking of it,
And she speaks for you stoutly : the Moor
    replies,
That he you hurt is of great fame in Cyprus
And great affinity and that in wholesome wisdom
He might not but refuse you. But he protests he loves
    you,
And needs no other suitor but his likings
To take the safest occasion by the front
To bring you in again.

50   CASSIO.   Yet, I beseech you,
If you think fit, or that it may be done,
Give me advantage of some brief discourse
With Desdemona alone.

    EMILIA.   Pray you, come in :
I will bestow you where you shall have time
To speak your bosom freely.

    CASSIO.   I am much bound to you.
                               (*Exeunt.*)

SCENE II.   *A room in the castle.*

(*Enter* OTHELLO, IAGO, *and* Gentlemen.)
    OTHELLO. These letters give, Iago, to the pilot ;
And by him do my duties to the senate :
That done, I will be walking on the works ;

41 *your displeasure,* your misfortune.
45 *great affinity,* well connected.
46 *He might not but refuse you,* he cannot help refusing you.
Scenes i. and ii. Stage directions. There is no reason for any
    change of place or break of scene, even on the modern
    stage. If Scene i. is played on the fore-stage, as if in front
    of Othello's quarters, it is conceivable that Iago goes in to
    get his morning's orders from the general and both come out
    together. *Scene iii.* then opens on the full stage, exact place
    not specified. There is nothing in the text to warrant
    " garden."

Repair there to me.

IAGO.   Well, my good lord, I'll do't.

OTHELLO. This fortification, gentlemen, shall we
    see't ?

GENTLEMEN. We'll wait upon your lordship.

                                        (*Exeunt.*)

SCENE III.   *The garden of the castle.*

(*Enter* DESDEMONA, CASSIO, *and* EMILIA.)

DESDEMONA. Be thou assured, good Cassio, I will do
All my abilities in thy behalf.

EMILIA. Good madam, do : I know it grieves my
    husband,
As if the case were his.

DESDEMONA. O, that's an honest fellow. Do not
    doubt, Cassio,
But I will have my lord and you again
As friendly as you were.

CASSIO.   Bounteous madam,
Whatever shall become of Michael Cassio,
He's never any thing but your true servant.

10   DESDEMONA. I know't ; I thank you. You do love
    my lord,
You have known him long, and be you well assur'd
He shall in strangeness stand no further off
Than in a politic distance.

CASSIO.   Ay, but, lady,
That policy may either last so long,
Or feed upon such nice and waterish diet,
Or breed itself so out of circumstance,
That, I being absent and my place supplied,
My general will forget my love and service.

---

3 *it grieves my husband,* a clue to Emilia's share in the plot. Iago
    has obviously been at work on her, too, and has deceived
    her into crediting his good intentions.
12 *He shall in strangeness . . . distance,* his coldness to you shall be
    no more than policy demands.

DESDEMONA. Do not doubt that ; before Emilia here
I give thee warrant of thy place ; assure thee,
If I do vow a friendship, I'll perform it
To the last article.   My lord shall never rest ;
I'll watch him tame and talk him out of patience ;
His bed shall seem a school, his board a shrift ;
I'll intermingle everything he does
With Cassio's suit : therefore be merry, Cassio ;
For thy solicitor shall rather die
Than give thy cause away.

(Enter OTHELLO and IAGO at a distance.)

EMILIA. Madam, here comes my lord.

CASSIO. Madam, I'll take my leave.

DESDEMONA. Why, stay, and hear me speak.

CASSIO. Madam, not now : I am very ill at ease,
Unfit for mine own purpose.

DESDEMONA. Well, do your discretion.

(Exit CASSIO.)

IAGO. Ha ! I like not that.

OTHELLO.   What dost thou say ?

IAGO. Nothing, my lord, or if—I know not what.

OTHELLO. Was not that Cassio parted from my wife ?

IAGO. Cassio, my lord ? No, sure, I cannot think it,
That he would steal away so guilty-like,
Seeing you coming.

OTHELLO.   I do believe 'twas he.

DESDEMONA. How now, my lord !
I have been talking with a suitor here,
A man that languishes in your displeasure.

OTHELLO. Who is't you mean ?

DESDEMONA. Why, your lieutenant, Cassio.   Good my lord,

---

23 *watch him tame*, metaphor from hawking.   Wild hawks were
    tamed by keeping them awake.   *Cf.* Petruchio's methods
    with Katharina, *Taming of the Shrew*.
24 *his board a shrift*, meal-times a penance.

73

If I have any grace or power to move you,
His present reconciliation take ;
For if he be not one that truly loves you,
That errs in ignorance and not in cunning,
50 I have no judgement in an honest face :
I prithee, call him back.
    Othello.   Went he hence now ?
    Desdemona. Ay, sooth ; so humbled
That he hath left part of his grief with me,
To suffer with him.   Good love, call him back.
    Othello. Not now, sweet Desdemona ; some other
    time.
    Desdemona. But shall't be shortly ?
    Othello.   The sooner, sweet, for you.
    Desdemona. Shall't be to-night at supper ?
    Othello.   No, not to-night.
    Desdemona. To-morrow dinner, then ?
    Othello.   I shall not dine at home ;
I meet the captains at the citadel.
60   Desdemona. Why, then, to-morrow night ; or
    Tuesday morn ;
On Tuesday noon, or night ; on Wednesday morn ;
I prithee, name the time, but let it not
Exceed three days : in faith, he's penitent ;
And yet his trespass, in our common reason—
Save that, they say, the wars must make examples
Out of their best—is not almost a fault
To incur a private check.   When shall he come ?
Tell me, Othello : I wonder in my soul,
What you would ask me, that I should deny,
70 Or stand so mammering on.   What ! Michael
    Cassio ?
That came a-wooing with you, and so many a time,

47 *His present reconciliation take*, forgive him now.
65 *wars must make examples . . . check*, were it not that military
    discipline demands his punishment, his fault would not
    deserve even private censure.
70 *mammering*, hesitating.

When I have spoke of you dispraisingly,
Hath ta'en your part, to have so much to do
To bring him in ? By'r lady, I could do much—

   OTHELLO. Prithee, no more : let him come when
    he will,
I will deny thee nothing.

   DESDEMONA.   Why, this is not a boon ;
'Tis as I should entreat you wear your gloves,
Or feed on nourishing dishes, or keep you warm,
Or sue to you to do a peculiar profit
To your own person : nay, when I have a suit
Wherein I mean to touch your love indeed,
It shall be full of poise and difficult weight
And fearful to be granted.

   OTHELLO.   I will deny thee nothing :
Whereon, I do beseech thee, grant me this,
To leave me but a little to myself.

   DESDEMONA. Shall I deny you ? no : farewell, my
    lord.

   OTHELLO. Farewell, my Desdemona, I'll come
    to thee straight.

   DESDEMONA. Emilia, come. Be as your fancies teach
    you ;
Whate'er you be, I am obedient.
                (*Exeunt* DESDEMONA *and* EMILIA.)

90   OTHELLO. Excellent wretch ! Perdition catch my
    soul,
But I do love thee, and when I love thee not,
Chaos is come again.

   IAGO. My noble lord,—

---

76 *Why, this is not a boon.* Throughout this speech Desdemona
    is playing straight into Iago's hand.
79 *peculiar*, relating to himself.
90 *wretch*, half-humorous endearment. *Cf.* "rogue," "you little
    rascal."
91 *and when I love thee not* . . . An ominous speech. Moulton
    places here the turning point of the play : "The tide of
    Othello's love has reached the height, and from here the
    ebb begins."

OTHELLO.　　　　　　　What dost thou say, Iago ?

IAGO. Did Michael Cassio, when you woo'd my lady,

Know of your love ?

OTHELLO. He did, from first to last : . . . why dost thou ask ?

IAGO. But for a satisfaction of my thought ;

No further harm.

OTHELLO.　　　　　Why of thy thought, Iago ?

IAGO. I did not think he had been acquainted with her.

100　OTHELLO. O yes ; and went between us very oft.

IAGO. Indeed !

OTHELLO. Indeed ! ay, indeed : discern'st thou aught in that ?

Is he not honest ?

IAGO.　　　　　　Honest, my lord ?

OTHELLO.　　　　　　　　Honest ! ay, honest.

IAGO. My lord, for aught I know.

OTHELLO. What dost thou think ?

IAGO.　　　　　　　　　　Think, my lord ?

OTHELLO. Think, my lord ! By heaven, he echoes me,

As if there were some monster in his thought

Too hideous to be shown. Thou dost mean something :

I heard thee say even now, thou lik'st not that,

110　When Cassio left my wife : what didst not like ?

And when I told thee he was of my counsel

In my whole course of wooing, thou criedst "Indeed !"

And didst contract and purse thy brow together,

As if thou then hadst shut up in thy brain

Some horrible conceit : if thou dost love me,

Show me thy thought.

IAGO. My lord, you know I love you.

---

115 *conceit*, idea, conception.

OTHELLO.   I think thou dost ;
And, for I know thou'rt full of love and honesty,
And weigh'st thy words before thou giv'st them
    breath,
Therefore these stops of thine fright me the more :
For such things in a false disloyal knave
Are tricks of custom ; but in a man that's just
They're close dilations, working from the heart
That passion cannot rule.
        IAGO.   For Michael Cassio,
I dare be sworn I think that he is honest.
        OTHELLO. I think so too.
        IAGO.   Men should be what they seem ;
Or those that be not, would they might seem none !
        OTHELLO. Certain, men should be what they seem.
        IAGO. Why, then, I think Cassio's an honest man.
        OTHELLO. Nay, yet there's more in this.
I prithee, speak to me as to thy thinkings,
As thou dost ruminate, and give the worst of thought
The worst of word.
        IAGO.   Good my lord, pardon me :
Though I am bound to every act of duty,
I am not bound to that all slaves are free to.
Utter my thoughts ? Why, say they are vile and
    false ;
As where's that palace whereinto foul things
Sometimes intrude not ? who has a breast so pure,
But some uncleanly apprehensions
Keep leets and law-days and in session sit
With meditations lawful ?

121 *false disloyal knave.* Note the dramatic irony.
123 *close dilations . . . cannot rule,* instinctive hesitations (*cf.*
    Latin *dilationes*) that come from genuine affection, un-
    stirred by prejudice or self-interest. First Quarto reads
    " denotements."
139 *uncleanly apprehensions . . . meditations lawful,* illicit thoughts
    occupy " the bench " alongside righteous judgments.
140 *Keep leets and law-days.* Cf. Sonnet 30, " When to the sessions
    of sweet silent thought." (*leet* = a citizens' court of justice.)

OTHELLO. Thou dost conspire against thy friend,
    Iago,
If thou but think'st him wrong'd and mak'st his
    ear
A stranger to thy thoughts.
    IAGO.   I do beseech you—
Though I perchance am vicious in my guess,
As, I confess, it is my nature's plague
To spy into abuses, and oft my jealousy
Shapes faults that are not—I entreat you then,
From one that so imperfectly conjects,
150 You'ld take no notice, nor build yourself a trouble
Out of my scattering and unsure observance.
It were not for your quiet nor your good,
Nor for my manhood, honesty, or wisdom,
To let you know my thoughts.
    OTHELLO.   'Zounds !
    IAGO. Good name in man and woman, dear my
        lord,
Is the immediate jewel of our souls :
Who steals my purse steals trash ; 'tis something,
    nothing ;
'Twas mine, 'tis his, and has been slave to thousands ;
But he that filches from me my good name
160 Robs me of that which not enriches him
And makes me poor indeed.
    OTHELLO. By heaven, I'll know thy thoughts.
    IAGO. You cannot, if my heart were in your hand ;
Nor shall not, whilst 'tis in my custody.
    OTHELLO. Ha !
    IAGO.   O beware, my lord, of jealousy ;
It is the green-eyed monster which doth mock
The meat it feeds on : that cuckold lives in bliss

163 *if my heart . . . hand.* Probably in reply to a threatening move
    of Othello's hand to his dagger. The Elizabethan would
    be as quick on the draw as a modern gangster with his
    gun. " If you cut out my heart it will tell you nothing."
    Othello's " Ha ! " is one of impatience at the cool reply.

Who, certain of his fate, loves not his wronger ;
But, O what damned minutes tells he o'er
70 Who dotes, yet doubts, suspects, yet strongly loves !
    OTHELLO. O misery !
    IAGO. Poor and content is rich, and rich enough,
But riches fineless is as poor as winter
To him that ever fears he shall be poor.
Good God, the souls of all my tribe defend
From jealousy !
    OTHELLO.   Why, why is this ?
Think'st thou I'ld make a life of jealousy,
To follow still the changes of the moon
With fresh suspicions ? No, to be once in doubt
80 Is once to be resolv'd : exchange me for a goat,
When I shall turn the business of my soul
To such exsufflicate and blown surmises,
Matching thy inference. 'Tis not to make me jealous
To say my wife is fair, feeds well, loves company,
Is free of speech, sings, plays and dances well ;
Where virtue is, these are more virtuous :
Nor from mine own weak merits will I draw
The smallest fear or doubt of her revolt ;
For she had eyes, and chose me. No, Iago ;
190 I'll see before I doubt ; when I doubt, prove,
And on the proof, there is no more but this :
Away at once with love or jealousy !
    IAGO. I am glad of it ; for now I shall have reason
To show the love and duty that I bear you
With franker spirit. Therefore, as I am bound,

168 *certain of his fate . . . strongly loves.* The man who knows he
    is betrayed, but does not love his wife, is happy ; but
    what misery for one who loves his wife and merely
    suspects her.
172 *fineless,* endless.
179 *once in doubt . . . resolv'd,* once my suspicions are aroused I
    lose no time before ascertaining the truth.
182 *exsufflicate,* inflated.
190 *I'll see before I doubt.* The whole of this speech is important
    in its revealing of Othello's character.

Receive it from me.   I speak not yet of proof.
Look to your wife, observe her well with Cassio,
Wear your eye thus, not jealous nor secure :
I would not have your free and noble nature,
200 Out of self-bounty, be abused ; look to't :
I know our country disposition well ;
In Venice they do let God see the pranks
They dare not show their husbands ; their best con-
     science
Is not to leave't undone, but keep't unknown.

OTHELLO. Dost thou say so ?

IAGO. She did deceive her father, marrying you ;
And when she seem'd to shake and fear your looks,
She loved them most.

OTHELLO.   And so she did.

IAGO.   Why, go to then ;
She that, so young, could give out such a seeming,
210 To seel her father's eyes up close as oak,
He thought 'twas witchcraft—But I am much to
     blame ;
I humbly do beseech you of your pardon
For too much loving you.

OTHELLO.   .   I am bound to thee for ever.

IAGO. I see this hath a little dash'd your spirits.

OTHELLO. Not a jot, not a jot.

IAGO.   I' faith, I fear it has.
I hope you will consider what is spoke
Comes from my love.   But I do see you're moved.
I am to pray you not to strain my speech
To grosser issues nor to larger reach
220 Than to suspicion.

200 *self-bounty*, because of its own good nature.
201 *our country disposition*, the character of our Venetian women.
203 *their best conscience . . . keep't unknown.*   The only command-
     ment they respect : Thou shalt not be found out.
210 *close as oak*, as closely grained as oak.
211 *He thought 'twas witchcraft*, she deceived him so completely that
     he thought it was witchcraft.   Iago cleverly leaves the sen-
     tence unfinished.

OTHELLO. I will not.

IAGO. Should you do so, my lord,
My speech should fall into such vile success
As my thoughts aim not at. Cassio's my worthy
    friend—
My lord, I see you're mov'd.

OTHELLO. No, not much mov'd :
I do not think but Desdemona's honest.

IAGO. Long live she so ! and long live you to think
    so !

OTHELLO. And yet, how nature erring from itself—

IAGO. Ay, there's the point : as—to be bold with
    you—
Not to affect many proposed matches
30 Of her own clime, complexion, and degree,
Whereto we see in all things nature tends—
Foh ! one may smell in such a will most rank,
Foul disproportion, thoughts unnatural.
But pardon me ; I do not in position
Distinctly speak of her ; though I may fear
Her will, recoiling to her better judgement,
May fall to match you with her country forms
And happily repent.

OTHELLO. Farewell, farewell :
If more thou dost perceive, let me know more ;
40 Set on thy wife to observe : leave me, Iago.

IAGO (going). My lord, I take my leave.

OTHELLO. Why did I marry ? This honest creature
    doubtless
Sees and knows more, much more, than he unfolds.

IAGO (returning). My lord, I would I might entreat
    your honour

222 *vile success*, unfortunate consequences.
229 *Not to affect . . . clime*, to have no inclination for suitors of
    her own country.
234 *I do not in position . . . her*, I do not in this particular instance
    refer definitely to Desdemona.
237 *fall to match you with her country forms*, compare you with those
    of her own country. 238 *happily*, haply, by chance.

To scan this thing no further ; leave it to time.
Though it be fit that Cassio have his place,
For, sure, he fills it up with great ability,
Yet, if you please to hold him off awhile,
You shall by that perceive him and his means :
250 Note, if your lady strain his entertainment
With any strong or vehement importunity ;
Much will be seen in that.   In the mean time,
Let me be thought too busy in my fears—
As worthy cause I have to fear I am—
And hold her free, I do beseech your honour.
   OTHELLO. Fear not my government.
   IAGO. I once more take my leave.   (*Exit.*)
   OTHELLO. This fellow's of exceeding honesty,
And knows all qualities, with a learned spirit,
260 Of human dealings.   If I do prove her haggard,
Though that her jesses were my dear heart-strings,
I'ld whistle her off and let her down the wind,
To prey at fortune.   Haply, for I am black
And have not those soft parts of conversation
That chamberers have, or for I am declin'd
Into the vale of years—yet that's not much—
She's gone.   I am abus'd ; and my relief
Must be to loathe her.   O curse of marriage,
That we can call these delicate creatures ours,

249 *and his means*, what means he will use to gain reinstatement.
250 *strain his entertainment*, persuade you to receive him.
255 *hold her free*, consider her innocent.
256 *government*, discretion.
260 *haggard . . . jesses*, sustained metaphor from falconry. A
    haggard was an untamed hawk ; *jesses*, two narrow strips
    of leather fastened one to each leg, the other ends attached
    to a swivel from which depended the lead ; when the hawk
    was flown, swivel and leash were broken off, but the jesses
    went with the bird.
262 *down the wind*, when a hawk flew " down the wind," *i.e.* with
    the wind behind her, she seldom returned.
265 *chamberer*, lady's man, *cf.* modern " lounge lizard."
267 *I am abus'd*, in spite of his protestations to Iago, Othello
    already half believes, without proof.

70 And not their appetites !   I had rather be a toad,
And live upon the vapour in a dungeon,
Than keep a corner in a thing I love
For others' uses. Yet, 'tis the plague of great ones ;
Prerogativ'd are they less than the base ;
'Tis destiny unshunnable, like death :
Even then this forked plague is fated to us
When we do quicken.   Desdemona comes :
            (*Re-enter* DESDEMONA *and* EMILIA.)
If she be false, O then heaven mocks itself !
I'll not believe't.

    DESDEMONA.   How now, my dear Othello !
80 Your dinner, and the generous islanders
By you invited, do attend your presence.

    OTHELLO. I am to blame.

    DESDEMONA.   Why do you speak so faintly ?
Are you not well ?

    OTHELLO. I have a pain upon my forehead here.

    DESDEMONA. 'Faith, that's with watching ; 'twill
      away again :
Let me but bind it hard, within this hour
It will be well.

    OTHELLO.   Your napkin is too little :
            (*He puts the handkerchief from him ; and it drops.*)
Let it alone. Come, I'll go in with you.

    DESDEMONA. I am very sorry that you are not well.
                    (*Exeunt* OTHELLO *and* DESDEMONA.)

290   EMILIA. I am glad I have found this napkin :
This was her first remembrance from the Moor :
My wayward husband hath a hundred times
Woo'd me to steal it ; but she so loves the token,

275 *Prerogativ'd . . . less than the base*, more open to such abuses
    than a poor man.
280 *generous*, well-born.
287 *Your napkin is too little*, *i.e.* her attentions cannot mend his
    real pain.
292 *wayward*, capricious. At least, so he seemed to Emilia to
    whom he did not reveal his motives.

83

For he conjur'd her she should ever keep it,
That she reserves it evermore about her
To kiss and talk to. I'll have the work ta'en out,
And give't Iago : what he will do with it
Heaven knows, not I ;
I nothing but to please his fantasy.

(Re-enter IAGO.)

300 IAGO. How now ! what do you here alone ?

EMILIA. Do not you chide ; I have a thing for
you.

IAGO. A thing for me ? It is a common thing—

EMILIA. Ha !

IAGO. To have a foolish wife.

EMILIA. O, is that all ? What will you give me
now
For that same handkerchief ?

IAGO.   What handkerchief ?

EMILIA. What handkerchief !
Why, that the Moor first gave to Desdemona ;
That which so often you did bid me steal.

310 IAGO. Hast stol'n it from her ?

EMILIA. No, 'faith ; she let it drop by negligence,
And, to the advantage, I, being here, took't up.
Look, here it is.

IAGO.   A good wench ; give it me.

EMILIA. What will you do with't, that you have
been
So earnest to have me filch it ?

IAGO *(snatching it)*. Why, what's that to you ?

EMILIA. If it be not for some purpose of import,
Give't me again : poor lady, she'll run mad
When she shall lack it.

IAGO. Be not acknown on't ; I have use for it.
320 Go, leave me.   *(Exit EMILIA.)*

---

296 *the work ta'en out*, the pattern copied. Notice Shakespeare's
careful pointing of Emilia's innocence.

312 *to the advantage*, by good luck.

320 *Be not acknown on't*. Pretend to know nothing about it.

84

I will in Cassio's lodging lose this napkin,
And let him find it.   Trifles light as air
Are to the jealous confirmations strong
As proofs of holy writ.   This may do something.
The Moor already changes with my poison :
Dangerous conceits are, in their natures, poisons,
Which at the first are scarce found to distaste,
But with a little act upon the blood
30 Burn like the mines of sulphur.   I did say so :
Look, where he comes !

(Re-enter OTHELLO.)

                           Not poppy, nor mandragora,
Nor all the drowsy syrups of the world,
Shall ever medicine thee to that sweet sleep
Which thou ow'dst yesterday.

    OTHELLO   Ha ! ha ! false to me, to me ?

    IAGO. Why, how now, general ! no more of that.

    OTHELLO. Avaunt ! be gone ! thou hast set me
      on the rack :
I swear 'tis better to be much abus'd
Than but to know't a little.

    IAGO.   How now, my lord !

    OTHELLO. What sense had I of her stol'n hours of
      lust ?
340 I saw't not, thought it not, it harm'd not me :
I slept the next night well, was free and merry ;
I found not Cassio's kisses on her lips :
He that is robb'd, not wanting what is stol'n,
Let him not know't, and he's not robb'd at all.

    IAGO. I am sorry to hear this.

326 *The Moor . . . poison.*   Omitted in First Quarto.
329 *with a little act,* after short action.
330 *I did say so.*   What did I tell you ?
331 *mandragora,* mandrake.   Referring to its use as a soporific.
    Cf. *Antony and Cleopatra* :
        " Give me to drink mandragora
          That I might sleep out this great gap of time——"
334 *ow'dst,* didst own.
339 *sense,* feelings.   I felt no disgrace when I knew nothing of it.

85

OTHELLO.   O now, for ever
Farewell the tranquil mind ! farewell content !
Farewell the plumed troop, and the big wars
That make ambition virtue !   O farewell !
Farewell the neighing steed, and the shrill trump,
350 The spirit-stirring drum, the ear-piercing fife,
The royal banner, and all quality,
Pride, pomp and circumstance of glorious war !
And, O you mortal engines, whose wide throats
The immortal Jove's dread clamour counterfeit,
Farewell !   Othello's occupation's gone !
    IAGO. Is't possible, my lord ?
    OTHELLO. Villain, be sure thou prove my love a
        whore,
Be sure of it, give me the ocular proof ;
Or, by the worth of man's eternal soul,
360 Thou hadst been better have been born a dog
Than answer my wak'd wrath !
    IAGO.   Is't come to this ?
    OTHELLO. Make me to see't ; or, at the least, so
        prove it,
That the probation bear no hinge nor loop
To hang a doubt on ; or woe upon thy life !
    IAGO. My noble lord,—
    OTHELLO. If thou dost slander her and torture me,
Never pray more ; abandon all remorse ;
On horror's head horrors accumulate ;
Do deeds to make heaven weep, all earth amaz'd ;
370 For nothing canst thou to damnation add
Greater than that.
    IAGO.   O grace ! O heaven forgive me !
Are you a man ? have you a soul or sense ?
God be wi' you ; take mine office. O wretched fool,

353 *mortal engines*, deadly instruments.
    wide throats, Folio gives " rude throats."
363 *probation*, evidence.
370 *For nothing canst thou to damnation add*, you can do nothing
    that more deserves damnation.
373 *O wretched fool*, apostrophizing himself.

That livest to make thine honesty a vice !
O monstrous world ! Take note, take note, O world,
To be direct and honest is not safe.
I thank you for this profit ; and from hence
I'll love no friend, sith love breeds such offence.

> (IAGO *moves as if to go out.*)

OTHELLO. Nay, stay : thou shouldst be honest.
380 IAGO. I should be wise, for honesty's a fool
And loses that it works for.
OTHELLO.   By the world,
I think my wife be honest and think she is not ;
I think that thou art just and think thou art not.
I'll have some proof.   Her name, that was as fresh
As Dian's visage, is now begrim'd and black
As mine own face.   If there be cords, or knives,
Poison, or fire, or suffocating streams,
I'll not endure it.   Would I were satisfied !
IAGO. I see, sir, you are eaten up with passion :
390 I do repent me that I put it to you.
You would be satisfied ?
OTHELLO.   Would ? nay, I will.
IAGO. And may : but, how ? how satisfied, my
    lord ?
It is impossible you should see this,
Were they as prime as goats, as hot as monkeys,
As salt as wolves in pride, and fools as gross
As ignorance made drunk.   But yet, I say,
If imputation and strong circumstances,

377 *this profit*, this lesson.
378 *hence . . . offence*, note finality of rhyme, to give impression that
    he is indeed leaving Othello.
379 *shouldst be honest*, as far as I can tell, you are honest.   Iago
    slightly changes meaning in his reply.
382 *be honest . . . is.* "Be" implies some doubt, "is" is em-
    phatic.   Notice the extra syllable in an important line.
    In these two lines Othello sums up his dilemma.   He is
    not yet jealous, but is tortured by the idea of jealousy.
    The whole of this speech is omitted in First Quarto.
388 *satisfied*, made certain of the truth (not revenged).

Which lead directly to the door of truth,
Will give you satisfaction, you may have't.

400   OTHELLO. Give me a living reason she's disloyal.
    IAGO. I do not like the office,
But, sith I am enter'd in this cause so far,
Prick'd to't by foolish honesty and love,
I will go on. I lay with Cassio lately ;
And, being troubled with a raging tooth,
I could not sleep.
There are a kind of men so loose of soul,
That in their sleeps will mutter their affairs ;
One of this kind is Cassio :
410 In sleep I heard him say " Sweet Desdemona,
Let us be wary, let us hide our loves ; "
And then, sir, would he gripe and wring my hand,
Cry " O sweet creature ! " and then kiss me hard,
As if he pluck'd up kisses by the roots
That grew upon my lips ; and sigh'd, and then
Cried " Cursed fate that gave thee to the Moor ! "
    OTHELLO. O monstrous ! monstrous !
    IAGO.   Nay, this was but his dream.
    OTHELLO. But this denoted a foregone conclusion :
    IAGO. 'Tis a shrewd doubt, though it be but a
    dream.
420 And this may help to thicken other proofs
That do demonstrate thinly.
    OTHELLO.   I'll tear her all to pieces.
    IAGO. Nay, but be wise : yet we see nothing done ;
She may be honest yet. Tell me but this,
Have you not sometimes seen a handkerchief

---

400 *living reason*, visible proof.
407 *so loose of soul*, incapable of keeping their thoughts to them-
    selves.
410 *In sleep I heard him.* Note the corroborative detail. Iago
    lies with imagination and artistry.
418 *a foregone conclusion*, something that had happened before.
419 *'Tis a shrewd doubt, . . . dream.* Folio and Second Quarto
    give this line to Othello.
420 *thicken other proofs*, support more slender evidence.

Spotted with strawberries in your wife's hand ?

   OTHELLO. I gave her such a one ; 'twas my first
     gift.

   IAGO. I know not that : but such a handkerchief—
I am sure it was your wife's—did I to-day
See Cassio wipe his beard with.

   OTHELLO.   If it be that—

   IAGO. If it be that, or any that was hers,
It speaks against her with the other proofs.

   OTHELLO. O that the slave had forty thousand
     lives !

One is too poor, too weak for my revenge.
Now do I see 'tis true. Look here, Iago ;
All my fond love thus do I blow to heaven.
'Tis gone.
Arise, black vengeance, from thy hollow cell !
Yield up, O love, thy crown and hearted throne
To tyrannous hate ! Swell, bosom, with thy fraught,
For 'tis of aspics' tongues !

   IAGO.   Yet be content.

   OTHELLO. O, blood, Iago, blood !

   IAGO. Patience, I say ; your mind perhaps may
     change.

   OTHELLO. Never, Iago. Like to the Pontic sea,
Whose icy current and compulsive course
Ne'er feels retiring ebb, but keeps due on
To the Propontic and the Hellespont,

---

434 *Now do I see 'tis true.* But Othello has not yet had the ocular
    proof he demanded.   Note that Iago is too clever to be
    satisfied until he *has* given such " proof " to Othello.

438 *hearted*, secure.

439 *fraught*, freight.

440 *aspic*, poisonous asp.

443-450 omitted in First Quarto.

443 *Pontic sea, cf.* translation of Pliny's *Natural History*, published
    1601 : " The Sea Pontus [*i.e.* the Black Sea] ever floweth
    and runneth out into Propontis [the Sea of Marmora],
    but the sea never retireth back again within Pontus."

446 *Hellespont*, the Dardanelles.

Even so my bloody thoughts, with violent pace,
Shall ne'er look back, ne'er ebb to humble love,
Till that a capable and wide revenge
450 Swallow them up.   Now, by yond marble heaven,
(*Kneels.*) In the due reverence of a sacred vow
I here engage my words.
      Iago.   Do not rise yet.
(*Kneels.*) Witness, you ever-burning lights above,
You elements that clip us round about,
Witness that here Iago doth give up
The execution of his wit, heart, hand,
To wrong'd Othello's service ! Let him command,
And to obey shall be in me remorse,
What bloody business ever.   (*They rise.*)
      Othello.   I greet thy love,
460 Not with vain thanks, but with acceptance bounteous,
And will upon the instant put thee to't :
Within these three days let me hear thee say
That Cassio's not alive.
      Iago. My friend is dead ; 'tis done at your request:
But let her live.
      Othello.   O damn her !
Come, go with me apart ; I will withdraw,
To furnish me with some swift means of death
For the fair devil.   Now art thou my lieutenant.
      Iago. I am your own for ever.   (*Exeunt.*)

---

449 *capable*, comprehensive, including both culprits.
    Iago kneels. Note that the terms of Iago's vow are more
      exact than those of Othello.
458 *remorse*, a point of conscience.
465 *But let her live.* Iago knows that Othello is in the mood for
      immediate action.   To press for a decision at such a
      moment was to assure Desdemona's sharing Cassio's fate.
468 *Now art thou my lieutenant.* Iago has now attained the pur-
      pose he first gave for his plot against Cassio.

SCENE IV.   *Before the castle.*

(*Enter* DESDEMONA, EMILIA, *and* Clown.)

DESDEMONA. Do you know, sirrah, where Lieutenant Cassio lies?

CLOWN. I dare not say he lies any where.

DESDEMONA. Why, man?

CLOWN. He's a soldier, and for one to say a soldier lies, is stabbing.

DESDEMONA. Go to: where lodges he?

CLOWN. To tell you where he lodges, is to tell you where I lie.

10 DESDEMONA. Can anything be made of this?

CLOWN. I know not where he lodges, and for me to devise a lodging and say he lies here or he lies there, were to lie in mine own throat.

DESDEMONA. Can you inquire him out, and be edified by report?

CLOWN. I will catechize the world for him; that is, make questions, and by them answer.

DESDEMONA. Seek him, bid him come hither: tell him I have moved my lord on his behalf, and 20 hope all will be well.

CLOWN. To do this is within the compass of man's wit, and therefore I will attempt the doing it. (*Exit.*)

DESDEMONA. Where should I lose that handkerchief, Emilia?

EMILIA. I know not, madam.

DESDEMONA. Believe me, I had rather have lost my purse Full of crusadoes: and, but my noble Moor

19 *tell him I have moved my lord, etc.* Even in this comedy scene Shakespeare wastes no time. Desdemona's message to Cassio keeps the audience in mind of the fate awaiting her.

26 *crusadoes,* a crusado was a Portuguese coin with a cross on it; worth about five shillings.

Is true of mind and made of no such baseness
As jealous creatures are, it were enough
To put him to ill thinking.

 EMILIA.   Is he not jealous?

30 DESDEMONA. Who, he? I think the sun where he
  was born
Drew all such humours from him.

 EMILIA.   Look, where he comes.

 DESDEMONA. I will not leave him now till Cassio
Be call'd to him.

     (Enter OTHELLO.)
     How is't with you, my lord?

 OTHELLO. Well, my good lady. *(Aside)* O, hardness to dissemble!—
How do you, Desdemona?

 DESDEMONA.   Well, my good lord.

 OTHELLO. Give me your hand: this hand is
  moist, my lady.

 DESDEMONA. It yet hath felt no age nor known no
  sorrow.

 OTHELLO. This argues fruitfulness and liberal
  heart:
Hot, hot, and moist: this hand of yours requires

40 A sequester from liberty; fasting and prayer,
Much castigation, exercise devout;
For here's a young and sweating devil here,
That commonly rebels. 'Tis a good hand,
A frank one.

 DESDEMONA.   You may, indeed, say so;
For 'twas that hand that gave away my heart.

31 *humours,* pun on the two meanings of character and moisture.
36 *this hand is moist,* a hot moist palm was supposed to denote
  sensual desires.
38 *fruitfulness and liberal heart. Cf.* note on p. 67, but Othello
  now means both this and "liberal" in a bad sense, *i.e.*
  loose, too free.
40 *sequester from liberty,* separation from liberty, *i.e.* captivity.
43 *'Tis a good hand, a frank one,* a plain hand to read. Desdemona misunderstands him.

OTHELLO. A liberal hand : the hearts of old gave
    hands ;
But our new heraldry is hands, not hearts.

DESDEMONA. I cannot speak of this. Come now,
    your promise.

OTHELLO. What promise, chuck ?

50 DESDEMONA. I have sent to bid Cassio come speak
    with you.

OTHELLO. I have a salt and sorry rheum offends
    me ;
Lend me thy handkerchief.

DESDEMONA.   Here, my lord.

OTHELLO. That which I gave you.

DESDEMONA.   I have it not about me.

OTHELLO. Not ?

DESDEMONA.   No, indeed, my lord.

OTHELLO.   That is a fault.
That handkerchief
Did an Egyptian to my mother give ;
She was a charmer, and could almost read
The thoughts of people : she told her, while she
    kept it,
'Twould make her amiable and subdue my father
60 Entirely to her love ; but if she lost it
Or made a gift of it, my father's eye
Should hold her loathed and his spirits should hunt
After new fancies : she, dying, gave it me ;
And bid me, when my fate would have me wive,
To give it her. I did so : and take heed on't ;

47 *hands, not hearts*, nowadays women give only their hands
    and not their hearts. Reference to heraldry is obscure.
    Probably inserted as a "topical gag" in 1611 when
    James I. inaugurated "a new dignitie between Barons and
    Knights." The holder was entitled to display the Red
    Hand of Ulster on his coat of arms.

55-75. Here Shakespeare gives us a short sample of
    Othello's story-telling which had first fascinated Desde-
    mona. *Cf.* V. ii. 219.

65 *To give it her, i.e.* to the woman I loved.

Make it a darling like your precious eye ;
To lose't or give't away were such perdition
As nothing else could match.

   DESDEMONA.   Is't possible ?

   OTHELLO. 'Tis true : there's magic in the web of it :
70 A sibyl, that had number'd in the world
The sun to course two hundred compasses,
In her prophetic fury sew'd the work ;
The worms were hallow'd that did breed the silk ;
And it was dyed in mummy which the skilful
Conserve of maidens' hearts.

   DESDEMONA.   Indeed ! is't true ?

   OTHELLO. Most veritable ; therefore look to't well.

   DESDEMONA. Then would to God that I had never
      seen't !

   OTHELLO. Ha ! wherefore ?

   DESDEMONA. Why do you speak so startingly and
      rash !

80 OTHELLO. Is't lost ? is't gone ? speak, is it out
      o' the way ?

   DESDEMONA. Heaven bless us !

   OTHELLO. Say you ?

   DESDEMONA. It is not lost ; but what an if it were ?

   OTHELLO. How !

   DESDEMONA. I say, it is not lost.

   OTHELLO.   Fetch't, let me see't.

   DESDEMONA. Why, so I can, sir, but I will not now.
This is a trick to put me from my suit :
Pray you, let Cassio be receiv'd again.

   OTHELLO. Fetch me the handkerchief : my mind
      misgives.

---

71 *The sun to course two hundred compasses*, two hundred years.

72 *prophetic fury*, whilst possessed by a god.

74 *mummy*, a preparation of wax or gum such as was used for
    embalming bodies.

85 *I say, it is not lost*, Desdemona lies in sudden and superstitious
    fear. *Cf.* Emilia's lie when Desdemona asks her about the
    handkerchief.

90 DESDEMONA. Come, come ;
You'll never meet a more sufficient man.
   OTHELLO. The handkerchief !
   DESDEMONA.   I pray, talk me of Cassio.
   OTHELLO. The handkerchief !
   DESDEMONA.   A man that all his time
Hath founded his good fortunes on your love,
Shared dangers with you,—
   OTHELLO. The handkerchief !
   DESDEMONA. In sooth, you are to blame.
   OTHELLO. 'Zounds !   (*Exit.*)
   EMILIA. Is not this man jealous ?
100 DESDEMONA. I ne'er saw this before.
Sure, there's some wonder in this handkerchief :
I am most unhappy in the loss of it.
   EMILIA. 'Tis not a year or two shows us a man :
They are all but stomachs, and we all but food ;
They eat us hungerly, and when they are full,
They belch us. Look you, Cassio and my husband !
                (*Enter* CASSIO *and* IAGO.)
   IAGO. There is no other way ; 'tis she must do't :
And, lo, the happiness ! go, and importune her.
   DESDEMONA. How now, good Cassio ! what's the
      news with you ?
110 CASSIO. Madam, my former suit : I do beseech you
That by your virtuous means I may again
Exist, and be a member of his love
Whom I with all the office of my heart
Entirely honour : I would not be delay'd.
If my offence be of such mortal kind
That nor my service past, nor present sorrows,

---

91 *sufficient,* capable, worthy.
104 *all but . . . all but,* nothing but.
   (*Enter Cassio and Iago.*) The audience would expect Emilia
      to confess about the handkerchief to Desdemona, even
      though it is understandable that she would not dare do so
      to Othello. So Cassio and Iago are brought on before there
      is time. That there might be time *off*-stage is no concern
      of a practical dramatist.

Nor purpos'd merit in futurity,
Can ransom me into his love again,
But to know so must be my benefit ;
120 So shall I clothe me in a forc'd content,
And shut myself up in some other course,
To fortune's alms.

    DESDEMONA.   Alas, thrice-gentle Cassio !
My advocation is not now in tune ;
My lord is not my lord ; nor should I know him,
Were he in favour as in humour alter'd.
So help me every spirit sanctified,
As I have spoken for you all my best
And stood within the blank of his displeasure
For my free speech ! you must awhile be patient :
130 What I can do I will ; and more I will
Than for myself I dare : let that suffice you.

    IAGO. Is my lord angry ?

    EMILIA.   He went hence but now
And certainly in strange unquietness.

    IAGO. Can he be angry ? I have seen the cannon,
When it hath blown his ranks into the air,
And, like the devil, from his very arm
Puff'd his own brother :—and can he be angry ?
Something of moment then : I will go meet him :
There's matter in't indeed, if he be angry.

140   DESDEMONA. I prithee, do so.   (*Exit* IAGO.)
                        Something, sure, of state,
Either from Venice, or some unhatch'd practice
Made demonstrable here in Cyprus to him,

---

117 *purposed merit in futurity*, resolution to behave myself in future.
119 *But to know so . . . benefit*, if my cause is beyond mending
    it is better that I know it.
124 *Were he in favour . . . altered.* If his looks had changed as
    much as his mood.
127 *within the blank*, the centre, bull's eye. (From "blanc "=
    white.)
134 *Can he be angry ?* Iago is enjoying himself.
141 *some unhatch'd practice . . . Cyprus*, the beginnings of some
    plot which he has discovered since he came to Cyprus.

Hath puddled his clear spirit ; and in such cases
Men's natures wrangle with inferior things,
Though great ones are their object.   'Tis even so ;
For let our finger ache, and it indues
Our other healthful members even to a sense
Of pain : nay, we must think men are not gods,
Nor of them look for such observances
As fit the bridal.   Beshrew me much, Emilia,
I was, unhandsome warrior as I am,
Arraigning his unkindness with my soul ;
But now I find I had suborn'd the witness,
And he's indicted falsely.

    EMILIA. Pray heaven it be state-matters, as you
        think,
And no conception nor no jealous toy
Concerning you.

    DESDEMONA. Alas the day ! I never gave him cause.

    EMILIA. But jealous souls will not be answer'd so ;
They are not ever jealous for the cause,
But jealous for they are jealous : 'tis a monster
Begot upon itself, born on itself.

    DESDEMONA. Heaven keep that monster from
        Othello's mind !

    EMILIA. Lady, amen.

    DESDEMONA. I will go seek him. Cassio, walk
        hereabout :
If I do find him fit, I'll move your suit
And seek to effect it to my uttermost.

    CASSIO. I humbly thank your ladyship.

                (*Exeunt* DESDEMONA *and* EMILIA.)
                (*Enter* BIANCA.)

---

143 *puddled*, stirred up and muddied.
144 *Men's natures . . . object*, we lose patience with trifles when we
     are obsessed by big worries.
149 *such observances . . . bridal*, a husband cannot always play
     the bridegroom.
152 *Arraigning his unkindness . . . falsely*. I was blaming him in
     my heart ; and now I admit I had allowed my selfishness
     to turn my thoughts against him.

(224)

7

BIANCA. Save you, friend Cassio !

CASSIO.   What make you from home ?
170 How is it with you, my most fair Bianca ?
I' faith, sweet love, I was coming to your house.

BIANCA. And I was going to your lodging, Cassio.
What, keep a week away ? seven days and nights ?
Eight score eight hours ? and lovers' absent hours,
More tedious than the dial eight score times ?
O weary reckoning !

CASSIO.   Pardon me, Bianca :
I have this while with leaden thoughts been press'd ;
But I shall, in a more continuate time,
Strike off this score of absence.   Sweet Bianca,
            (*Giving her* DESDEMONA'S *handkerchief.*)
180 Take me this work out.

BIANCA.   O Cassio, whence came this ?
This is some token from a newer friend :
To the felt absence now I feel a cause :
Is't come to this ?   Well, well.

CASSIO.   Go to, woman !
Throw your vile guesses in the devil's teeth,
From whence you have them.   You are jealous now
That this is from some mistress, some remembrance :
No, in good troth, Bianca.

BIANCA.   Why, whose is it ?

CASSIO. I know not, sweet : I found it in my
     chamber.
I like the work well : ere it be demanded—
190 As like enough it will—I'ld have it copied :
Take it, and do't ; and leave me for this time.

BIANCA. Leave you ? wherefore ?

CASSIO. I do attend here on the general ;
And think it no addition, nor my wish,

---

175 *More tedious than the dial*, far longer than clock-measured time.
178 *more continuate time*, uninterrupted.
182 *To the felt absence . . . cause*, your absence hurt me, now the
     cause of that absence (*i.e.* another woman) hurts.
194 *no addition*, no recommendation.

To have him see me woman'd.

BIANCA.   Why, I pray you?

CASSIO. Not that I love you not.

BIANCA.   But that you do not love me.
I pray you, bring me on the way a little,
And say if I shall see you soon at night.

CASSIO. 'Tis but a little way that I can bring you;
For I attend here: but I'll see you soon.

BIANCA. 'Tis very good; I must be circumstanc'd.
                              (*Exeunt.*)

201 *I must be circumstanc'd*, I must put up with circumstances.

ACT IV

SCENE I.　*Cyprus.　Before the castle.*

(*Enter* Othello *and* Iago.)

IAGO. Will you think so?

OTHELLO.　　　　　　　　　Think so, Iago!

IAGO.　　　　　　　　　　　　　　　　What,
To kiss in private?

OTHELLO.　　　　　　An unauthoriz'd kiss.

IAGO. Or to be naked with her friend abed
　　An hour or more, not meaning any harm?

OTHELLO. Naked abed, Iago, and not mean any
　　harm?
It is hypocrisy against the devil:
They that mean virtuously, and yet do so,
The devil their virtue tempts, and they tempt heaven.

IAGO. So they do nothing, 'tis a venial slip:
10 But if I give my wife a handkerchief—

OTHELLO. What then?

IAGO. Why, then, 'tis hers, my lord; and, being
　　hers,
She may, I think, bestow't on any man.

OTHELLO. She is protectress of her honour too:
May she give that?

IAGO. Her honour is an essence that's not seen;

Enter Othello and Iago. Note the speed with which this scene
　　opens.　*Cf.* Bradley, "The Othello of Act Four is Othello
　　in his fall.　Chaos has come."

　6 *hypocrisy against the devil.* An appearance of evil is as much a
　　form of hypocrisy as a deceitful appearance of goodness.

　9 *venial*, pardonable.

They have it very oft that have it not :
But, for the handkerchief—

    OTHELLO. By heaven, I would most gladly have
      forgot it.
Thou said'st—O, it comes o'er my memory,
As doth the raven o'er the infected house,
Boding to all—he had my handkerchief.

    IAGO. Ay, what of that ?

    OTHELLO.   That's not so good now

    IAGO.   What
If I had said I had seen him do you wrong ?
Or heard him say—as knaves be such abroad,
Who having, by their own importunate suit,
Or by the voluntary dotage of some mistress,
Convinced or supplied them, cannot chose
But they must blab—

    OTHELLO.   Hath he said anything ?

    IAGO. He hath, my lord ; but be you well assur'd,
No more than he'll unswear.

    OTHELLO.   What hath he said ?

    IAGO. 'Faith, that he did—I know not what he
      did.

    OTHELLO. What ?   what ?—Handkerchief—con-
fessions—handkerchief !—To confess, and be hanged
for his labour ;—first, to be hanged, and then to

---

16 *They have it very oft . . . not,* they often appear to have it who
    have lost it.

21 *raven . . . house.*   The raven was a bird of ill-omen, and its
    presence over a plague-stricken house boded death.

26 *Who having . . . convinced or supplied,* having either persuaded
    (some mistress) by their importunities or complied with a
    mistress's own desires.

29 *But they must blab.*   *Cf.* with Iago's earlier reference to Cassio
    as being " loose of soul."

34 *To confess . . . O devil !*   These lines (34–40) are omitted in the
    First Quarto.

    confess, and be hanged.   A proverb. Othello may mean that
      Cassio is already as good as dead. But Shakespeare is
      working up for the " trance," and the rest of Othello's
      speech is not coherent.

confess.—I tremble at it. Nature would not invest
herself in such shadowing passion without some
instruction. It is not words that shake me thus.
Noses, ears, and lips.—Is't possible?—Confess—
40 handkerchief!—O devil!   (*Falls in a trance.*)

    Iago. Work on,
My medicine, work! Thus credulous fools are
    caught,
And many worthy and chaste dames even thus,
All guiltless, meet reproach. (*He sees* Cassio *approach-
    ing.*) What, ho! my lord!
My lord, I say! Othello!
            (*Enter* Cassio.)
                    How now, Cassio!

    Cassio. What's the matter?

    Iago. My lord is fall'n into an epilepsy:
This is his second fit; he had one yesterday.

    Cassio. Rub him about the temples.

    Iago.   No, forbear;
50 The lethargy must have his quiet course:
If not, he foams at mouth and by and by
Breaks out to savage madness. Look, he stirs:
Do you withdraw yourself a little while,
He will recover straight: when he is gone,
I would on great occasion speak with you.
                    (*Exit* Cassio.)
How is it, general? have you not hurt your head?

    Othello. Dost thou mock me?

    Iago.   I mock you! no, by heaven.

---

36 *Nature would not invest herself . . . instruction.* My passions could
    not be so stirred by mere dreams or hearsay. My instincts
    tell me she is guilty.
    (*Enter Cassio.*) Note how chance favours Iago. If Cassio
    had arrived a moment earlier Othello would have accused
    him to his face.
48 *he had one yesterday.* This to prevent Cassio seeking some
    special cause, or getting help. Another clever lie.
56 *have you not hurt your head? Cf.* Hazlitt: " Iago's indifference
    . . . is perfectly diabolical."

Would you would bear your fortune like a man !

   OTHELLO. A horned man's a monster and a beast.

IAGO. There's many a beast then in a populous city,

And many a civil monster.

   OTHELLO. Did he confess it ?

   IAGO.   Good sir, be a man ;

Think every bearded fellow that's but yok'd

May draw with you : there's millions now alive

That nightly lie in those unproper beds

Which they dare swear peculiar : your case is better.

O, 'tis a spite of hell, the fiend's arch-mock,

To lip a wanton in a secure couch,

And to suppose her chaste !   No, let me know ;

And knowing what I am, I know what she shall be.

   OTHELLO. O thou art wise ; 'tis certain.

   IAGO.   Stand you awhile apart ;

Confine yourself but in a patient list.

Whilst you were here o'erwhelmed with your grief—

A passion most unsuiting such a man—

Cassio came hither : I shifted him away,

And laid good 'scuse upon your ecstasy,

Bade him anon return and here speak with me ;

The which he promis'd.   Do but encave yourself,

And mark the fleers, the gibes, and notable scorns,

That dwell in every region of his face ;

59 *horned man*, popular expression for a husband who has been betrayed.

65 *unproper*, not private property. *Cf.* proper noun, a person's own name.

66 *peculiar*, their own (see note, III. iii. 79).

69 *No, let me know . . . what she shall be.* I would rather know for certain that I am betrayed, then I would know how to deal with my wife.

72 *Confine yourself . . . list*, keep your patience within limits (list= a confined space).

74 *most unsuiting.* Note Iago's constant gibe that Othello is not behaving " like a man."

78 *encave*, hide. Probably back-stage under the gallery.

79 *notable scorns*, obvious contempt.

For I will make him tell the tale anew,
Where, how, how oft, how long ago, and when
He hath, and is again to cope your wife :
I say, but mark his gesture.   Marry, patience ;
Or I shall say you are all in all in spleen,
And nothing of a man.

    OTHELLO.   Dost thou hear, Iago ?
I will be found most cunning in my patience ;
But—dost thou hear ?—most bloody.

    IAGO.   That's not amiss ;
But yet keep time in all.   Will you withdraw ?

                        (OTHELLO retires.)

90 Now will I question Cassio of Bianca,
A housewife that by selling her desires
Buys herself bread and clothes : it is a creature
That dotes on Cassio ; as 'tis the strumpet's plague
To beguile many and be beguil'd by one :
He, when he hears of her, cannot refrain
From the excess of laughter.   Here he comes :

               (Re-enter CASSIO.)

As he shall smile, Othello shall go mad ;
And his unbookish jealousy must construe
Poor Cassio's smiles, gestures and light behaviour,
100 Quite in the wrong.   How do you now, lieutenant ?

    CASSIO. The worser that you give me the addition
Whose want even kills me.

    IAGO. Ply Desdemona well, and you are sure on't.
(Speaking lower.) Now, if this suit lay in Bianca's power,

---

83 *cope*, encounter.
85 *all in all in spleen*, obsessed by sudden, capricious anger rather
    than a man's steady resolution.
89 *keep time in all*, act with care and precision, to an ordered
    plan.
91 *housewife*, in a derogatory sense, hussy.
93 *'tis the strumpet's plague*, it is the fate of a loose woman eventu-
    ally to fall sincerely in love and be despised.
98 *unbookish*, unreasoning, lacking knowledge of the world. The
    implied metaphor followed up by "construe," meaning
    "interpret."
101 *addition*, title of lieutenant.

Iow quickly should you speed !

CASSIO. Alas, poor caitiff !

OTHELLO. Look, how he laughs already !

IAGO. I never knew woman love man so.

CASSIO. Alas, poor rogue ! I think, i' faith, she loves me.

OTHELLO. Now he denies it faintly, and laughs it out.

IAGO. Do you hear, Cassio ?

OTHELLO. Now he importunes him To tell it o'er : go to ; well said, well said.

IAGO. She gives it out that you shall marry her : Do you intend it ?

CASSIO. Ha, ha, ha !

OTHELLO. Do you triumph, Roman ? Do you triumph ?

CASSIO. I marry her ! What ? A customer ! Prithee, bear some charity to my wit ; do not think it so unwholesome. Ha, ha, ha !

OTHELLO. So, so, so, so : they laugh that win.

IAGO. 'Faith, the cry goes that you shall marry her.

CASSIO. Prithee, say true.

IAGO. I am a very villain else.

OTHELLO. Have you scored me ? Well.

CASSIO. This is the monkey's own giving out : she is persuaded I will marry her, out of her own love and flattery, not out of my promise.

OTHELLO. Iago beckons me ; now he begins the story.

CASSIO. She was here even now ; she haunts me in every place. I was the other day talking on the sea-bank with certain Venetians ; and thither comes

---

115 *Roman.* Reference to racial difference between Moor and Italian. Dr. Johnson points out association between " Roman " and " triumph."

116 *customer,* one who sells her favours. Common term for harlot.

123 *scored,* branded.

the bauble, and, by this hand, she falls me thus abou
my neck—

OTHELLO. Crying " O dear Cassio ! " as it were
his gesture imports it.

CASSIO. So hangs, and lolls, and weeps upon me
so hales, and pulls me : ha, ha, ha !

OTHELLO. Now he tells how she plucked him to
my chamber. O, I see that nose of yours, but no
140 that dog I shall throw it to.

CASSIO. Well, I must leave her company.

IAGO. Before me ! look, where she comes.

CASSIO. 'Tis such another fitchew ! marry, a per-
fumed one.

(Enter BIANCA.)

What do you mean by this haunting of me ?

BIANCA. Let the devil and his dam haunt you !
What did you mean by that same handkerchief you
gave me even now ? I was a fine fool to take it.
I must take out the work ? A likely piece of work,
150 that you should find it in your chamber, and not
know who left it there ! This is some minx's token,
and I must take out the work ? There ; give it your
hobby-horse : wheresoever you had it, I'll take out
no work on't.

CASSIO. How now, my sweet Bianca ! how now !
how now !

OTHELLO. By heaven, that should be my handkerchief !

BIANCA. An you'll come to supper to-night, you
160 may ; an you will not, come when you are next
prepared for.   *(Exit.)*

IAGO. After her, after her.

CASSIO. 'Faith, I must ; she'll rail in the street else.

IAGO. Will you sup there ?

132 *bauble*, toy, plaything.
143 *fitchew*, polecat, reputed to be particularly lecherous. But this
      one is perfumed, *i.e.* has not the polecat's offensive smell.
(*Enter Bianca.*)   Again chance plays into Iago's hand.

CASSIO. 'Faith, I intend so.

IAGO. Well, I may chance to see you : for I would very fain speak with you.

CASSIO. Prithee, come ; will you ?

IAGO. Go to ; say no more. (*Exit* CASSIO.)

OTHELLO (*advancing*). How shall I murder him, Iago ?

IAGO. Did you perceive how he laughed at his vice ?

OTHELLO. O Iago !

IAGO. And did you see the handkerchief ?

OTHELLO. Was that mine ?

IAGO. Yours, by this hand : and to see how he prizes the foolish woman your wife ! she gave it him, and he hath given it his whore.

OTHELLO. I would have him nine years a-killing. A fine woman ! a fair woman ! a sweet woman !

IAGO. Nay, you must forget that.

OTHELLO. Ay, let her rot, and perish, and be damned to-night ; for she shall not live. No, my heart is turned to stone ; I strike it, and it hurts my hand. O, the world hath not a sweeter creature : she might lie by an emperor's side and command him tasks.

IAGO. Nay, that's not your way.

OTHELLO. Hang her ! I do but say what she is : so delicate with her needle, an admirable musician. O she will sing the savageness out of a bear : of so high and plenteous wit and invention !——

IAGO. She's the worse for all this.

OTHELLO. O, a thousand thousand times : and then, of so gentle a condition !

IAGO. Ay, too gentle.

OTHELLO. Nay, that's certain : but yet the pity of it, Iago ! O Iago, the pity of it, Iago !

170 *How shall I murder him?* Note the simplicity of resolution compared with Othello's earlier speeches.
197 *too gentle*, Iago twists the meaning : too easily swayed.

200   IAGO. If you are so fond over her iniquity, give her patent to offend ; for, if it touch not you, it comes near nobody.

OTHELLO. I will chop her into messes.

IAGO. O, 'tis foul in her.

OTHELLO. With mine officer !

IAGO. That's fouler.

OTHELLO. Get me some poison, Iago, this night. I'll not expostulate with her, lest her body and beauty unprovide my mind again : this night, Iago.

210   IAGO. Do it not with poison, strangle her in her bed, even the bed she hath contaminated.

OTHELLO. Good, good, the justice of it pleases, very good.

IAGO. And for Cassio, let me be his undertaker : you shall hear more by midnight.

OTHELLO. Excellent good.   (*A trumpet within.*) What trumpet is that same ?

IAGO. Something from Venice, sure. 'Tis Lodovico Come from the duke : and, see, your wife is with him.

(*Enter* LODOVICO, DESDEMONA, *and* Attendants.)

LODOVICO. Save you, worthy general !

OTHELLO.   With all my heart, sir.

220   LODOVICO. The duke and senators of Venice greet you.   (*Gives him a letter.*)

OTHELLO. I kiss the instrument of their pleasures. (*He kisses the seal, then opens the letter, and reads.*)

DESDEMONA. And what's the news, good cousin Lodovico ?

IAGO. I am very glad to see you, signior ; Welcome to Cyprus.

LODOVICO. I thank you. How does Lieutenant Cassio?

---

200 *If you are . . . nobody*, if you are so foolishly tolerant of her sin, give her full permission to be unfaithful, for it concerns no one but yourself.

203 *messes*, small pieces.

209 *unprovide my mind*, weaken my resolution.

210 *strangle her*. Here Shakespeare departs from the original story.

214 *let me be his undertaker*, I undertake to dispose of him.

IAGO. Lives, sir.

DESDEMONA. Cousin, there's fall'n between him and
my lord

An unkind breach : but you shall make all well.

OTHELLO. Are you sure of that ?

DESDEMONA. My lord !

OTHELLO (*reads*). " This fail you not to do, as you
will—"

LODOVICO. He did not call ; he's busy in the paper

Is there division 'twixt my lord and Cassio ?

DESDEMONA. A most unhappy one : I would do
much

To atone them, for the love I bear to Cassio.

OTHELLO. Fire and brimstone !

DESDEMONA. My lord ?

OTHELLO. Are you wise ?

DESDEMONA. What, is he angry ?

LODOVICO. May be the letter mov'd him;

For, as I think, they do command him home,

Deputing Cassio in his government.

DESDEMONA. Trust me, I am glad on't.

OTHELLO. Indeed !

DESDEMONA. My lord ?

OTHELLO. I am glad to see you mad.

DESDEMONA. Why, sweet Othello,—

OTHELLO (*striking her with the letter*). Devil !

DESDEMONA. I have not deserv'd this.

LODOVICO. My lord, this would not be believ'd in
Venice,

Though I should swear I saw't : 'tis very much :

Make her amends ; she weeps.

235 *atone*, reconcile.
236 *Are you wise ?* In acting, these words are sometimes given to
Iago, spoken to Othello. This certainly seems more suitable. On the other hand, spoken by Othello to Desdemona, they would mean, " Are you mad (to betray yourself
so openly) ? " (*Cf.* below, " I am glad to see you mad.")
241 *mad*, mad enough to admit your gladness in my being super-
seded by Cassio.

OTHELLO.   O devil, devil !
If that the earth could teem with woman's tears,
Each drop she falls would prove a crocodile.
Out of my sight !

DESDEMONA. I will not stay to offend you.   (*Going.*)

250   LODOVICO. Truly, an obedient lady :
I do beseech your lordship, call her back.

OTHELLO. Mistress !

DESDEMONA.   My lord ?

OTHELLO.   What would you with her, sir ?

LODOVICO. Who, I, my lord ?

OTHELLO. Ay ; you did wish that I would make
   her turn :
Sir, she can turn, and turn, and yet go on,
And turn again ; and she can weep, sir, weep ;
And she's obedient, as you say, obedient,
Very obedient.   Proceed you in your tears.
      (*Speaking alternately to* LODIVICO *and* DESDEMONA.)
Concerning this, sir,—O well-painted passion !—

260 I am commanded here. . . .   Get you away ;
I'll send for you anon. . . .   Sir, I obey the mandate,
And will return to Venice. . . .   Hence, avaunt !
                              (*Exit* DESDEMONA.)
Cassio shall have my place.   And, sir, to-night,
I do entreat that we may sup together :
You are welcome, sir, to Cyprus. . . .   Goats and
   monkeys !   (*Exit.*)

LODOVICO. Is this the noble Moor whom our full
   senate
Call all in all sufficient ?   This the noble nature
Whom passion could not shake ? whose solid virtue
The shot of accident, nor dart of chance,

270 Could neither graze nor pierce ?

247 *If that the earth . . . crocodile,* if the earth could be made
      fertile (teem) by women's tears, hers would produce
      crocodiles. (*Cf.* The old myth of crocodiles luring men
      to death by crying.)
255 *turn, and turn,* in the bad sense of unfaithfulness.

IAGO.   He is much chang'd.

LODOVICO. Are his wits safe ? Is he not light of
brain ?

IAGO. He's that he is : I may not breathe my
censure

What he might be : if what he might he is not,

I would to heaven he were !

LODOVICO.   What, strike his wife !

IAGO. 'Faith, that was not so well ; yet would I
knew

That stroke would prove the worst !

LODOVICO.   Is it his use ?

Or did the letters work upon his blood,

And new-create this fault ?

IAGO.   Alas, alas !

It is not honesty in me to speak

280 What I have seen and known. You shall observe him,

And his own courses will denote him so

That I may save my speech : do but go after,

And mark how he continues.

LODOVICO. I am sorry that I am deceiv'd in him.

(*Exeunt.*)

SCENE II.   *A room in the castle.*

(*Enter* OTHELLO *and* EMILIA.)

OTHELLO. You have seen nothing then ?

EMILIA. Nor ever heard, nor ever did suspect.

OTHELLO. Yes, you have seen Cassio and she together.

272 *censure*, private opinion.
273 *if what he might . . . he were.* If he is not all he might be
(*i.e.* sane), I wish he were. Here, and in the next speech,
Iago is mystery-mongering, implying that there is something sadly wrong but loyalty forbids him to speak.
Enter Othello and Emilia. Othello at last takes an obvious step.
But it is too late. The poison has done its work, and
Othello now seeks, not the truth, but confirmation of his
suspicions.

EMILIA. But then I saw no harm, and then I heard
Each syllable that breath made up between them.

OTHELLO. What, did they never whisper?

EMILIA. Never, my lord.

OTHELLO. Nor send you out o' the way?

EMILIA. Never.

OTHELLO. To fetch her fan, her gloves, her mask,
nor nothing?

10 EMILIA. Never, my lord.

OTHELLO. That's strange.

EMILIA. I durst, my lord, to wager she is honest,
Lay down my soul at stake : if you think other,
Remove your thought ; it doth abuse your bosom.
If any wretch have put this in your head,
Let heaven requite it with the serpent's curse !
For, if she be not honest, chaste, and true,
There's no man happy ; the purest of her sex
Is foul as slander.

OTHELLO. Bid her come hither : go.
(*Exit* EMILIA.)

20 She says enough ; yet she's a simple bawd
That cannot say as much. This is a subtle whore,
A closet lock and key of villanous secrets :
And yet she'll kneel and pray ; I have seen her do't.
(*Enter* DESDEMONA *with* EMILIA.)

DESDEMONA. My lord, what is your will?

OTHELLO. Pray, chuck, come hither.

DESDEMONA. What is your pleasure?

OTHELLO. Let me see your eyes . . .
Look in my face.

DESDEMONA. What horrible fancy's this?

OTHELLO (*to* EMILIA). Some of your function,
mistress,

---

20 *she's a simple bawd . . . pray,* she's a poor fool if she doesn't lie
to save her mistress. This Emilia pretends to be pious, but
she stands guard over my wife's guilty secrets. (Iago has
already poisoned Othello against putting any trust in
Venetian women.)

Leave procreants alone, and shut the door ;
Cough, or cry " hem," if any body come :
Your mystery, your mystery : nay, dispatch.

(*Exit* EMILIA.)

 DESDEMONA. Upon my knees, what doth your
  speech import ?
I understand a fury in your words,
But not the words.

 OTHELLO. Why, what art thou ?

 DESDEMONA. Your wife, my lord ; your true and
  loyal wife.

 OTHELLO. Come, swear it, damn thyself ;
Lest, being like one of heaven, the devils themselves
Should fear to seize thee : therefore be double
 damn'd.
Swear thou art honest.

 DESDEMONA.   Heaven doth truly know it.

 OTHELLO. Heaven truly knows that thou art false
 as hell.

 DESDEMONA. To whom, my lord ? With whom ?
  How am I false ?

 OTHELLO. O Desdemona ! away ! away ! away !

 DESDEMONA. Alas the heavy day ! Why do you
  weep ?
Am I the motive of these tears, my lord ?
If haply you my father do suspect
An instrument of this your calling back,
Lay not your blame on me. If you have lost him,
Why, I have lost him too.

 OTHELLO.   Had it pleas'd heaven
To try me with affliction ; had they rain'd
All kinds of sores and shames on my bare head,
Steep'd me in poverty to the very lips,

---

30 *Your mystery*, carry on with your trade, *i.e.* that of a procuress.
 Othello behaves as if he were a stranger visiting a brothel.
 Desdemona cannot understand. *Cf.* below, " Am I that
 name, Iago ? "
36 *damn thyself*, by taking a false oath.

(224)   8

Given to captivity me and my utmost hopes,
I should have found in some place of my soul
A drop of patience.   But, alas, to make me
A fixed figure for the time of scorn
To point his slow unmoving finger at. . . .
Yet could I bear that too ; well, very well :
But there, where I have garner'd up my heart,
Where either I must live, or bear no life ;
60 The fountain from the which my current runs,
Or else dries up ; to be discarded thence,
Or keep it as a cistern for foul toads
To knot and gender in ! Turn thy complexion there,
Patience, thou young and rose-lipp'd cherubin.—
Ay, there, look grim as hell !

   DESDEMONA. I hope my noble lord esteems me
   honest.

   OTHELLO. O ay ; as summer flies are in the
   shambles,

That quicken even with blowing.
O thou black weed, why art so lovely fair ?

55 *A fixed figure . . . finger at.* A heavily disputed passage.
   On the face of it (taking both Quartos' reading, " unmoving " instead of Folio's " and moving ") the meaning
   seems to be : I am made a fixed figure (like a figure on a
   clock) at which the slowly moving (apparently unmoving)
   hand points.   Note the slowly moving *hour* hand, or the
   unmoving finger of a sun-dial, gives the " time of day " ;
   transfer this to time of scorn.   But the secret of poetry is
   that you feel its force rather than examine its logic ; and
   this is the poet's presentation of an unsettled brain,
   " Sweet bells jangled, out of tune."

62 *Or keep it . . . knot and gender in,* either to discard my love, or
   keep it, knowing it to be a foul, polluted thing.

63 *Turn thy complexion,* lose colour at the horror of it.

68 *quicken even with blowing,* come to life as soon as the eggs are
   laid.   Actually the comparison is not with the flies, but
   with the polluted food.

69 *O thou black weed . . . aches at thee.* Folio reads :

                    " O thou weed
   Who art so lovely fair, and smell'st so sweet
   That the sense aches at thee,—"

70 Thou smell'st so sweet that the sense aches at thee;
  Would thou hadst ne'er been born!

    DESDEMONA. Alas, what ignorant sin have I com-
       mitted?

    OTHELLO. Was this fair paper, this most goodly
      book,

Made to write " whore " upon?   What committed?
Committed!   O thou public commoner!
I should make very forges of my cheeks,
That would to cinders burn up modesty,
Did I but speak thy deeds.   What committed?
Heaven stops the nose at it and the moon winks,
80 The bawdy wind that kisses all it meets
Is hush'd within the hollow mine of earth,
And will not hear it.   What committed?
Impudent strumpet!

    DESDEMONA.   By heaven, you do me wrong.

    OTHELLO. Are not you a strumpet?

    DESDEMONA.   No, as I am a Christian:

If to preserve this vessel for my lord
From any other foul unlawful touch
Be not to be a strumpet, I am none.

    OTHELLO. What, not a whore?

    DESDEMONA.   No, as I shall be sav'd.

    OTHELLO. Is't possible?

90   DESDEMONA. O heaven forgive us!

    OTHELLO.   I cry you mercy, then:

I took you for that cunning whore of Venice
That married with Othello. (*Raising his voice.*) You,
    mistress,

That have the office opposite to Saint Peter,
And keep the gate of hell!

               (*Re-enter* EMILIA.)

               You, you, ay, you!

We have done our course; there's money for your
    pains:

       75 *public commoner*, harlot.
       78 omitted in First Quart

I pray you, turn the key and keep our counsel. (*Exit.*)

EMILIA. Alas, what does this gentleman conceive?
How do you, madam? how do you, my good lady?

DESDEMONA. 'Faith, half asleep.

100   EMILIA. Good madam, what's the matter with my
        lord?

DESDEMONA. With who?

EMILIA. Why, with my lord, madam.

DESDEMONA. Who is thy lord?

EMILIA.   He that is yours, sweet lady.

DESDEMONA. I have none: do not talk to me,
        Emilia;
I cannot weep; nor answer have I none,
But what should go by water.   Prithee, to-night
Lay on my bed my wedding sheets, remember;
And call thy husband hither.

EMILIA.   Here's a change indeed!
                                    (*Exit.*)

DESDEMONA. 'Tis meet I should be us'd so, very
        meet.

110 How have I been behav'd, that he might stick
The small'st opinion on my greatest abuse?

        (*Re-enter* EMILIA *with* IAGO.)

IAGO. What is your pleasure, madam? How is't
        with you?

DESDEMONA. I cannot tell.   Those that do teach
        young babes
Do it with gentle means and easy tasks:
He might have chid me so; for, in good faith,
I am a child to chiding.

IAGO.   What's the matter, lady?

99 *half asleep*, dazed.
106 *go by water*, be said by weeping.
111 *The small'st opinion . . . abuse.* Folio gives "my least mis-
        use."   Present reading implies, "take the least exception
        even to my greatest fault."
116 *I am a child to chiding*, I am like a child when I am scolded.

EMILIA. Alas, Iago, my lord hath so bewhor'd her,
Thrown such despite and heavy terms upon her,
As true hearts cannot bear.

20 DESDEMONA. Am I that name, Iago ?

IAGO.   What name, fair lady ?

DESDEMONA. Such as she says my lord did say I
    was.

EMILIA. He call'd her whore : a beggar in his drink
Could not have laid such terms upon his callet.

IAGO. Why did he so ?

DESDEMONA. I do not know ; I am sure I am none
    such.

IAGO. Do not weep, do not weep. Alas the day !

EMILIA. Hath she forsook so many noble matches,
Her father and her country and her friends,
To be call'd whore ? Would it not make one weep ?

30 DESDEMONA. It is my wretched fortune.

IAGO.   Beshrew him for't :
How comes this trick upon him ?

DESDEMONA.   Nay, heaven doth know.

EMILIA. I will be hang'd, if some eternal villain,
Some busy and insinuating rogue,
Some cogging, cozening slave, to get some office,
Have not devised this slander ; I'll be hang'd else.

IAGO. Fie, there is no such man ; it is impossible.

DESDEMONA. If any such there be, heaven pardon
    him !

EMILIA. A halter pardon him ! and hell gnaw his
    bones !
Why should he call her whore ? Who keeps her
    company ?

117 *bewhor'd*, thrown the word at her in accusation. In this scene
    the " silent " Emilia begins to come into her own.
123 *callet*, lowest of terms for a loose woman.
132 *eternal*, outrageous. Notice how Shakespeare uses this passage
    for a double purpose : (a) dramatic irony ; (b) to show
    Emilia's innocence of her husband's plot.
134 *cogging*, cheating.

140 What place ? what time ? what form ?   What likeli-
      hood ?
The Moor's abus'd by some outrageous knave,
Some base notorious knave, some scurvy fellow.
O heaven, that such companions thou'ldst unfold,
And put in every honest hand a whip
To lash the rascal naked through the world
Even from the east to the west !
    Iago.   Speak within door.
    Emilia. O fie upon them ! Some such squire he
      was
That turn'd your wit the seamy side without,
And made you to suspect me with the Moor.
150 Iago. You are a fool ; go to.
    Desdemona.   O good Iago,
What shall I do to win my lord again ?
Good friend, go to him ; for, by this light of heaven,
I know not how I lost him.   Here I kneel :
If e'er my will did trespass 'gainst his love,
Either in discourse of thought or actual deed,
Or that mine eyes, mine ears, or any sense,
Delighted them in any other form ;
Or that I do not yet, and ever did,
And ever will—though he do shake me off
160 To beggarly divorcement—love him dearly,
Comfort forswear me ! Unkindness may do much ;
And his unkindness may defeat my life,
But never taint my love.   I cannot say " whore : "

143 *companions*, low fellows, *cf*. boon companions.
     unfold, reveal.
146 *Speak within door*, keep your voice down.
147 *Some such squire*, a reminder of one of Iago's motives.
148 *turn'd your wit . . . without*. *Cf.* II. iii. 54, "Whom love
     hath turned almost the wrong side out."
153 *Here I kneel* to l. 166 : omitted in First Quarto.
157 *Delighted them . . . form*, interested themselves in any other
     man's appearance.
161 *Comfort forswear me*, may all peace of mind desert me.
162 *defeat*, unmake, destroy.

It doth abhor me now I speak the word ;
To do the act that might the addition earn
Not the world's mass of vanity could make me.

    IAGO. I pray you, be content ; 'tis but his humour :
The business of the state does him offence,
And he does chide with you.

170 DESDEMONA. If 'twere no other,—

    IAGO.   'Tis but so, I warrant.
                          (*Trumpets within.*)

Hark, how these instruments summon to supper !
The messengers of Venice stay the meat :
Go in, and weep not ; all things shall be well.
            (*Exeunt* DESDEMONA *and* EMILIA.)
            (*Enter* RODERIGO.)

How now, Roderigo !

    RODERIGO. I do not find that thou dealest justly
with me.

    IAGO. What in the contrary ?

    RODERIGO. Every day thou daffest me with some
device, Iago ; and rather, as it seems to me now,
180 keepest from me all conveniency than suppliest me
with the least advantage of hope. I will indeed no
longer endure it, nor am I yet persuaded to put up
in peace what already I have foolishly suffered.

    IAGO. Will you hear me, Roderigo ?

    RODERIGO. 'Faith, I have heard too much, for
your words and performances are no kin together.

    IAGO. You charge me most unjustly.

    RODERIGO. With nought but truth. I have wasted
myself out of my means. The jewels you have had
190 from me to deliver to Desdemona would half have
corrupted a votarist. You have told me she hath
received them and returned me expectations and
comforts of sudden respect and acquaintance, but I
find none.

<hr/>

165 *addition*, title. (See elsewhere.)
178 *daff*, put off. *Cf.* doff (the hat).
191 *votarist*, a nun.   193 *sudden*, immediate.

Iago. Well ; go to ; very well.

Roderigo. Very well ? Go to ? I cannot go to, man ; nor 'tis not very well. Nay, I think it is scurvy, and begin to find myself fobbed in it.

Iago. Very well.

200 Roderigo. I tell you 'tis not very well. I will make myself known to Desdemona : if she will return me my jewels, I will give over my suit and repent my unlawful solicitation ; if not, assure yourself I will seek satisfaction of you.

Iago. You have said now.

Roderigo. Ay, and said nothing but what I protest intendment of doing.

Iago. Why, now I see there's mettle in thee, and even from this instant do build on thee a better 210 opinion than ever before. Give me thy hand, Roderigo. Thou hast taken against me a most just exception ; but yet, I protest, I have dealt most directly in thy affair.

Roderigo. It hath not appeared.

Iago. I grant indeed it hath not appeared, and your suspicion is not without wit and judgement. But, Roderigo, if thou hast that in thee indeed, which I have greater reason to believe now than ever, I mean purpose, courage, and valour, this night 220 show it. If thou the next night following enjoy not Desdemona, take me from this world with treachery and devise engines for my life.

Roderigo. Well, what is it ? Is it within reason and compass ?

Iago. Sir, there is especial commission come from Venice to depute Cassio in Othello's place.

Roderigo. Is that true ? Why, then Othello and Desdemona return again to Venice.

198 *fobbed*, " fobbed off," cheated with feeble excuses.
205 *You have said now*, Have you quite finished ?
222 *engines*, means of destruction.
228 *return again to Venice*. This would suit Roderigo's plans very well.

IAGO. O no ; he goes into Mauritania and takes away with him the fair Desdemona, unless his abode be lingered here by some accident ; wherein none can be so determinate as the removing of Cassio.

RODERIGO. How do you mean, removing of him ?

IAGO. Why, by making him uncapable of Othello's place ; knocking out his brains.

RODERIGO. And that you would have me to do ?

IAGO. Ay, if you dare do yourself a profit and a right. He sups to-night with a harlot, and thither will I go to him : he knows not yet of his honourable fortune. If you will watch his going thence, which I will fashion to fall out between twelve and one, you may take him at your pleasure. I will be near to second your attempt, and he shall fall between us. Come, stand not amazed at it, but go along with me ; I will show you such a necessity in his death that you shall think yourself bound to put it on him. It is now high supper-time, and the night grows to waste. About it.

RODERIGO. I will hear further reason for this.

IAGO. And you shall be satisfied. (*Exeunt.*)

SCENE III. *Another room in the castle.*

(*Enter* OTHELLO, LODOVICO, DESDEMONA, EMILIA, *and* Attendants.)

LODOVICO. I do beseech you, sir, trouble yourself no further.

OTHELLO. O pardon me ; 'twill do me good to walk.

229 *he goes into Mauritania*, a lie. *Cf.* IV. i. 238, 263.
    (*Mauritania*, the land of the Moors.)
247 *high supper time*, fully supper time. " It is high time " is still idiomatic English.

LODOVICO. Madam, good night ; I humbly thank
    your ladyship.

DESDEMONA. Your honour is most welcome.

OTHELLO.   Will you walk, sir ?

O—Desdemona,—

DESDEMONA. My lord ?

OTHELLO. Get you to bed on the instant ; I will
be returned forthwith : dismiss your attendant there :
look it be done.

260 DESDEMONA. I will, my lord.

       (*Exeunt* OTHELLO, LODOVICO, *and* Attendants.)

EMILIA. How goes it now ? he looks gentler than
    he did.

DESDEMONA. He says he will return incontinent :
He hath commanded me to go to bed,
And bade me to dismiss you.

EMILIA.   Dismiss me ?

DESDEMONA. It was his bidding ; therefore, good
    Emilia,
Give me my nightly wearing, and adieu :
We must not now displease him.

EMILIA. I would you had never seen him !

DESDEMONA. So would not I : my love doth so
    approve him,
270 That even his stubbornness, his checks and frowns—
Prithee, unpin me—have grace and favour in them.

EMILIA. I have laid those sheets you bade me on
    the bed.

DESDEMONA. All's one. Good faith, how foolish
    are our minds !
If I do die before thee, prithee, shroud me
In one of those same sheets.

EMILIA.   Come, come, you talk.

DESDEMONA. My mother had a maid call'd Barbara :

---

261 *he looks gentler than he did.* " Shakespeare has here put into
    half a line what some authors would have spun out into
    ten set speeches."—Hazlitt.
262 *incontinent*, immediately.

She was in love, and he she lov'd prov'd mad
And did forsake her: she had a song of
    " willow ";
An old thing 'twas, but it express'd her fortune,
30 And she died singing it: that song to-night
Will not go from my mind; I have much to do,
But to go hang my head all at one side,
And sing it like poor Barbara. Prithee, dispatch.
    EMILIA. Shall I go fetch your night-gown?
    DESDEMONA.   No, unpin me here.
This Lodovico is a proper man.
    EMILIA. A very handsome man.
    DESDEMONA. He speaks well.
    EMILIA. I know a lady in Venice would have
walked barefoot to Palestine for a touch of his nether
90 lip.

    DESDEMONA (*singing*). *The poor soul sat sighing by a*
        sycamore tree,
    Sing all a green willow:
    Her hand on her bosom, her head on her knee,
        Sing willow, willow, willow:
    The fresh streams ran by her, and murmur'd her
        moans;
        Sing willow, willow, willow;
    Her salt tears fell from her, and soften'd the
        stones;—
(Lay by these)
(*Singing*) *Sing willow, willow, willow;*
300 (Prithee, hie thee; he'll come anon)
(*Singing*) *Sing all a green willow must be my garland.*
    Let nobody blame him; his scorn I approve,—
Nay, that's not next.—Hark! who is't that
    knocks?
    EMILIA. It's the wind.

277 *he she lov'd prov'd mad.* This, in conjunction with the willow
    song, is reminiscent of *Hamlet.*
281 *I have much to do . . .* to 303, *Nay, that's not next,* and the
    whole of the song, omitted in First Quarto.

DESDEMONA (*singing*). *I call'd my love false love ;
but what said he then ?*
   Sing willow, willow, willow :
   *If I court moe women, you'll couch with moe
men.—*

So, get thee gone ; good night.   Mine eyes do itch ;
Doth that bode weeping ?

EMILIA.   'Tis neither here nor there.

310 DESDEMONA. I have heard it said so.   O these
men, these men !

Dost thou in conscience think,—tell me, Emilia—
That there be women do abuse their husbands
In such gross kind ?

EMILIA.   There be some such, no question.

DESDEMONA. Wouldst thou do such a deed for all
the world ?

EMILIA. Why, would not you ?

DESDEMONA.   No, by this heavenly light !

EMILIA. Nor I neither by this heavenly light ;
I might do't as well i' the dark.

DESDEMONA. Wouldst thou do such a deed for all
the world ?

EMILIA. The world's a huge thing : it is a great
price

320 For a small vice.

DESDEMONA. In troth, I think thou wouldst
not.

EMILIA. In troth, I think I should ; and undo't
when I had done.   Marry, I would not do such a
thing for a joint-ring, nor for measures of lawn, nor
for gowns, petticoats, nor caps, nor any petty exhibition ; but, for the whole world,—why, who would

315 *by this heavenly light.*   Emilia purposely twists Desdemona's
   meaning both here and in the next line.
322 *and undo't when I had done*, once in possession of the whole
   world I could right the wrong done my husband.
324 *joint-ring*, a ring in which the circle was held together by
   clasped hands.   325 *exhibition*, reward.

not make her husband a cuckold to make him a
monarch? I should venture purgatory for't.

DESDEMONA. Beshrew me, if I would do such a
wrong
For the whole world.

EMILIA. Why, the wrong is but a wrong i' the
world; and having the world for your labour, 'tis
a wrong in your own world, and you might quickly
make it right.

DESDEMONA. I do not think there is any such
woman.

EMILIA. Yes, a dozen; and as many to the vantage
As would store the world they played for.
But I do think it is their husbands' faults
If wives do fall: say that they slack their duties,
And pour our treasures into foreign laps,
Or else break out in peevish jealousies,
Throwing restraint upon us; or say they strike us,
Or scant our former having in despite;
Why, we have galls, and though we have some grace,
Yet have we some revenge. Let husbands know
Their wives have sense like them: they see and smell
And have their palates both for sweet and sour,
As husbands have. What is it that they do
When they change us for others? Is it sport?
I think it is: and doth affection breed it?
I think it doth: is't frailty that thus errs?
It is so too: and have not we affections,
Desires for sport, and frailty, as men have?
Then let them use us well: else let them know,

330 *The wrong . . . make it right,* such behaviour is only wrong in
the eyes of the world, and if you owned the world you
could make your own rules.
335 *to the vantage,* in addition.
336 *store,* people (with their children).
337–354 omitted in First Quarto.   339 *foreign,* strangers'.
342 *scant our former having,* reduce our allowances.
343 *galls,* tempers.
349 *affection,* passion, desire, or appetite.

The ills we do, their ills instruct us to.

    DESDEMONA. Good night, good night : heaven me
      such uses send,

Not to pick bad from bad, but by bad mend.

(Exeunt.)

354 *their ills instruct us to.* *Cf.* Shylock, " The villainy you teach
     us we will execute, and it shall go hard but we will better
     the instruction."

356 *Not to pick bad . . . mend.* Not to learn evil from bad example,
     but, having suffered through it, to learn to live better.

ACT V

SCENE I. *Cyprus. A street.*

(*Enter* IAGO *and* RODERIGO.)

IAGO. Here, stand behind this bulk ; straight will
　　he come :
Wear thy good rapier bare, and put it home,
Quick, quick ; fear nothing ; I'll be at thy elbow :
It makes us, or it mars us, think on that,
And fix most firm thy resolution.

RODERIGO. Be near at hand ; I may miscarry in't.

IAGO. Here, at thy hand : be bold, and take thy
　　stand.　　　　　　　　　　　　(*Retires.*)

RODERIGO. I have no great devotion to the deed ;
And yet he hath given me satisfying reasons :
'Tis but a man gone.　Forth, my sword : he dies.

IAGO. I have rubb'd this young quat almost to the
　　sense,
And he grows angry.　Now, whether he kill Cassio,
Or Cassio him, or each do kill the other,
Every way makes my gain : live Roderigo,
He calls me to a restitution large
Of gold and jewels that I bobb'd from him,
As gifts to Desdemona ;
It must not be : if Cassio do remain,
He hath a daily beauty in his life

---

1 *bulk,* buttress or projection.
3 *put it home, i.e.* into Cassio's body.
11 *quat,* pimple or spot ; *to the sense,* to the quick.
16 *bobb'd from him,* cheated him of.

127

20 That makes me ugly ; and, besides, the Moor
May unfold me to him ; there stand I in peril :
No, he must die.   But so : I hear him coming.
(Enter CASSIO.)

RODERIGO. I know his gait, 'tis he.—Villain, thou
    diest !   (Makes a pass at CASSIO.)
CASSIO. That thrust had been mine enemy indeed,
But that my coat is better than thou know'st :
I will make proof of thine.
(Draws, and wounds RODERIGO.)

RODERIGO.   O, I am slain !
(IAGO from behind wounds CASSIO in the leg, and exit.)
CASSIO. I am maim'd for ever.   Light, ho ! murder !
    murder !   (Falls.)
(Enter OTHELLO.)

OTHELLO. The voice of Cassio : Iago keeps his
    word.
RODERIGO. O villain that I am !
OTHELLO.   It is even so.
30 CASSIO. O help, ho ! light ! a surgeon !
OTHELLO. 'Tis he :—O brave Iago, honest and
    just,
That hast such noble sense of thy friend's wrong !
Thou teachest me.   Minion, your dear lies dead,
And your unblest fate hies : strumpet, I come.
Forth of my heart those charms, thine eyes, are blotted ;
Thy bed, lust-stain'd, shall with lust's blood be
    spotted.   (Exit.)
(Enter LODOVICO and GRATIANO.)

CASSIO. What, ho ! no watch ? no passage ?
    murder ! murder !

---

25 *my coat is better*, Cassio, as an officer, would be wearing a
    leather jerkin.   Iago wisely thrusts lower.
(*Enter Othello*), probably on the gallery above the main stage.
    He is obviously out of the action.
33 *Minion*, a loose woman.   *Cf.* French *mignon*, darling (in a bad
    sense).
37 *no passage ?*   No passer-by ?

Gratiano. 'Tis some mischance; the cry is very direful.

Cassio. O help!

Lodovico. Hark!

Roderigo. O wretched villain!

Lodovico. Two or three groan: it is a heavy night: These may be counterfeits, let's think 't unsafe To come in to the cry without more help.

Roderigo. Nobody come? then shall I bleed to death.

Lodovico. Hark!

(*Re-enter* Iago, *with a light.*)

Gratiano. Here's one comes in his shirt, with light and weapons.

Iago. Who's there? Whose noise is this that cries on murder?

Lodovico. We do not know.

Iago.   Did not you hear a cry?

Cassio. Here, here! for heaven's sake, help me!

Iago.   What's the matter?

Gratiano. This is Othello's ancient, as I take it.

Lodovico. The same indeed; a very valiant fellow.

Iago. What are you here that cry so grievously?

Cassio. Iago? O, I am spoil'd, undone by villains! Give me some help.

Iago. O me, lieutenant! what villains have done this?

Cassio. I think that one of them is hereabout, And cannot make away.

Iago.   O treacherous villains! (*To* Lodovico *and* Gratiano) What are you there? Come in, and give some help.

Roderigo. O help me here!

---

42 *heavy,* dark.
43 *counterfeits,* a trap laid by thieves to draw us into the shadow.

CASSIO. That's one of them.

IAGO.   O murderous slave ! O villain !
                              (*Stabs* RODERIGO.)

RODERIGO. O damn'd Iago ! O inhuman dog !

IAGO. Kill men i' the dark !—Where be these
  bloody thieves ?

How silent is this town !—Ho ! murder ! murder !—
What may you be ?   Are you of good or evil ?

LODOVICO. As you shall prove us, praise us.

IAGO. Signior Lodovico ?

LODOVICO. He, sir.

IAGO. I cry you mercy.   Here's Cassio hurt by
  villains.

70 GRATIANO. Cassio !

IAGO. How is't, brother ?

CASSIO. My leg is cut in two.

IAGO.   Marry, heaven forbid !
Light, gentlemen : I'll bind it with my shirt.
                    (*Enter* BIANCA.)

BIANCA. What is the matter, ho ?   Who is't that
  cried ?

IAGO. Who is't that cried !

BIANCA. O my dear Cassio ! my sweet Cassio !
O Cassio, Cassio, Cassio !

IAGO. O notable strumpet ! Cassio, may you suspect

Who they should be that have thus mangled you ?

80 CASSIO. No.

GRATIANO. I am sorry to find you thus : I have
  been to seek you.

(*Stabs* RODERIGO.) This extra murder of Iago's is often overlooked.   There is nothing tragic in Roderigo's death, but
  the ruthless murder of the poor dupe must be taken into
  account in assessing Iago's character.   It also helps to delay
  the resolution of the plot.

66 *praise us*, appraise, decide whether we are " of good or evil."

74 *Who is't that cried ?*   Repeated by Iago in a tone implying,
  "As if you didn't know ! "

IAGO. Lend me a garter. So. O for a chair,
To bear him easily hence !
    BIANCA. Alas, he faints ! O Cassio, Cassio,
      Cassio !
    IAGO. Gentlemen all, I do suspect this trash
To be a party in this injury.
Patience awhile, good Cassio. Come, come ;
Lend me a light. Know we this face or no ?
Alas, my friend and my dear countryman ;
Roderigo ? no :—yes, sure :—O heaven ! Roderigo.
    GRATIANO. What, of Venice ?
    IAGO. Even he, sir : did you know him ?
    GRATIANO.   Know him ? ay.
    IAGO. Signior Gratiano ? I cry you gentle pardon;
These bloody accidents must excuse my manners,
That so neglected you.
    GRATIANO.   I am glad to see you.
    IAGO. How do you, Cassio ? O, a chair, a chair !
    GRATIANO. Roderigo !
    IAGO. He, he, 'tis he. (*A chair brought in.*) O that's
      well said ; the chair.
Some good man bear him carefully from hence ;
I'll fetch the general's surgeon. (*To* BIANCA) For
    you, mistress,
Save you your labour. He that lies slain here, Cassio,
Was my dear friend : what malice was between
    you ?
    CASSIO. None in the world ; nor do I know the
    man.
    IAGO (*to* BIANCA). What, look you pale ? O bear
    him out o' the air.
            (CASSIO *and* RODERIGO *are borne off.*)
Stay you, good gentlemen. Look you pale, mistress ?
Do you perceive the gastness of her eye ?

---

82 *a garter*, to use as tourniquet.
85 *trash*, good-for-nothing woman.
101 *Save you your labour*, Bianca has probably been trying to
    dress Cassio's wound.   106 *gastness*, ghastliness, terror.

Nay, if you stare, we shall hear more anon.
Behold her well ; I pray you, look upon her :
Do you see, gentlemen ? Nay, guiltiness will speak,
110 Though tongues were out of use.

(*Enter* EMILIA.)

EMILIA. 'Las, what's the matter? what's the
matter, husband ?
IAGO. Cassio hath here been set on in the dark
By Roderigo and fellows that are 'scaped :
He's almost slain, and Roderigo dead.
EMILIA. Alas, good gentleman ! Alas, good Cassio !
IAGO. This is the fruit of whoring. Pray,
Emilia,
Go know of Cassio where he supp'd to-night.
(*To* BIANCA) What, do you shake at that ?
BIANCA. He supp'd at my house ; but I therefore
shake not.
120   IAGO. O did he so ? I charge you, go with me.
EMILIA. Fie, fie upon thee, strumpet !
BIANCA. I am no strumpet ; but of life as honest
As you that thus abuse me.
EMILIA.   As I ! foh ! fie upon thee !
IAGO. Kind gentlemen, let's go see poor Cassio
dress'd.
Come, mistress, you must tell's another tale.
Emilia, run you to the citadel,
And tell my lord and lady what hath happ'd.
(*To* LUDOVICO *and* GRATIANO) Will you go on afore ?
(*Aside*) This is the night
That either makes me or fordoes me quite. (*Exeunt.*)

107 *if you stare*, although you may stare in silence we shall find
means (*i.e.* by torture) to make you talk. First Quarto
reads, " if you stir."
109 *guiltiness will speak, etc.* Her guilt is betrayed by her face

SCENE II.   *A bedchamber in the castle :* DESDEMONA
in bed asleep.

(*Enter* OTHELLO *with a light.*)
   OTHELLO. It is the cause, it is the cause, my soul,
Let me not name it to you, you chaste stars !
It is the cause.   Yet I'll not shed her blood ;
Nor scar that whiter skin of hers than snow,
And smooth as monumental alabaster.
Yet she must die, else she'll betray more men.
Put out the light, and then put out the light :
If I quench thee, thou flaming minister,
I can again thy former light restore,
10 Should I repent me : but once put out thine,
Thou cunning'st pattern of excelling nature,
I know not where is that Promethean heat
That can thy light relume.   When I have pluck'd the
      rose,
I cannot give it vital growth again,
It must needs wither : I'll smell it on the tree.
                              (*Kisses her.*)
Ah, balmy breath, that dost almost persuade
Justice herself to break her sword ! Once more :
Be thus when thou art dead, and I will kill thee,
And love thee after.   One more, and this the last :
20 So sweet was ne'er so fatal.   I must weep,
But they are cruel tears : this sorrow's heavenly ;
It strikes where it doth love.   She wakes.

---

1 *It is the cause,* this is not a crime of passionate revenge, but
     the stroke of justice, " else she'll betray more men."
7 *Put out the light.*   " Thy " is sometimes preferred to " the "
     in the second clause.   It spoils the metaphor by over-
     explaining, and robs the second " light " of its meaning
     for Othello himself.   He put out his own light in killing
     Desdemona.   Both Quartos and the First Folio give " the."
8 *flaming minister,* the light carried by Othello.
12 *Promethean heat,* fire stolen from heaven.
21 *this sorrow's heavenly,* " Whom the Lord loveth he chasteneth."

133

DESDEMONA. Who's there ?   Othello ?
OTHELLO.   Ay, Desdemona.
DESDEMONA. Will you come to bed, my lord ?
OTHELLO. Have you pray'd to-night, Desdemona ?
DESDEMONA.   Ay, my lord.
OTHELLO. If you bethink yourself of any crime
Unreconcil'd as yet to heaven and grace,
Solicit for it straight.

    DESDEMONA. Alas, my lord, what do you mean by
    that ?

30 OTHELLO. Well, do it, and be brief ; I will walk
    by :
I would not kill thy unprepared spirit ;
No ; heaven forfend ! I would not kill thy soul.
    DESDEMONA. Talk you of killing ?
    OTHELLO.   Ay, I do.
    DESDEMONA.   Then heaven
Have mercy on me !
    OTHELLO.   Amen, with all my heart !
    DESDEMONA. If you say so, I hope you will not
    kill me.
    OTHELLO. Hum !
    DESDEMONA. And yet I fear you ; for you are fatal
    then
When your eyes roll so : why I should fear I know not,
Since guiltiness I know not ; but yet I feel I fear.

40 OTHELLO. Think on thy sins.
    DESDEMONA.   They are loves I bear to you.
    OTHELLO. Ay, and for that thou diest.
    DESDEMONA. That death's unnatural that kills for
    loving.
Alas, why gnaw you so your nether lip ?
Some bloody passion shakes your very frame :
These are portents ; but yet I hope, I hope,
They do not point on me.

37 *fatal*, deadly.
41 *Ay, and for that thou diest*, because you once loved me (and then
    deceived me).

OTHELLO.　　　　　　　　Peace, and be still!

DESDEMONA.　I will so.　What's the matter?

OTHELLO.　That handkerchief which I so lov'd and
gave thee
Thou gavest to Cassio.

DESDEMONA.　　　　　　No, by my life and soul!
Send for the man, and ask him.

OTHELLO.　　　　　　　　Sweet soul, take heed,
Take heed of perjury; thou art on thy death-bed.

DESDEMONA.　Ay, but not yet to die.

OTHELLO.　　　　　　　　　　Yes, presently:
Therefore confess thee freely of thy sin;
For to deny each article with oath
Cannot remove nor choke the strong conception
That I do groan withal.　Thou art to die.

DESDEMONA.　Then Lord have mercy on me!

OTHELLO.　　　　　　　　　I say, amen.

DESDEMONA.　And have you mercy too!
I never did offend you in my life;
Never lov'd Cassio,
But with such general warranty of heaven
As I might love; I never gave him token.

OTHELLO.　By heaven, I saw my handkerchief in's
hand.
O perjur'd woman! thou dost stone my heart,
And makest me call what I intend to do
A murder, which I thought a sacrifice:
I saw the handkerchief.

DESDEMONA.　　　　　　He found it then;
I never gave it him: send for him hither;
Let him confess a truth.

OTHELLO.　　　　　　　He hath confess'd.

DESDEMONA.　What, my lord?

---

52 *presently*, at once.
55 *conception*, conviction (of your guilt).
65 *makest me call . . . sacrifice*, your protestations are rousing me
　　to anger so that I kill in passion, not from an impersonal
　　sense of justice.

OTHELLO. That he hath . . . us'd thee.

DESDEMONA.   How ? unlawfully ?

OTHELLO. Ay.

DESDEMONA. He will not say so.

OTHELLO.   No, his mouth is stopp'd ;
Honest Iago hath ta'en order for't.

DESDEMONA. My fear interprets then. . . .   What,
is he dead ?

OTHELLO. Had all his hairs been lives, my great
revenge
Had stomach for them all.

DESDEMONA. Alas ! he is betray'd and I undone.

OTHELLO. Out, strumpet ! weep'st thou for him
to my face ?

80   DESDEMONA. O banish me, my lord, but kill me
not !

OTHELLO. Down, strumpet !

DESDEMONA. Kill me to-morrow : let me live to-
night !

OTHELLO. Nay, if you strive—

DESDEMONA. But half an hour !

OTHELLO.   Being done, there is no pause.

DESDEMONA. But while I say one prayer !

OTHELLO.   It is too late.
                    (*He stifles her.*)

EMILIA (*within*). My lord, my lord ! what, ho !
my lord, my lord !

OTHELLO. What noise is this ? Not dead ? not
yet quite dead ?
I that am cruel am yet merciful ;
I would not have thee linger in thy pain . . .
90 So, so.

EMILIA (*within*). What, ho ! my lord, my lord !

---

84 *Being done*, once started.
    He stifles her.   First Quarto gives Desdemona a line here :
    "O how, how, how !"

89 *I would not have thee linger . . . So, so.* On the question as to
    how Othello gives the *coup de grâce*, see p. 155.

OTHELLO. Who's there?

EMILIA (*within*). O good my lord, I would speak
a word with you!

OTHELLO. Yes: 'tis Emilia. By and by. She's
dead.
'Tis like she comes to speak of Cassio's death.—
The noise was here. Ha! no more moving?
Still as the grave. Shall she come in? were't
good?—
I think she stirs again:—no. What's best to do?
If she come in, she'll sure speak to my wife:
My wife, my wife, what wife? I have no wife.
O insupportable! O heavy hour!
Methinks it should be now a huge eclipse
Of sun and moon, and that the affrighted globe
Should yawn at alteration.

EMILIA (*within*). I do beseech you I may speak
with you,
O good my lord!

OTHELLO. I had forgot thee: O, come in, Emilia:
Soft; by and by. Let me the curtains draw.
Where art thou? (*Unlocks the door.*)
(*Enter* EMILIA.)
What's the matter with thee now?

EMILIA. O my good lord, yonder's foul murders
done!

OTHELLO. What, now?

EMILIA. But now, my lord.

OTHELLO. It is the very error of the moon;
She comes more nearer earth than she was wont,
And makes men mad.

EMILIA. Cassio, my lord, hath kill'd a young
Venetian

---

101 *a huge eclipse,* "—and then put out the light."
102 *globe should yawn at alteration,* the earth should gape in horror
at the change.
110 *What, now?* Othello is taken by surprise and thinks only of
his own crime.

Call'd Roderigo.

OTHELLO.   Roderigo kill'd !
And Cassio kill'd !

EMILIA.   No, Cassio is not kill'd.

OTHELLO. Not Cassio kill'd ! Then murder's out
of tune,
And sweet revenge grows harsh.

120 DESDEMONA. O, falsely, falsely murder'd !

EMILIA.   O Lord, what cry is that ?

OTHELLO. That ? what ?

EMILIA. Out, and alas ! that was my lady's voice.
Help ! help, ho ! help ! O lady, speak again !
Sweet Desdemona ! O sweet mistress, speak !

DESDEMONA. A guiltless death I die.

EMILIA. O, who hath done this deed ?

DESDEMONA. Nobody ; I myself. Farewell :
Commend me to my kind lord : O, farewell ! (*Dies.*)

OTHELLO. Why, how should she be murder'd ?

EMILIA.   Alas, who knows ?

130 OTHELLO. You heard her say herself, it was not I.

EMILIA. She said so : I must needs report the
truth.

OTHELLO. She's like a liar gone to burning hell :
'Twas I that kill'd her.

EMILIA.   O the more angel she,
And you the blacker devil !

OTHELLO. She turn'd to folly, and she was a whore.

EMILIA. Thou dost belie her, and thou art a devil.

OTHELLO. She was false as water.

EMILIA.   Thou as rash as fire,
To say that she was false : O she was heavenly true !

OTHELLO. O I were damn'd beneath all depth in
hell,

140 But that I did proceed upon just grounds
To this extremity. Thy husband knew it all.

EMILIA. My husband ?

---

128 *Commend me*, formal phrase (*cf.* remember me to —).

138

OTHELLO. Thy husband.

EMILIA. That she was false to wedlock ?

OTHELLO. Ay, with Cassio. Nay, had she been
    true,
If heaven would make me such another world
Of one entire and perfect chrysolite,
I'ld not have sold her for it.

EMILIA. My husband ?

OTHELLO.   Ay, 'twas he that told me first :
An honest man he is, and hates the slime
That sticks on filthy deeds.

EMILIA.   My husband ?

OTHELLO. What needs this iteration, woman ? I
    say thy husband.

EMILIA. O mistress, villany hath made mocks with
    love !
My husband say that she was false !

OTHELLO.   He, woman ;
I say thy husband : dost understand the word ?
My friend, thy husband, honest, honest Iago.

EMILIA. If he say so, may his pernicious soul
Rot half a grain a day ! he lies to the heart :
She was too fond of her most filthy bargain.

OTHELLO. Ha !

EMILIA. Do thy worst :
This deed of thine is no more worthy heaven
Than thou wast worthy her.

OTHELLO.   Peace, you were best.

EMILIA. Thou hast not half the power to do me
    harm
As I have to be hurt. O gull ! O dolt !

147 *chrysolite*, green-coloured, semi-precious stone.
151 *My husband*. Note how the dramatist helps Emilia to build
    up, ready for her " big scene."
153–156 omitted in First Quarto.
160 *Ha !* Othello draws his sword.
164 *Thou hast not half the power . . . hurt*, I can bear much more
    than you can ever inflict.

As ignorant as dirt ! thou hast done a deed—
I care not for thy sword ; I'll make thee known,
Though I lost twenty lives.—Help ! help, ho ! help !
The Moor hath kill'd my mistress ! Murder ! murder !
        (*Enter* MONTANO, GRATIANO, IAGO, *and others.*)

170 MONTANO. What is the matter ?   How now,
        general !

    EMILIA. O, are you come, Iago ?   you have done
        well,
That men must lay their murders on your neck.

    GRATIANO. What is the matter ?

    EMILIA. Disprove this villain, if thou be'st a man :
He says thou told'st him that his wife was false :
I know thou didst not, thou'rt not such a villain.
Speak, for my heart is full.

    IAGO. I told him what I thought, and told no more
Than what he found himself was apt and true.

180 EMILIA. But did you ever tell him she was false ?

    IAGO. I did.

    EMILIA. You told a lie ; an odious, damned lie ;
Upon my soul, a lie, a wicked lie.
She false with Cassio ! Did you say with Cassio ?

    IAGO. With Cassio, mistress.   Go to, charm your
        tongue.

    EMILIA. I will not charm my tongue ; I am bound
        to speak :
My mistress here lies murder'd in her bed,—

    ALL. O heavens forfend !

    EMILIA. And your reports have set the murder on.

190 OTHELLO. Nay, stare not, masters : it is true,
        indeed.

    GRATIANO. 'Tis a strange truth.

    MONTANO. O monstrous act !

    EMILIA.   Villany, villany, villany !

---

171 *You have done well . . . neck,* you have managed things well to
        get the blame for other people's murders.   Emilia does not
        yet fully believe Othello's story that Iago is responsible.
185 *charm your tongue,* be silent.

I think upon't—I think . . . I smell't . . . O villany !
I thought so then—I'll kill myself for grief :—
O villany, villany !

   IAGO. What, are you mad ? I charge you, get
you home.

   EMILIA. Good gentlemen, let me have leave to
speak :
'Tis proper I obey him, but not now.
Perchance, Iago, I will ne'er go home.

   OTHELLO. O ! O ! O !   (*He falls on the bed.*)

   EMILIA.   Nay, lay thee down and roar ;
For thou hast kill'd the sweetest innocent
That e'er did lift up eye.

   OTHELLO (*rising*).   O, she was foul !
I scarce did know you, uncle : there lies your niece,
Whose breath, indeed, these hands have newly
stopp'd :
I know this act shows horrible and grim.

   GRATIANO. Poor Desdemona ! I am glad thy
father's dead :
Thy match was mortal to him, and pure grief
Shore his old thread in twain. Did he live now,
This sight would make him do a desperate turn,
Yea, curse his better angel from his side,
And fall to reprobation.

   OTHELLO. 'Tis pitiful ; but yet Iago knows
That she with Cassio hath the act of shame
A thousand times committed. Cassio confess'd it,

---

194 *I thought so then*, see IV. ii. 132, also III. iii. 315–319, but it is
     doubtful whether Emilia has yet remembered the hand-
     kerchief ; note her exclamation when Othello speaks of it
     (below, l. 220).
207 *mortal*, fatal.
208 *shore his old thread*, a reference to the Greek myth. The three
     Fates presided over the life of man—Clotho drew the thread
     from the distaff, Lachesis spun it from birth to death,
     Atropos cut the thread off at death.
211 *fall to reprobation*, commit an act which would cause his
     damnation.

And she did gratify his amorous works
With that recognizance and pledge of love
Which I first gave her.   I saw it in his hand :
It was a handkerchief, an antique token
My father gave my mother.

220 EMILIA. O God ! O heavenly God !

IAGO.   'Zounds, hold your peace.

EMILIA. 'Twill out, 'twill out : I peace !
No, I will speak as liberal as the north :
Let heaven and men and devils, let them all,
All, all, cry shame against me, yet I'll speak.

IAGO. Be wise, and get you home.

EMILIA.   I will not.

(IAGO *offers to stab* EMILIA.)

GRATIANO.   Fie !

Your sword upon a woman ?

EMILIA. O thou dull Moor ! that handkerchief thou
    speak'st of
I found by fortune and did give my husband ;
For often, with a solemn earnestness,

230 More than indeed belong'd to such a trifle,
He begg'd of me to steal it.

IAGO.   Villanous whore !

EMILIA. She give it Cassio ? No, alas, I found it,
And I did give't my husband.

IAGO.   Filth, thou liest !

EMILIA. By heaven, I do not, I do not, gentlemen.
O murderous coxcomb ! what should such a fool
Do with so good a woman ?

OTHELLO.   Are there no stones in heaven
But what serve for the thunder ? Precious villain !

(*He runs at* IAGO ; IAGO, *from behind, stabs* EMILIA,
    and exit.)

---

222 *as liberal as the north*, as freely (and with the same devastating
    effect) as the north wind.   First Quarto : " as the air."
235 *coxcomb*, fool (metonymy, the fool's cap for the person).
236 *no stones . . . thunder*, *i.e.* none to spare for the destruction of
    Iago.

GRATIANO. The woman falls ; sure, he hath kill'd
his wife.

EMILIA. Ay, ay : O lay me by my mistress's side.

GRATIANO. He's gone, but his wife's kill'd.

MONTANO. 'Tis a notorious villain. Take you this
weapon,
Which I have here recover'd from the Moor :
Come, guard the door without ; let him not pass,
But kill him rather. I'll after that same villain,
For 'tis a damned slave.

(Exeunt all but OTHELLO *and* EMILIA.)

OTHELLO. I am not valiant neither,
But every puny whipster gets my sword.
But why should honour outlive honesty ?
Let it go all.

EMILIA. What did thy song bode, lady ?
Hark, canst thou hear me ? I will play the swan,
And die in music. *(Singing) Willow, willow, willow.*—
Moor, she was chaste ; she lov'd thee, cruel Moor ;
So come my soul to bliss, as I speak true ;
So speaking as I think I die, I die. *(Dies.)*

OTHELLO. I have another weapon in this chamber ;
It is a sword of Spain, the ice-brook's temper :—
O, here it is. *(Calling)* Uncle, I must come forth.

GRATIANO *(within)*. If thou attempt it, it will cost
thee dear :
Thou hast no weapon, and perforce must suffer.

OTHELLO. Look in upon me then and speak with me,
Or, naked as I am, I will assault thee.

(Re-enter GRATIANO.)

GRATIANO. What is the matter ?

OTHELLO. Behold, I have a weapon ;
A better never did itself sustain
Upon a soldier's thigh : I have seen the day,

241 *notorious*, notable, gross. Not modern meaning.
246 *whipster*, stripling, whipper-snapper.
248 *What did thy song bode*, etc. These lines referring to the
willow song are, of course, cut in First Quarto.

That, with this little arm and this good sword,
I have made my way through more impediments
Than twenty times your stop.   But, O vain boast !
Who can control his fate ?   'Tis not so now.
Be not afraid, though you do see me weapon'd ;
Here is my journey's end, here is my butt,
270 And very sea-mark of my utmost sail.
Do you go back dismay'd ?   'Tis a lost fear ;
Man but a rush against Othello's breast,
And he retires.   Where should Othello go ?
Now, how dost thou look now ?   O ill-starr'd wench !
Pale as thy smock ! when we shall meet at compt,
This look of thine will hurl my soul from heaven,
And fiends will snatch at it.   Cold, cold, my girl,
Even like thy chastity.   O cursed slave !
Whip me, ye devils,
280 From the possession of this heavenly sight !
Blow me about in winds ! roast me in sulphur !
Wash me in steep-down gulfs of liquid fire !
O Desdemona ! Desdemona, dead !
O ! O ! O !

(*Enter* Lodovico, Montano, Cassio *carried in a chair,
            and* Officers *with* Iago, *prisoner.*)

  Lodovico. Where is this rash and most unfortunate
    man ?
  Othello. That's he that was Othello : here I am.
  Lodovico. Where is that viper ? bring the villain
    forth.

---

266 *your stop*, any resistance you could offer.
269 *butt*, aim (archery).
270 *very sea-mark*, the final beacon to which I steer.   *Cf.* Romeo :
            " Thou desperate pilot, now at once run on
            The dashing rocks thy sea-sick weary bark."
271 *'Tis a lost fear*, unnecessary fear.
272 *Man but a rush*, attack me with nothing stronger than a rush.
275 *at compt*, the final judgement.
279 *Whip me, ye devils*, cf. in *Measure for Measure*, Claudio's descrip-
            tion of damned souls, and both with Dante's *Inferno*.

OTHELLO. I look down towards his feet ; but that's a fable.
If that thou be'st a devil, I cannot kill thee.

(Wounds IAGO.)

LODOVICO. Wrench his sword from him.

IAGO.   I bleed, sir ; but not kill'd.

OTHELLO. I am not sorry neither : I'ld have thee live ;
For, in my sense, 'tis happiness to die.

LODOVICO. O thou Othello, that wert once so good,
Fall'n in the practice of a damned slave,
What shall be said to thee ?

OTHELLO.   Why, any thing :
An honourable murderer, if you will ;
For nought I did in hate, but all in honour.

LODOVICO. This wretch hath part confess'd his villany :
Did you and he consent in Cassio's death ?

OTHELLO. Ay.

CASSIO. Dear general, I never gave you cause.

OTHELLO. I do believe it, and I ask you pardon.
Will you, I pray, demand that demi-devil
Why he hath thus ensnar'd my soul and body ?

IAGO. Demand me nothing : what you know, you know :
From this time forth I never will speak word.

LODOVICO. What, not to pray ?

GRATIANO.   Torments will ope your lips.

OTHELLO. Well, thou dost best.

LODOVICO. Sir, you shall understand what hath befall'n,
Which, as I think, you know not. Here is a letter
Found in the pocket of the slain Roderigo ;
And here another : the one of them imports

288 *towards his feet*, expecting the cloven hoof.
292 *in my sense*, in my opinion and mood.
307 *Torments*, torture.

The death of Cassio to be undertook
By Roderigo.

OTHELLO.　O villain !

CASSIO.　　　　Most heathenish and most gross !

LODOVICO.　Now here's another discontented paper,
Found in his pocket too ; and this, it seems,
Roderigo meant to have sent this damned villain ;
But that belike Iago in the nick
320 Came in and satisfied him.

OTHELLO.　　　　O the pernicious caitiff !
How came you, Cassio, by a handkerchief
That was my wife's ?

CASSIO.　　　　I found it in my chamber :
And he himself confess'd but even now
That there he dropp'd it for a special purpose
Which wrought to his desire.

OTHELLO.　　　　O fool ! fool ! fool !

CASSIO. There is besides in Roderigo's letter,
How he upbraids Iago, that he made him
Brave me upon the watch, whereon it came
That I was cast : and even but now he spake,
330 After long seeming dead, Iago hurt him,
Iago set him on.

LODOVICO. You must forsake this room, and go
　　with us :
Your power and your command is taken off,
And Cassio rules in Cyprus. For this slave,
If there be any cunning cruelty
That can torment him much and hold him long,
It shall be his. You shall close prisoner rest,
Till that the nature of your fault be known
To the Venetian state. Come, bring him away.
340　OTHELLO. Soft you ; a word or two before you go.

316 *discontented paper*, a letter of complaint.
319 *nick*, in the nick of time.
320 *satisfied him*, paid him in full. Ironic, referring to Iago's
　　murder of Roderigo.
329 *cast*, dismissed.

I have done the state some service, and they know't.
No more of that. I pray you, in your letters,
When you shall these unlucky deeds relate,
Speak of me as I am ; nothing extenuate,
Nor set down aught in malice. Then must you
    speak
Of one that loved not wisely but too well ;
Of one not easily jealous, but, being wrought,
Perplex'd in the extreme ; of one whose hand,
Like the base Indian, threw a pearl away
50 Richer than all his tribe ; of one whose subdued
    eyes,
Albeit unused to the melting mood,
Drop tears as fast as the Arabian trees
Their med'cinable gum. Set you down this ;
And say besides, that in Aleppo once,
Where a malignant and a turban'd Turk
Beat a Venetian and traduc'd the state,
I took by the throat the circumcised dog,
And smote him, thus.   (*Stabs himself.*)
    LODOVICO. O bloody period !
    GRATIANO.   All that's spoke is marr'd.
60   OTHELLO. I kiss'd thee ere I kill'd thee : no way
    but this ;

347 *being wrought*, worked upon.
348 *Perplex'd*, deeply stirred and thrown into confusion. (Much
    stronger than modern meaning.)
349 *base Indian*, First Folio gives Judean, but the association
    between " pearl " and " Indian " seems stronger. Pro-
    bably in those early days of trading there would be current
    many stories of the natives' ignorance of the value of their
    goods.
353 *med'cinable*, medicinal.
354 *Aleppo*, a stronghold of Mohammedanism.
355 *malignant*, anti-Christian. *Cf.* Puritan use of the term in
    reference to Cavaliers.
359 *period*, conclusion.
    All that's spoke is marr'd, all our arrangements are wasted ; or,
    more probably, the apparently reasonable speech is de-
    stroyed by such an ending.

Killing myself, to die upon a kiss.

(Falls on the bed, and dies.)

Cassio. This did I fear, but thought he had no
    weapon ;
For he was great of heart.

Lodovico *(to* Iago*)*.   O Spartan dog,
More fell than anguish, hunger, or the sea !
Look on the tragic loading of this bed ;
This is thy work : the object poisons sight,
Let it be hid. Gratiano, keep the house,
And seize upon the fortunes of the Moor,
For they succeed on you. To you, lord governor,
370 Remains the censure of this hellish villain ;
The time, the place, the torture : O, enforce it !
Myself will straight aboard ; and to the state
This heavy act with heavy heart relate.

(Exeunt.)

361 *to die upon a kiss. Cf.* Romeo, Mark Antony.
363 *Spartan,* double reference both to Iago's silence and to the
    savagery of Spartan hounds.
367 *Let it be hid,* the signal for the curtains to be drawn across the
    inner stage, so dispensing with a funeral procession.
369 *lord governor,* Cassio.
370 *censure,* judgement upon.

AFTER A FIRST READING

ABOUT THE CHARACTERS

As we read one of Shakespeare's plays we find ourselves believing in the reality of the people he has drawn. We identify ourselves with some in their sorrows, others we hate for their evil-doing, as we should pity or hate them were we to meet them in real life. They cease to be puppets of which one man, Shakespeare, pulls the strings ; they become the stuff of life itself and the creator is lost sight of in the convincing reality of his creation.

It is right that this should be so. Belief in the independent existence of his characters is the highest tribute that can be paid to a writer, just as " complete illusion " in the theatre (*i.e.* forgetting that the players are " only acting ") is the finest compliment that can be paid to actors. For the characters of a play are alive in the mind of the poet as he writes ; they live again in the mind of the actor who must portray them ; and every reader of the play is potentially the actor of all or any of the parts as he reads. The actor who is to play Othello or Iago must read and re-read the play until, as he acts, he *is* Othello or Iago.

But here a word of warning. In his play Shakespeare has no time, not even the time granted to a novelist, to reveal all the details of his characters (this, apart from the fact that much that a novelist must do the playwright can safely leave to his actors). Nor does photographic reality suit the purpose of the playwright. A dramatist gives us only what is essential to the theme of his play ; to draw a comparison with the cinema, he chooses the particular " camera angle " that will suit his purpose. Sometimes, in our enthusiasm, we are tempted to give the characters a more specious reality than Shakespeare intended them to have, to superimpose a petty and frivolous decoration upon the original. It is as if we were to take crayons or paint and clumsily colour in a finely conceived etching or the heads and figures in the sketch books of Leonardo da Vinci. In so doing we drag art back to reality and undo all that the artist has done to give his work significance. For Truth is greater than Reality ; it is the patterning of everyday stuff by a master-mind.

This sense of the truth of Shakespeare's characterization does not always come at a first reading. How many of us could, after meeting a person for the first time, give more than a general account of him ? We could say whether he was gay or surly, likable or repulsive, tender or harsh in manner. But to find motives for his behaviour, weigh good qualities against bad, excuse faults and give exact merit to virtues would take years of acquaintanceship. So a first swift reading of *Othello* will give us only a general impression. We can say, " Iago is a villain," and perhaps, with Emilia, that Desdemona was " too fond of her most filthy bargain," or with Othello himself that he " loved not wisely, but too well." But only after several careful readings can we begin to estimate the characters or to appreciate Shakespeare's craftsmanship in drawing portraits so true in so few lines.

The best way to study the characterization in a play is to tackle it in the same way that a producer prepares for its presentation. The play is read through several times, as many times as there are leading characters, and at each reading he concentrates upon one particular character as if he were preparing to play the part himself. This does not mean that he reads only the lines of the character concerned, but that he reads the whole play from the " angle " of the particular character concerned. For example, the scene between Othello and Iago, Act IV. scene i., must be read twice, once from the point of view of Othello, and again from that of Iago. The difference between the two " sub-texts " (or mental backgrounds) will be obvious. As we read for Othello we must wipe from our minds all knowledge of Desdemona's innocence, of Emilia's theft of the handkerchief, of Iago's schemes. We must see Iago as Othello sees him, a frank and loyal servant. Only then can we get " under the skin " of Othello's agony, agony so intense that it drives him into a fit. Then, as we turn to study Iago, we must forget our own natural pity—for Iago had none—and despise this black-faced, credulous, middle-aged fool ; we must feel pride in our skill and trickery and appraise with cold curiosity the Moor's despair. Only then can we understand Iago as he watches the stricken general, only then appreciate his " diabolical indifference."

The following comments on the principal characters are intended as assistance, perhaps provocation, to the student who is engaged upon such a detailed study. There is no attempt to insist upon editorial preconceptions ; they are the expression of an individual opinion based upon study of the play and observation of human beings in general. Similarly, the quotations from standard authorities are given amongst the essay questions and intended rather as an invitation to discussion than as *ex cathedra* statements. For the only estimate of any character, whether in fiction or in real life, that can be true for each of us is that which we have arrived at from our own experience and reactions. Let us learn to know Shakespeare's people for ourselves, not from report, or from the judgment, however wise or authoritative, of others.

OTHELLO

(It is suggested that the study of Othello should come first because, if we concentrate first on, say, Iago, it will be impossible to clear from our minds the knowledge of his intrigues and an obsession with his evil.) We have many comments on Othello's character from other people in the play. Iago tells us that the general is

> . . . of a free and open nature
> That thinks men honest that but seem to be so.

Desdemona, too, bears witness that he is

> . . . true of mind and made of no such baseness
> As jealous creatures are.

And when he first betrays his jealousy she finds him so changed that

> Were he in favour as in humour altered
> I should not know him.

But let us look at Othello for ourselves. We first meet him when Iago warns him against the coming of Brabantio and Roderigo. He is calm and prepared to answer for his actions. He receives an urgent summons to the Senate ; faces a blustering father ; quells a threatened brawl with a snub to hot-heads who would fight on any pretext : " Were it my cue to fight, I should have known it without a prompter." Then he quietly departs to face the Senate and Brabantio's accusations. In this short scene we meet a man of courage, dignity, iron self-control, and honourable pride.

AFTER A FIRST READING

The scene in the Senate House develops further this first glimpse of his steadfast and open nature, and adds to it his loyalty to his employers, his love for Desdemona, and his trust in his servant, Iago. We learn all we need to know of his past life and adventures, and of how he wooed Desdemona only after she had given him obvious encouragement. His speech to the Senate gives us also a first glimpse of Othello's sensitive imagination, of the poet that is in him : " . . . antres vast and deserts idle . . . hills whose heads touch heaven."

But to call Othello a poet does not mean only that he has a happy knack of choosing words and rhythms that please the ear. After all, one might argue that this was only Shakespeare letting his pen run away with him. A poet is more than a versifier ; he is a man who " sees life steadily and sees it whole." He patterns not only phrases, but life itself. Of speech he makes a poem ; of life a composition, a picture. The Othello of Act I. is a " whole " man, a man whose life has pattern and purpose. Into this pattern he has woven his courage, his faith in his fellow-men, his pride of race, and now—the golden thread which completes the design—his love and idealization of Desdemona. We are reminded of this in Act II. when he first greets his wife. Here, in one sentence, he gives complete expression to this sense of " wholeness " :

> If it were now to die
> 'Twere now to be most happy.

The further study of Othello concerns itself with the breaking up of this unity. He himself gives us warning of it :

> When I love thee not, chaos is come again.

Immediately upon this Iago plants in his mind a seed

of doubt. It is only doubt. Othello's first agony is that he has lost his peace of mind :

> I swear 'tis better to be much abus'd
> Than but to know a little.

He is, as yet, by no means convinced of his wife's guilt. The shame of suspecting her eats at his heart. He must have proof. But this very need of proof has destroyed his self-respect. He no longer feels himself a leader of men, constant, unmoved :

> Farewell the tranquil mind . . . Othello's occupation's gone.

When he loses his peace of mind he ceases to be a soldier ; but when damning evidence has been brought by one whom he trusts and he loses his faith in Desdemona, he ceases to be a man :

> A horned man's a monster and a beast !

Chaos has come again.

The "chaos" shows three distinct phases of development. First, the torture so works upon Othello that he is thrown into a fit of epilepsy. But close on this comes his conviction of Cassio's guilt. He resolves on Cassio's murder, and for a few moments regains stature : " How shall I murder him, Iago ? " A second phase shows itself when, in sudden uncontrollable anger and misery, he strikes Desdemona. But this sudden break of self-control, simple and natural enough in any ordinary man who is convinced of his wife's guilt (however shocking in one of Othello's calibre and reputation) is sanity itself compared with the scene that follows. The Othello of Act IV. Scene ii. is a madman, in the very depth of his " chaos." Bradley, in discussing " the distaste for *Othello*," shows how many people take exception to the brutality of striking Desdemona ; but the

nauseating mental cruelty of the "brothel" scene
would be unendurable were it not for the poetry in
which Othello's despair finds expression :

> O thou black weed, why art so lovely fair?
> Thou smell'st so sweet that the sense aches at thee

The soldier and the lover have gone, but the poet still
remains, even now when all else is "perplexed in
the extreme." Though in this scene Othello comes
nearest to alienating all sympathy, he still holds us
to him by his poetry. A man whose despair finds such
expression cannot be contemptible.

From now onward we watch the reintegrating of
Othello's character. When we next see him he has
regained his dignity, "He looks gentler than he did."
He has managed to sublimate personal jealousy into
a "cause"; his idealism has triumphed. The
Othello of Act V. is once more of heroic stature.
Desdemona must die, not as punishment, not to
satisfy Othello's lust for revenge, but lest "she
betray more men" — more men like Cassio, once
Othello's closest friend, as well as more men like
himself.

If this final mood is properly understood, the
suggestion that Othello gives the *coup de grâce* to
Desdemona (ll. 89–90) with a dagger is seen to violate
both dramatic and psychological truth. A sudden
return to the physical brutality necessary for a dagger-
thrust is impossible at this moment, a gross anticlimax. Othello completes his murder with bare
hands on Desdemona's throat. To quote against this
Othello's line, "White as thy smock," with medical
evidence on death by strangulation, or even, as some
have done, to argue in return that if Othello had used
a dagger the smock would have been blood-stained
and not white, is an insult to Shakespeare and to all
who have ever played Othello. It is as if one con-

sulted an ornithologist on Shelley's *Skylark*. Does not the Oxford English Dictionary state, in flat contradiction to the poet, that a skylark *is* a bird?

For a little while this reintegration of Othello is threatened; but he moves through the clamour of Emilia's accusation and scorn, through the horror of his discovery of Iago's treachery, to his final speech. Here he shows himself complete once more, with whatever dross was in him purged away. The soldier, the lover, the poet, and more than this, a man whose suffering has shown him life's complete pattern. He is greater than when we first met him, the play's poetic purpose has been served, and with his own sword Othello puts "Finis" to the poem that was his life.

IAGO

When we were studying the character of Othello we found that it was necessary to ignore the true nature of Iago, and to look upon the trusted servant with the eyes of the deceived general. But it is impossible to concentrate upon Iago without taking into account the characters, not only of Othello, but of all the other principals, for all are pawns in Iago's game of revenge. Iago was under no misapprehension (except as regards Emilia) as to the kind of people who surrounded him; his whole management of the central intrigue springs from his shrewd knowledge. But Iago's understanding of Othello in particular is of paramount importance, for the unity of the play can be fully appreciated only when we realize that Othello's character is the mainspring and motive of Iago's behaviour.

All that is base and evil in Iago is challenged by all that is noble in Othello. Iago's villainy is not motiveless. It is the expression of evil, which, of its very nature, must seek to destroy good. In the hatred of evil for good lies the motive. If the study of Othello is the study of the break-up and final reintegration of a noble mind, the study of Iago fails unless it answers the question, " Why did he seek to destroy Othello ? "

Long before the end of Act I. (where Iago conveniently confides something of his plans to the audience) one significant point of contrast between the two men has been made clear. Iago (like Shakespeare, if we credit Bernard Shaw) " loves a shindy." He hounds on Roderigo and Brabantio, and, when these two and their followers encounter Othello, is eager for a fight. It is Othello, calm and self-secure, who prevents a brawl from breaking out. It should be remarked in passing that it is the *creating* of a shindy that most delights Iago, not the participation in it. (Note also Act II. Scene iii., and Act V. Scene i.)

Here, then, are the two main pillars upon which the playwright is to build : the Moor, " of a constant loving disposition," and Iago, a stirrer-up of " shindies," an instigator of hate and passion ; Iago, a self-confessed hater of the man he serves, Othello " a man not easily jealous " ; Iago, cold and calculating in his hatred, Othello, " being moved, perplexed in the extreme."

" I hate the Moor." Is not this motive enough ? " Hates any man the thing he would not kill ? " And, again to quote Shylock, " Affection [*i.e.* instinctive feeling], mistress of passion, sways it to the mood of what it likes or loathes." It is true that Iago himself takes pains to dig out motives for this hatred. He suspects Othello of overfamiliarity with Emilia, albeit the suspicion is uncertain ; he is angry that Othello should give precedence to Cassio, a " theoretician," when Iago has seen active service at Othello's side ; he himself loves Desdemona. But these motives, protests the decent man, are not strong enough to justify the horror that Iago brings upon

his master. Of course not. But Iago is not a
" decent " man. No-one knows better than Iago
that these " reasons " are only thought up *after* the
determination to destroy Othello has been taken.
These are excuses, not motives. Like many men who
despise the control of passion over human behaviour,
and exalt the supremacy of reason above the emotions
(" We have reason to cool our raging motions, our
carnal stings, our unbitted lusts "), he rationalizes
his own emotion of hatred in order to justify to himself his indulgence of it. To admit to himself that his
hatred of Othello is an instinctive passion, not based
on reason, would be to deny the truth of his own
philosophy.

Iago is bitterly jealous of Othello's superiority.
" Were I the Moor, I would not be Iago," that is,
" had I Othello's position and respect, I should not
need to cloak my hatred under an apparent devotion."
Added to this is a racial scorn of the coloured man.
This Iago betrays again and again, *e.g.* " His Moorship's ancient."

The question of Iago's love for Desdemona is a
vexed one. " Now I do love her too " (Act II.
Scene i. l. 292). Again, the decent man would argue
that if Iago loves Desdemona he would, surely,
though seeking to destroy Othello, make every effort
to save Desdemona's life. Yet it is Iago who suggests
the means of Desdemona's murder, and, worse still,
can look unmoved upon her distress at the end of Act
IV. Scene ii. The word " sadism " probably answers
this problem best. He enjoys the torture of the thing
he loves, particularly since he has no hope of possessing
it himself. We must also take into account here the
original source of Shakespeare's plot (see p. 188). In
Cinthio's story the ensign's love of Desdemona and
her refusal of his overtures are the main motive for
the plot against Othello. Shakespeare's genius for character creation almost dispenses with " plot " in the

ordinary sense, and he seems here to drag in this motive as something of an afterthought. For the sake of the conventional story it is mentioned as one of the motives, but immediately the statement is qualified and Shakespeare re-emphasizes the central conflict of character between the two men. Iago will be even with Othello " wife for wife." For Iago to confess physical desire for Desdemona would again be a denial of his philosophy that reason can control passion. Love is " merely a lust of the blood and a permission of the will. . . . Ere I would drown myself for the love of a guinea-hen, I would change my humanity with a baboon." Moreover, for Shakespeare to have allowed Iago's love for Desdemona as the main motive for Iago's villainy would have brought the play down to the crude level of " triangle drama " and fogged the central dramatic issue. Iago's insistence that his love for Desdemona is rather the result than the cause of his hatred for Othello maintains the unity of the central theme of jealousy, and this is given extra emphasis by Emilia's outburst :

> Some such squire he was
> That turned your wit the seamy side without
> And made you to suspect me with the Moor.

Incidentally, Shakespeare here cleverly clears the spectator's (and reader's) mind of any suspicion as to the justification of Iago's jealousy (he had merely listened to some silly tale), and at the same time underlines the aptness of Iago's revenge, for Othello's suspicions, too, are founded on hearsay and cozening.

Can we then dismiss Iago's character as the personification of evil, finding particular expression in a passion of jealousy, jealousy of the Moor's social and military superiority and of his happy choice of bride ? By no means. Shakespeare drew men, not "humours." Iago, in spite of his villainy, compels a certain grudging admiration, much as Milton's Satan "steals the show" in *Paradise Lost*. Unfortunately, there are many human qualities which can be esteemed as good or bad only when considered in the light of the uses to which they are put. The devil himself has been praised for perseverance. Iago has a cool head in a crisis; he knows when to take the initiative and when to let events follow their own course; admirable qualities, considered in the abstract. But, in Iago, this entails the cold-blooded murder of the wounded Roderigo, the accusation of Bianca as being party to the attempted murder of Cassio. Iago is quick-witted enough to take advantage of chance opportunities: " 'Tis here, but yet confused; knavery's plain face is never seen till used." But he is a master of strategy as well as tactics. He plans his campaign with a shrewd knowledge of his enemy and of attendant circumstances, taking care that all shall serve his turn. The uneasy state of the town and the susceptibility to insult of the local gentry will, he knows, turn what might elsewhere be forgiven as a mere lapse on Cassio's part into a serious military offence. He knows Desdemona well enough to be sure that she will help Cassio; knows Cassio well enough to be certain that he will seize upon the suggestion of using her as his mediator. To put it bluntly: Iago is no fool. He shares not only Caius Cassius's jealous, grudging disposition ("Upon what meat does this our Cæsar feed that he is grown so great?"), but another characteristic feared by Cæsar: "He thinks too much," and, like Cassius, he is therefore dangerous.

Iago's twenty-eight years of life, having failed to make of him more than an ensign, have turned him into a cynic. He despises Cassio for his courtier's manners, despises Othello for his ingenuousness and trusting disposition. Women he holds wholly in contempt. His scathing rhymes for Desdemona's amusement are not mere badinage, nor merely an illustration of his ready wit. Nor is Shakespeare only playing for time in this brief scene. Women, to Iago, are wantons and chattels, the worthiest of them fit only to " suckle fools and chronicle small beer." It is this cynicism, this inability to recognize the existence of positive goodness and its power to take action, that proves Iago's undoing. He despises Emilia ; but it is her righteous indignation, her love for her mistress and scorn of personal safety, that finally reveal his villainy.

Iago's cleverness is not mere criminal cunning. His speeches show him to be a man who, from reading and from observation of life, has worked out for himself a clear personal philosophy. His insistence upon reason as guiding force, his scorn of emotion, his inability to recognize the ideals which prompt the behaviour of others, are all in keeping with the doctrines of ruthless self-interest and power-seeking that have (somewhat unfairly) been laid at the door of the Florentine, Machiavelli. To the blunt English-men of Shakespeare's day the subtle Italian philoso-phy was as alien, and yet as much discussed and misinterpreted by them, as Freud's psychological theories were to the healthy-minded and determinedly non-introspective Englishman of the nineteen-twen-ties. Iago *as a type* was of topical interest to the Elizabethan audience. In Shakespeare's hands the type becomes an all-round human being, and we learn from a study of Iago that a man chooses and distorts to his own uses the current philosophy that fits his inherent qualities. Iago, a villain by nature, looks for a creed that will seem to justify him ; much as certain undisciplined natures seized upon the psychologist's theories on " inhibitions " and " com-plexes " as a grandiose excuse for self-indulgence.

Iago, like Othello, has a poet's imagery and a

power over words. He loves to elaborate a lie with neat corroborative detail. He takes a keen intellectual pleasure in playing with half-truths and using them to better effect than a downright lie. He is, in fact, an artist, a superb actor, with an intense joy in exercising his abilities. He is a conscious, intellectual artist ; Othello, an instinctive one.

In modern psychological terms, Iago is a megalomaniac. That is, the mainspring of his actions is the need to assert his power over his fellow creatures. He must know himself supreme ; others must dance to his piping, must submit to his experiments upon them. As a Toscanini, a Wagner, or a Shakespeare, as a surgeon or an engineer, he would have found satisfaction and a harmless outlet for his creative genius. But he is only an ensign with a lust for power and a greed for sensation. To express this magnificence within himself he must use the material that Providence has given him : his general, Desdemona, Emilia, Cassio, Roderigo. In the closing lines of *Tess of the D'Urbervilles* Thomas Hardy writes, " The President of the Immortals had ended his sport with Tess." So would Iago have played with his victims. But he is not President of the Immortals. He is human, more tied to earth, indeed, than those out of whom he has tried to fashion his masterpiece. Shakespeare maintains the consistency of his character-drawing to the very end. Here we have no eleventh-hour repentance, no Edmund trying, too late, to remedy the wrong he has done. Nor does Shakespeare allow Iago the dignity of self-inflicted death. Iago ends as he began, refusing to " wear his heart upon his sleeve."

> Demand me nothing ; what you know you know.
> From this time forth I never will speak word.

One doubts whether the threatened torture will ever

open those lips. Disgust at his own failure will be torture enough. Farewell the stirring-up of shindies ; farewell the thrill of lying like an artist ; farewell the joy of watching weaker mortals tortured to madness by his subtle poison. He, the invincible, the paragon of villainy, has failed. Iago's occupation's gone.

Though the theme of *Othello* is particularly concerned with the conflict of character between Iago and his general, we cannot dismiss the rest of the *dramatis personæ* under the slick generalization of " full supporting cast." Desdemona, Emilia, Roderigo, Cassio, Bianca—not only is each of these characters essential to the mechanics of the plot, but Shakespeare has taken the pains to give to each of them a full human reality.

It is impossible here to give more than a brief indication as to how these characters may be approached, but the questions on page 215 also bring up some of the main problems.

DESDEMONA

The central fact that matters about Desdemona is her love for Othello, the Moor. The glamour of his life and adventures first awakens this love ; and mingled with it is, perhaps, a little fear, for the essence of glamour is mystery, and the step between the mysterious and the frightening is a short one. That Desdemona had seen Othello in the grip of anger, and had learnt to fear him in such moods, is revealed by her line :

> And yet I fear you, for you are fatal then
> When your eyes roll so.

It is this fear of Othello (combined with a belief in

his story of the supernatural) that prompts the lie about the lost handkerchief. Desdemona's nerve fails her. However perfect her love, it has not cast out fear. This loss of nerve is in strong contrast to her courage in facing her father and the assembled Senate. Then, proud of her love and conscious of Othello's support, she firmly maintains her right of choice.

Both Brabantio and Iago lay great stress upon the " unnaturalness " of her choice of the Moor. But Desdemona is not a silly young girl attracted by a bizarre adventure, so spoilt, as a rich man's daughter, that she must find some utterly new and startling sensation (though Iago hints to Othello that such are her reasons for choosing so strange a match). In Desdemona's love there is the essential quality of pity and of " mothering."

> She loved me for the dangers I had passed,
> And I loved her that she did pity them.

There is, too, a deep admiration for Othello's noble qualities which far outweighs any prejudice of colour.

> I saw Othello's visage in his mind.

This is the Desdemona who so readily takes up the cause of the dismissed Cassio ; it is the same Desdemona who, once having vowed her obedience to Othello, answers his cruel blow with the simple, " I have not deserved this." In no scene is the steadiness of her love for Othello and her own crystal innocence more apparent than in Act IV. Scene ii. Othello's wild accusations are met with dignity, not with loud and weeping protest :

> If to preserve this vessel for my lord
> From any hated foul unlawful touch
> Be not to be a strumpet, I am none.

And later, in strong contrast with Emilia's frank speech, we find her quietly asking, " Am I—that name, Iago ? " In those five words Shakespeare probably tells us all we need to know of Desdemona.

Once Desdemona realizes that she has lost Othello's love and respect, she is changed. She drifts along the stream, helpless in the current of tragedy. " A child to chiding," she can no longer see her way clear. She is almost consciously preparing for her death, but indifferent to her fate, until, at the last minute, a physical reaction to the horror of it prompts her to plead for mercy, steadily protesting her innocence. The second and last lie we hear from Desdemona's lips is the final proof of her unchanged love for Othello :

> EMILIA : Oh, who hath done this deed?
> DESDEMONA : Nobody. I myself . . . farewell.
> Commend me to my kind lord. Oh—farewell.

Desdemona could have no better epitaph than that spoken by Emilia :

> Oh, she was heavenly true !

EMILIA

Iago's wife is not only the confidante and foil to Desdemona, but in her hands is the all-important " discovery " scene at the end. Emilia is at first described by Desdemona as too silent (though Iago warns Desdemona that she is mistaken) ; the first share in the *action* taken by Emilia is her theft of the handkerchief for Iago. This would suggest that the central idea in Emilia's development is the transference of her loyalty from Iago to Desdemona. Emilia is a woman of the world, of coarser texture than her mistress, frankly spoken, and generoushearted ; and the gentle Desdemona wins her devotion.

That Emilia is innocent of Iago's plot there can be no doubt. She certainly suggests that *someone* is cozening Othello, but she suspects nobody in particular. She feels some uneasiness when Iago snatches from her the handkerchief she intended only to copy ; we wonder a little at her silence when Desdemona shows obvious distress at its loss. There seems little doubt that, until the moment of supreme courage in the last scene, Emilia is afraid of Iago, or, at any rate, is completely controlled by him. Shakespeare also gives us every reason to believe that she was completely deceived in him. The " build-up " of her realization of his treachery is a fine example of Shakespeare's inside knowledge of the player's art : " My husband ? " thrice repeated, with longer speeches of Othello between.

The contrast between Emilia and Desdemona balances that between the two husbands. Emilia is honest enough, up to a point, but is under no illusion as to her own standards or motives. Prepared to admit that there are wantons in the world (this the gentle-hearted Desdemona cannot bear to believe), she owns herself to be of steadier stuff. In the last scene with Desdemona Emilia tries, by her frank chatter and airy belittling of the sin which Desdemona thinks is impossible, to prevent her mistress from becoming morbid and depressed.

Many of the apparent contradictions and inconsistencies of Emilia's behaviour have to be accounted for by the exigencies of the plot. Had she dared to scold Othello for his suspicions as roundly in Act IV. as in the last scene all might have been well—but there would have been no play. Emilia does her best to persuade Othello of Desdemona's innocence, but at this moment Othello is beyond argument or reasoning. Any sane man would need but to look at Desdemona to know her to be true. Iago, too, had skilfully prepared Othello for any such pleading from

Emilia, by telling him that all Venetian women were born liars.

Emilia's character stands out in this play with refreshing straightforwardness and lack of subtlety. She is the sanest of them all ; the nearest to common-sense life. Two loyalties guide her actions, the one to her husband, the other to her mistress. When she finds these to be irreconcilable her sense of justice triumphs, and she sacrifices herself for her mistress's good name.

CASSIO

To arrive at a true estimate of the character of Cassio we must try to study him apart from the intrigues of Iago. From Iago, indeed, we can accept the fact that this newly-appointed lieutenant has not seen a great amount of active service ; but against Iago's scorn of Cassio as a mere " counter-caster " we must weigh the fact that Othello, an experienced general, thought him fit for the post, and that later the Venetian Council appointed him to replace Othello.

What else do we know of Cassio ? That he acted as go-between in Othello's courtship ; that he was to be trusted with a secret—witness his pretended ignorance of the marriage (always presuming that this is not a playwright's slip). Iago's scorn of his gallantry and " drawing-room manners " should not lead us to over-emphasize this side of Cassio's character. So far as dialogue shows he merely observes the ordinary rules of etiquette of an experienced courtier. He betrays something of the catch-phrase habits of a fashion-follower in his over-use of the word " exquisite."

His respect and admiration for Desdemona are obvious and sincere, but there is no hint of anything beyond this, though Iago tries to persuade himself that Cassio is in love with her. Cassio's affair with Bianca merely stamps him as being "a man of the world," though, in passing, it might be said that a man who was eating his heart out for the love of a woman like Desdemona would hardly be so frankly amused and boisterous about the attentions of a mistress of whom he was growing tired.

Cassio is most alive and authentic (less a mere pawn of the playwright) in the third scene of Act II. His frank admission that he has no head for strong drink, his gentle protestations that he should be excused from the evening's debauchery, find an interesting echo in a description of Shakespeare by the son of a fellow-actor : "he [Shakespeare] was not a company keeper . . . would not be debauched, and if invited to, writ, 'he was in pain.'" When Cassio, in spite of his attempt at refusal, has been well primed with liquor we get another sidelight on his character. Something of a Puritan Shakespeare must have intended him (to say nothing of the playwright's temptation to "set on some of the lower sort to laugh"), for while he is in the disputatious stage of drunkenness Cassio holds forth on predestination, with an amusing persistence on salvation by military precedence. This tendency to moralize is present when he is sober : "O that men should put an enemy in their mouths to steal away their brains!" "Reputation" means much to this quiet young gentleman. His humility and shame before Othello proclaims his unbounded respect for his friend.

Cassio is no weakling, no mere court-butterfly. Like the virile young courtiers of Shakespeare's acquaintance he could hold his own with the sword as well as with the tongue. The real nobility of the young man who so narrowly escapes adding his name to the list of Iago's victims is probably most shrewdly revealed by a single line of gentle reproach :

AFTER A FIRST READING

Lodovico : . . . Did you and he consent in Cassio's death?
Othello : Ay!
Cassio : Dear general, I did never give you cause.

Roderigo

This wretched gentleman of Venice is a puppet that dances entirely to Iago's manipulation. He is a witless fellow with an *idée fixe*—his sentimental attachment to Desdemona. He is Iago's " purse," to be fobbed off with plausible excuses whenever he asks for results. He is also, to some extent, Iago's weapon. Unfortunately (for himself) he fumbles his main job, and Iago in all his villainy is nowhere more contemptible than when he gives the death-stroke to this poor dupe. It is perhaps worth while observing that though, as a general rule, *nothing* that Iago says to another character should be credited without careful investigation, he often comes near the truth when talking to Roderigo—he despises him so thoroughly. Many a man (and woman) tells the truth when talking to a dog. Shakespeare makes full use of this psychological fact in the early expository scenes.

The minor characters of the play have life and authenticity, and all are conceived in a manner which serves to underline the urgency and ruthlessness of the central action. Brabantio banishes Desdemona from his sight, yet dies of grief for the loss of her ; Bianca, loose-living but devoted to Cassio, is suddenly the victim of Iago's opportunist villainy. The Doge and the Senators are interrupted in the midst of urgent state affairs by the appeal of Brabantio, and the very speed with which the matter is settled underlines their preoccupation.

It is interesting to note that neither in *Othello* nor to any appreciable extent in the preceding tragedy, *Hamlet*, is there a satisfactory part for a comedian. This coincides with a certain " interregnum." Kempe (the creator of Peter in *Romeo and Juliet*, and of Falstaff) had left the company towards the end of 1599, according to some reports because his fellow-actors objected to his gagging.* Robert Arnim, who took his place, was a comedian of a different style, and we find him at the height of his powers in *King Lear*. Except for an obvious " fill-in " at the opening of Act III., the play *Othello* is without comic relief. This fact is a reminder that Shakespeare was writing for a familiar company of actors, and that he created his characters with these living instruments well in mind.

SHAKESPEARE'S STAGE AND ACTORS

The Stage

THE first recorded performance of *Othello* took place in the banqueting hall of Whitehall on November 1, 1604, though possibly the play was already an established success in the public theatre. Such presentations in the private theatres of the king or the wealthier nobles were very frequent ; often they were semi-public, admission costing half a crown in contrast with the cheaper prices (from one penny to a shilling) in theatres like The Swan, The Globe, The Fortune.

It was primarily for the stage of the public theatres that Shakespeare wrote his plays, and for the stage alone, with no thought of publication, until the unauthorized sale of " pirated " copies made this advisable. It will not be waste of time, then, to recall some of the differences between the stage for which Shakespeare wrote and that of our own day.

The playhouses were small ; for example, The

---

* *Cf. Hamlet* : Let those that play your clowns speak no more than is set down for them.

Fortune (1600), which was square, had outer walls about eighty feet long. Many of the other theatres were circular, *e.g.* The Swan, The Globe (the theatre used by Shakespeare's company). The tiers of boxes and galleries were built round the sides, still retaining a resemblance to the inn yards where the strolling players had been accustomed to set up their stages. The stage end carried a higher roof than the tiled or thatched covering that ran round the galleries, and from this stage roof the flag was hoisted when a performance was to take place. A second roof (called " the heaven " by the actors) covered the main area of the large, out-jutting stage. This main playing area projected (at The Fortune) twenty-seven and a half feet into the " pit," where the groundlings stood, and was forty-three feet wide. Greater playing depth was gained by use of the " inner stage," a curtained alcove beneath the back gallery (see note to l. 367, Act V. Scene ii). The gallery above was also used on occasion; for example, for Othello's brief appearance during the first scene of the last act.

CONTINUITY OF PLAYING

Performances took place in broad daylight, at two o'clock in winter, three in summer, and except for the stage and the tiers of boxes, were open to the sky. There was no proscenium curtain, and the action carried on without pauses between scenes. The present division of the plays into acts and scenes is the arbitrary work of scholar-editors, or found its way in to the text as " scenes " so marked for the convenience of the players. A " scene " started when a fresh group of actors came on the stage, or when the imaginary site of the action was changed. The scene ended with the exit of the actors, such ending often being marked by a rhymed tag or couplet. This method of scene indication is still used in the text of French plays ; and the present-day producer of a modern three-act play usually divides the thirty or forty minutes of a continuous act into "scenes"— for convenience in rehearsal—though the audience will be quite unconscious of any such division when the play is performed. Perhaps the best modern analogy with the Shakespearean scene is the film "sequence." During the two hours' run of a film (and the Shakespearean performance lasted about two hours) the action moves from scene to scene without interruption or "curtain" ; very rarely nowadays do we even get a complete "black-out"— scene dissolves into scene and the rhythm of these sequences is part of the artistry of good "cinema."

It is important when reading *Othello* to bear in mind this uninterrupted continuity, so that it may be realized how the speed of presentation affords no time for the audience to query inconsistencies that may come to light when the play is read and re-read in the study. There are many things in Shakespeare's plays that reward the student for his close attention and private study, but the hunting out of "mistakes," anachronisms, and contradictions of fact, the wonderings as to what may have happened off-stage (Mrs. Siddons as Lady Macbeth spent her spare time drinking porter) are petty and unprofitable pursuits. The reward of close study should be the realization of how and why Shakespeare became the world's foremost dramatist (that is incontrovertible fact) ; and the art of the dramatist lies in this very skill of ignoring logic and possibility just up to the point when the audience will not be shocked out of its "willing suspension of disbelief." Dramatic technique might well be summed up in the two colloquial phrases : "putting it across" and "getting away with it."

If we inquire too closely into Shakespeare's time

sequence in *Othello*, we make the uncomfortable discovery that from the night when Othello married Desdemona to Iago's first whispering of his suspicions there has been not a single opportunity for Cassio and Othello's wife to commit the misdeeds of which they are accused. But how many people seeing or reading the play for the first time realize this ? And how many of us, when this has been pointed out, are not prepared to brush aside time's petty measurement rather than sacrifice our belief in the play. Shakespeare is no metronome musician.

INTIMACY OF PRESENTATION

Some of the spectators in the " boxes " were less than ten feet away from the stage, the " groundlings " were close at the players' feet, and no part of the auditorium was more than thirty feet away from the actors. Moreover, the actors were visible " in the round," and not presented in a " picture frame." This partly explains the speed with which the actors were able to speak their lines and still be intelligible. Consider also the absence of heavy stage lighting, footlights, etc., which nowadays builds up so fierce a barrier between players and audience. Aside and soliloquy were then no mere conventions, and the identification of actor with audience was as easy as that of a teller of a fireside story with his friend in the opposite chair.

There was no attempt, in our modern sense, to " set " the scene. Rich trappings and curtainings were used ; easily shifted furniture helped to give some indication of the setting. The actors wore rich and outstanding garments suitable to the parts they played, but the stage set was the playwright's job. Shakespeare painted his own settings in his poetry. No painted backcloth, flying clouds projected on to a cyclorama, or the most earnest off-stage pebble-shaking can conjure up the storm at the opening of Act II. more vividly than Shakespeare's first seventeen lines.

THE ACTORS

The companies or fellowships of players worked rather on the lines of a modern repertory company. They played together for many years, and were not, as in the modern West End theatres, recruited for some special play, to disperse when the " run " is over. The King's Players (as Shakespeare's company was called after the accession of James I.) were prepared to play on the " Sunday after Hollowmas, *The Merry Wives of Windsor* ; Hollowmas, *The Moore of Venice* ; St. Stephen's Night, *Measure for Measure*." Richard Burbage played " lead " in this company—Hamlet, Richard III., Othello, Lear. Boys, of course, played the women's parts ; this is one of the reasons why, in the comedies, it was so simple a matter for a girl to " disguise " herself credibly as a boy.

The theatre was run as a co-operative concern, the senior actors holding shares in the business. When The Globe opened in 1599 Shakespeare held a tenth share both in the profits and in the responsibility. By 1604, owing to the sharing out amongst fresh actors (and the bequeathing of shares to heirs outside the profession by former shareholders who had died), the dramatist held a little less than a tenth. His share of the profits during these early years of the century would, on a rough estimate, work out at about £150 per year (modern value perhaps £800 or £900).* From this one can assume that the leading players of the time were in fairly comfortable circumstances.

The theatres were not playing all the year round,

---

* This, of course, was not Shakespeare's only source of income. See p. 176. For full details see Sir Sidney Lee's *Life of Shakespeare*.

and there were frequent closings during outbreaks of the plague. At such times the company would take to the road and tour the provinces.*

The reason that many people find a play by Shakespeare rather a tough proposition on the modern stage is partly because great acting has become a minor attraction compared with stage presentation and the mere " story " that is told. The Elizabethan audience went to the theatre to see *acting* ; to hear the music of language finely spoken. Shakespeare's lines call for the best of an actor's art and a keen dramatic sense from the audience. To the modern conception of Shakespeare as a " highbrow " it may seem strange that the people who first applauded his genius and filled The Globe to listen to his poetry and approve Burbage's " Hamlet " and " Othello," crowded with the same eager interest to watch the hanging and disembowelling of their fellow citizens. But is this so very surprising when we consider the plot of some of Shakespeare's tragedies ? Shakespeare catches up into poetry the brutality they witnessed every day. The Elizabethan audience could be carried away by swift and bloody action borne on a flood of poetry, could be made drunken with grand verse ; rejoiced, indeed, to find their own brutality made magnificent. Small wonder that plays written for such conditions have stood the test of centuries, and that the English-speaking actor who would learn his job thoroughly finds in Shakespeare's plays his best training school.

THE MAN WHO WROTE *OTHELLO*

SHAKESPEARE wrote *Othello* when he was about forty years old. The main facts of his life up to this point (if the student is not already acquainted with them)

* Shakespeare's Company are known to have played in Bath, Oxford, and Mortlake in 1604.

can be learnt from the brief summary given on pages 231-32. What most interests us here is the sort of man he was, and the life that he was probably leading during the time that he was writing this play, rehearsing it with his fellow-actors, and playing it before the London public and his royal and aristocratic patrons.

As far as worldly position and reputation went, Shakespeare was by now well established. He had made his name as a poet and playwright—particularly as a master of comedy. He was well in favour at the court ; earlier in the year of *Othello's* first performance (1604) the leading players of his company (now the King's Servants) had been made Grooms of the Chamber, and were in receipt of a small allowance for this office. James I. was a good friend to actors ; previously, as James VI. of Scotland, he had even dared to champion a travelling company of English players against the Kirk Sessions of Edinburgh. In August 1604 Shakespeare and his friends were called upon to attend certain Spanish envoys who were in London on a diplomatic mission. They do not appear to have given a dramatic performance for the benefit of these gentlemen.

In addition to his income from the Globe Theatre and his salary as Groom of the Chamber, Shakespeare was in receipt of certain sums from the performance of his plays in public, at court, and in the private theatres of the nobility. He was the owner of New Place, the largest house in Stratford ; he had at last established his right to a coat of arms, and in this either set or followed the fashion of many other actors of repute. In short, Shakespeare, like his Merchant Antonio of Venice, was a "sufficient man."

He seems normally to have lived in Southwark, near his theatre, but during 1604 (except for about three weeks at Somerset House, where the Spaniards were lodged) he was living in Silver Street, near Wood Street, Cheapside, at a wig-maker's, where he was instrumental in bringing about a marriage between a reluctant apprentice and his host's daughter. Nor was he the only member of his family in London ; there was, too, his younger brother, Edmund, "also a player," who was buried in Southwark in 1607.

From first establishing himself in the theatre up to the year 1601 Shakespeare had been writing plays and preparing scripts for the stage at the rate of three a year. Until he left London in 1611 he was working regularly as an actor. Of the rôles he played there is little record. His elder brother, Gilbert, mentions having seen him as Adam, in *As You Like It*, and he is reputed to have played the Ghost in his own *Hamlet*. In Ben Jonson's *Every Man in His Humour* he played the Elder Knowell. Something of the dramatist's voice and bearing may be gathered from this. He seems to have been a competent actor, according to the critics of his day, and it was certainly as an actor that he first established himself with a reputable company of players.

If eccentricity and a difficult temperament are, as many believe, the hallmark of genius, Shakespeare did not run true to type. Except for Greene's embittered outburst about the " upstart crow " and some sneers from the rough-tongued Ben Jonson (and these were at his work rather than his character) all contemporary comments on Shakespeare praise his courtesy and gentleness of manner. The epithet " sweet Shakespeare " was first used by his contemporaries ; the publisher Chettle, who first took up the cudgels on his behalf, described his demeanour as " no less civil than he excellent in the quality that he professes,* besides divers of worship have reported his uprightness of dealing, which argues his honesty,

---

* *i.e.* the profession he follows.

and his facetious grace in writing that approves his art." And whatever Ben Jonson may have said about him in their days of rivalry is out-balanced by his words : " I loved the man and do honour his memory, on this side idolatry, as much as any. He was, indeed, honest and of an open and free nature."

Success did not spoil Shakespeare. " He would not be debauched, and when invited writ, He was in pain." How far this was polite excuse, how far it points to a physique not over-robust is not known. Certain it is, that no man could get through the amount of work that Shakespeare set himself and have much time to spare for careless company. Webster pays tribute to " the right happy and copious industry of Mr. Shakespeare." But he was no recluse. We are told that he was " good company, and of a very ready and pleasant smooth wit." He was a frequent visitor to the Mermaid Tavern, where Ben Jonson presided over the " lyric feasts." Fuller described the " wit combats between Shakespeare and Ben Jonson . . . like a Spanish galleon and an English man-of-war ; Master Jonson (like the former) was built far higher in learning, solid, but slow in his performance. Shakespeare, with the English man-of-war, lesser in bulk, but lighter in sailing, could turn with all tides, tack about, and take advantage of all winds by the quickness of his wit and invention." Perhaps, like Cassio, he took care that his wine was " craftily qualified " and so kept his wit the nimbler.

Yet Shakespeare was writing his highest tragedies—*Othello*, *Macbeth*, *Lear*—when the Mermaid's Poets' Club was at its heyday. Raleigh had founded the club in 1603, but a few months later he was a prisoner in the Tower. The tavern still remained the meeting-place of the poets, and we can imagine Shakespeare leaving a half-written *Othello* at his lodgings that he might seek refreshment of body and wits in argument and back-back-chat with Jonson, Donne, Chapman,

Michael Drayton. Then back home through the dark or moonlit streets of London, one or two friends with him, his sword at his side ; and, were it his cue to fight, he would no doubt know it without a prompter. Certainly one Londoner of the time, " a certain loose person of no reckoning or value," claimed legal security against the dramatist and his friends " for fear of death or mutilation of his limbs."

Hamlet was written in 1601 (to be rewritten and patched later). This play heralded Shakespeare's " tragic period," though *Twelfth Night* and the so-called comedy *Measure for Measure* belong to this time, and an earlier draft of a play, *Love's Labours Won*, was rewritten as *All's Well that Ends Well*. These comedies offer proof enough that the dramatist was now seeing " the web of life " as " a mingled yarn, good and ill together." The carefree foolery of the early comedies was gone.

The web of a man's art is also of mingled yarn : part, like the spider, he must spin from out himself, but unless he reinforces this with strands drawn from the life around him it will prove too frail a thing. To talk of *Shakespeare's* tragic period and to ignore the mood of the dying age of Elizabeth and the " squalid peace " of James I. is to deny the very source of a poet's inspiration. Shakespeare was of his own age, as well as for all time. Ben Jonson was turning his hand from " pot-boiling " tragedies to comedy with a purpose :

> With an armed and resolved hand,
> I'll strip the ragged follies of the time
> Naked as at their birth.

But whilst Jonson, like the Bedlam keepers of his day, scourged lunatic humanity with the whip of ridicule, Shakespeare "kept watch o'er man's mortality," not in reforming zeal, or in sentimental pity, but with an artist's burning necessity to find truth In the ruthless pursuit of this he went down to hell.

OTHELLO

The mood of the Elizabethan eighties and nineties (the days of the Armada, of gay adventure, of quick glory and quicker disgrace, of joyous living and easy dying) had given place to one of disillusionment, cynicism, a preoccupation with the morbid. The seventeenth century opened with a spiritual " hangover " from the intoxication of Elizabeth's " spacious days." Shakespeare, too, was now a little declined into the vale of years (yet that not much) ; certainly he was of an age when a man looks back and weighs experience. But his was not the temperament for mild and melancholy retrospect. He was supreme in one medium, comedy ; the fashion of the times, his own deeper insight, the need to sharpen his skill on fresh problems, all pointed the way to experiment in writing tragedy. It has been suggested * that the death of Essex deeply affected the poet. How large a part some private emotional crisis may have played we do not know ; but if any such experience came his way it would serve rather to underline than to originate his new mood. " It was not possible for a man of his powers to observe the political and moral conduct of his contemporaries without perceiving that they were incapable of dealing with the problems raised by their own civilization, and that their attempt to carry out the codes of law and practise the religions offered to them by great prophets and lawgivers were, and still are, so foolish that we now call for the superman, virtually a new species, to rescue the world from mismanagement. This is the real sorrow of great men ; and in the face of it the notion that when a great man speaks bitterly or looks melancholy he must be troubled by a disappointment in love seems to me sentimental trifling." So Bernard Shaw accounts for Shakespeare's tragic period.

Meanwhile the artist's public called for tragedy, for sensational murder, intrigue, new and more

* See J. Dover Wilson, *The Essential Shakespeare.*

exquisite cruelties. Many lesser dramatists gave just this. Shakespeare, being Shakespeare, gave his public more. His insight into individual character had already taught him that there is " a soul of goodness in things evil." From striving to find this good in individuals he now turns to a deeper search, a search for " good " or, at least, an aiming towards good, in the conduct of the universe itself ; a search for some spark of life on the " sterile promontory."

He broods over his problem, ruthless as a scientist in his laboratory. Iago is allowed to work his will, for the search for truth condemns the dramatist to pitiless logic and " Iago's plot is Iago's character in action." Goneril, Regan, Edmund the bastard, Macbeth, and the evil let loose by the hero himself . . . Shakespeare, like Hamlet, follows the ghost, the ghost of human evil : " I'll cross it, though it blast me ! " And how near Shakespeare's fine mind came to destruction can be seen in *Timon of Athens*. With something of Iago's impersonal curiosity he watches humanity on the rack. Unlike Iago, he finds an answer to Othello's question, " Why he hath thus ensnared my soul and body ? " He did it to " find out," and he reaches the answer. Orpheus brought Eurydice back from hell ; Shakespeare returns with understanding and compassion—to say nothing of five of the greatest plays ever written.

His two last plays, *The Winter's Tale* and *The Tempest*, show us a Shakespeare purged through the pity and terror of his own imagination's experience.

> The clouds that gather round the setting sun
> Do take a sober colouring from an eye
> That hath kept watch o'er man's mortality . . .
> Thanks to the human heart by which we live,
> Thanks to its tenderness, its joys, and fears,
> To me the meanest flower that blows can give
> Thoughts that do often lie too deep for tears.

AFTER A SECOND READING

THE TEXT OF THE PLAY

WHEN Bernard Shaw or any other well-known dramatist writes a new play the first we hear of it will probably be through a Press notice of its performance. Sooner or later we shall be able to buy a copy of it at the bookseller's, and we shall find that, with the addition of a few stage directions and possibly descriptions of some of the characters, the text is as the play was performed at one of the London theatres (*not* necessarily the text that was used on the first night). It is unlikely that it is the same as the first script that was put into the producer's hands. Many alterations will have been made during rehearsal : whole scenes may have been cut out and new ones written in, lines inserted or cut in the individual actors' parts, and indeed the entire interpretation of a character changed. The Prompt Book (the script of the play as it has been amended and annotated during rehearsal) is a very precious thing ; it is the record of the *making* of a play, a composite work of author, producer, actors, and stage technicians. A copy of this will be prepared for the publishers, the type will be checked and rechecked, the printed pages carefully corrected by the author himself, and then thousands, perhaps tens of thousands of copies of the play will be issued for sale. When a copy comes into our hands we can be certain that this is the version of the play that the author wants us to take as final.

AFTER A SECOND READING

Things were very different in Shakespeare's day. To begin with, there was no such thing as law of copyright. The scripts of plays were the property of the company of players performing them. Shakespeare gained his first experience as a playwright by botching up, improving, and modernizing the work of other men. Nobody thought of challenging his right to do this. Later, when the whole play was his own work, he would hand over the finished manuscript to the theatre manager, and from this several copies would be transcribed for the actors' use. Perhaps one or two extra fair copies would be made for presentation to patrons of the theatre or friends of the author or manager. In rehearsal the same thing would happen to these scripts as happens to the typescripts in the modern theatre : stage directions scribbled in, lines cut out, odd words changed, extra lines written in. Something of this cutting might occur even before the actors' copies were made, and the full script never reach the actors' hands at all.

It was during Shakespeare's lifetime that printers began to realize that money could be made from the sale of copies of popular plays. But the managers of the theatres and the chief actors jealously guarded their property, and the playwrights themselves considered publication with reluctance. When they did publish it was usually in self-defence. But copies of the plays did get into the hands of the printers, and were published whether the authors liked it or not.

The two most common methods of securing the " copy " were by " pirating " and by secret buying of the actors' copies. " Pirating " consisted in sending trained shorthand writers * to performances of the play. Considering the speed with which the Elizabethan actor spoke his lines, the task could have been no easy one. Blanks had often to be filled in from

* *Characterie : an arte of shorte scripte, and secrete writing by character,* by Timothy Bright, 1588.

memory or invention ; perhaps, after a drink or two at a near-by tavern, some minor actor (a Second Soldier or inconspicuous Montagu) could be flattered into an individual rendering of a speech by Henry V. or Romeo (the First Quartos of both these plays were from pirated scripts). The omissions would then be made good from an unskilled actor's vague recollection of a part that was not his own. It can be imagined how little reliable were the editions published from such sources. These are known to scholars as the " bad Quartos."

A much more reliable, albeit more expensive, method was to purchase an actor's script. In 1608 certain actors were dismissed from the Whitefriars Theatre and fined forty pounds for selling copies of plays to printers. But even then—because of hasty and careless type-setting, mistakes in deciphering the handwriting, and the absence of authoritative correction—editions printed from such sources are under some suspicion. Though a great number of Shakespeare's plays were published in his lifetime it is more than doubtful whether he himself ever checked a copy.

These first copies of the plays, sold at fivepence or sixpence each, are known as the "Quartos"; and the " good Quartos," those taken from genuine acting scripts, are probably the nearest we can come to the actual stage version of Shakespeare's plays.

The *First Quarto* edition of *Othello* (Q_1) was not published until 1622, and shows every sign of having been taken from a reliable stage script. In 1630 a second Quarto (Q_2) was printed in which many corrections of obvious misprints were made, and since the *First Folio* had appeared in the meantime, many corrections and additions were incorporated from this later text.

The First Folio (published in 1623) was an authoritative edition of thirty-six of Shakespeare's plays,

under the nominal supervision of two of his fellow-
actors, John Heminge and Henry Condell. For the
Othello in this collection the printers seem to have had
access to a more complete copy of the play than Q_1,
probably a script that had not been submitted to the
maulings of rehearsal ; but, as we shall see, this was
certainly not an exact copy of Shakespeare's original
manuscript.   This folio version contains about
160 more lines than Q_1, and most of the quarto
omissions can readily be seen to be " production
cuts." But there is another very important difference
between this version and Q_1. In 1606 an Act was
passed restraining the use of oaths and blasphemous
expressions on the stage. If the Folio had been edited
by a bench of bishops it could not have been more
carefully combed of everything that might conceivably
fall within the meaning of this Act. In Q_1 oaths
blossom freely, and from this we can be safely assured
that it was taken from a version of the play in use
before 1606. Here is an example of the Folio's careful
expurgation :

First Quarto :

OTHELLO : . . . It was a handkerchief, an antique
   token
My father gave my mother.
   EMILIA : O God !   O heavenly God !
   IAGO :   'Zounds !   Hold your peace !

First Folio :

OTHELLO : (as Q_1).
   EMILIA : O heaven !   O heavenly powers !
   IAGO :   Come, hold your peace.

Except, then, for certain discrepancies due to mis-
reading and misprinting (and certainly the Folio was
the more carefully printed of the two) here lies the

difference between the two versions : the Folio, in
the main, is the more *literary*, including many passages
of poetic beauty which Q_1 lacks ; the Quarto is the
nearer to the original *stage* version. It is unlikely,
except in one or two negligible instances, that the extra
lines of the Folio were later *additions*. It is the Quarto
that *omits*, not the Folio that adds. Our preference for
one or other version will probably be decided according to the relative value we give to Shakespeare as
a writer and as a practical man of the theatre. For
if these cuts were made in an *acting* version before
1606, we can be allowed to suspect that Shakespeare
was present when they were made. We can conjure
up for ourselves some such scene as this :

BURBAGE [*rehearsing*] : . . . *Her name, that was as
fresh*
As Dian's visage, is now begrim'd and black—
Will ! This speech is too long.
? ?   [*playing* IAGO] : And it leaves me here
neither on stage nor off.
BURBAGE : Why not cut it and let Iago go straight
on. He can come instage again on " *You would
be satisfied ?* "
SHAKESPEARE : What ? Cut out " *cords, knives,
poison or fire or suffocating streams* " ?
BURBAGE : I tell you it's holding up the action !
You're letting your poetry run away with you.
SHAKESPEARE : Very well—cut it, cut it ! I suppose you'll be wanting to cut the " Pontic sea "
speech next.
BURBAGE : Well—er—as a matter of fact . . . I
was going to suggest—O yes, I know it's *good* . . .
but——

Thanks to the Folio we have both speeches.

Even after the compromise of Q_2 the editors had
not finished with *Othello*. The eighteenth century

AFTER A SECOND READING

brought a crop of careful editings, but the work of chief note is that of Nicholas Rowe (1674–1718), poet laureate to George I. His chief contribution was to " tidy " the text and bring it into line with the dramatic method of his day. This meant division into acts and scenes, and the defining of an exact place for the action (" before the castle " ; " a room in the castle," etc.), with the insertion of exits and entrances where they had previously been omitted. In short, the editors of the eighteenth century made a brave attempt to push the play behind the proscenium arch. Amongst men of literary fame who issued editions of Shakespeare were Pope and Dr. Johnson, but their chief work lay in textual criticism and discussions on alternative readings.

The outstanding achievement of the early nineteenth century was the publication of the Third Variorum Edition, edited by James Boswell, son of Dr. Johnson's Boswell. This collates the various readings of the plays and incorporates the extensive Shakespearean research of Edmund Malone (1741–1812) and others.

But ultimately, for the text of *Othello*, all editors are driven back to a choice between the readings of Q_1 and the First Folio, with the considerable assistance of three centuries of patient scholarship. The text printed here conforms on the whole to what is nowadays accepted as the " standard " text, with a leaning, in cases of doubt, to Q_1. The oaths of Q_1 are retained because they were undoubtedly part of the original text. Where there are heavy discrepancies between Q_1 and the Folio attention is drawn to this in a footnote ; this will prevent confusion should a student be faced with another editor's preference.

One word as to punctuation. The Quartos were punctuated in a style all their own, with the enforcement of rhythm rather than clarity of thought as the object. The Folio and the eighteenth-century editor revised the punctuation according to the literary rules of their day, but not always helpfully to the actor or the modern reader. Accordingly some slight re-editing has been done in the present text, largely in the direction of using the full stop in the place of indiscriminate semicolons, and, in order to restore some of the Elizabethan speed, the omission of commas where the sense is obvious without them.

SHAKESPEARE'S WORKSHOP

1. SOURCE OF THE PLAY

" SHAKESPEARE, with all his gifts, never found the inspiration to write an original play." When Bernard Shaw wrote this he meant by " original " a play of which the author had invented the plot for himself. If Shakespeare is to be condemned because he borrowed his stories from other people, we must rule out also from the list of great dramatists all the Greek tragic poets and, indeed, most of the writers of tragedy before Ibsen and Chekhov. The idea that tragic playwrights should make up their own stories is of comparatively recent date.

The story of the Moor of Venice, *Un Capitano Moro*, was published in 1566 in a collection of short Italian stories called *Hecatomithi*. The author was Giraldi Cinthio. It is unlikely that Shakespeare worked with a copy of this book at his elbow, and there is no record of there having been any English translation of the story available. It is possible that he heard the story at second-hand : one thing is certain ; that the many differences found between Cinthio's original story and Shakespeare's play are changes which a practical man of the theatre would make in preparing the story for the stage. If they are not Shakespeare's own hey are from an earlier play of which all trace has disappeared.

The only named character in Cinthio's story is Desdemona. Othello is simply the Moor ; Iago, the Ensign ; Cassio, the Captain ; the Ensign's wife is unnamed. The story begins with the courtship of Desdemona by the Moor, and their marriage against the wishes of her parents. For some time the two live happily in Venice. Then the Moor is sent to Cyprus ; Desdemona accompanies him, as do also the Captain, the Ensign, and the Ensign's wife and little daughter. The wife and daughter become very friendly with Desdemona ; the Ensign falls madly in love with her.

When Desdemona ignores the Ensign's advances he determines to be revenged upon her, and also upon the Captain, to whom Desdemona has shown more signs of friendship than to himself. The Captain is cashiered by the Moor for brawling and Desdemona pleads his cause with her husband. The Ensign uses this as a means of persuading the Moor that his wife is unfaithful to him. The Ensign then steals Desdemona's handkerchief (her first gift from the Moor) when she is playing with the little girl, and he finds means to place it on the Captain's bed. The Captain's wife is intrigued by the design of the embroidery, and is copying it when the Ensign draws the Moor's attention to her possession of the handkerchief. This convinces the Moor of his wife's guilt with the Captain, and he prepares to take revenge.

The Ensign is commissioned to dispatch the Captain, but only succeeds in maiming him. Desdemona's distress when she hears of the Captain's loss of a limb is interpreted by the Moor as further proof of her guilt. He plots with the Ensign, and together they carry out the murder. Desdemona is beaten to death by the Ensign, in the Moor's presence, with a stocking filled with sand ; they then pull the roof down on the bed and the body, so that it may appear that Desdemona has been killed by a roof-fall. Later, the Moor, half-mad with grief, dismisses the Ensign—too constant a reminder of their joint crime. The Captain has now recovered and the Ensign seeks revenge for his own dismissal by denouncing the Moor. The Captain hands on the information to the Venice Signory, and the Moor is summoned to Venice to stand his trial. In spite of the most severe torture he remains silent and admits nothing. He is condemned to banishment, but Desdemona's kinsfolk kill him. Later the Ensign, arrested for other crimes, and dying under torture, confesses the whole truth.

The original story is given here at length so that Shakespeare's reshaping of it can be more carefully examined. The changes he made were not haphazard or the mere slips of a faulty memory. To begin with, the dramatist was faced with the problem of making the Moor an heroic figure, worthy of tragedy. For this, two things were necessary : Othello must win and hold the sympathy of the audience, and he must not be punished like a common murderer, but must put an end to his own life. The motive for the murder of Desdemona had to be changed from mere desire for revenge to an idealist's sense of justice— " It is the cause ! " For the brutality of the original murder Shakespeare substituted the stifling with a pillow, and a " heavenly sorrow " that " strikes where it doth love."

In Cinthio's story, the Moor never discovers the way he has been duped by the Ensign. Shakespeare reveals the truth to his hero and thus not only gives him a reason for self-murder, but completes Othello's own purging by sorrow and full self-knowledge. It is interesting to note, in passing, that in the Italian version Cinthio asserts that he had the story direct from the widow of the Ensign concerned, and that

AFTER A SECOND READING

Shakespeare gives to Emilia the task of enlightening Othello.

Many of the other changes can be attributed to Shakespeare's deeper interest in character, particularly in the character of Iago. According to Cinthio the whole plot hinges on the Ensign's passion for Desdemona ; the man is typical of the Renaissance passion-ridden villain. In the play this incentive is almost negligible, and that Shakespeare intended it to be so may be argued from the fact that he creates an *entirely new* character, Roderigo, to fill the rôle of the importunate lover. He also contrives to use Roderigo as a useful lay figure to whom Iago can reveal his plot, and finally as a victim for Iago's wanton murder. This important addition to the *dramatis personæ*, and the changes resulting from it, help Shakespeare to build up the " passionless malignity " of Iago, and raise the central conflict to a far higher plane than that of Cinthio's story. Note, too, that he transfers the idea of silence under torture from Othello (in whose case it is now useless) to Iago.

The chief changes that any dramatist has to make in adapting a story for the stage are those dictated by the need of concentration. Any discussion of this is apt to trespass upon the ground of dramatic form, but it is worth while pointing out here that in the original story the action covers several months, whereas in the play the events are crowded into one night in Venice and thirty-six hours in Cyprus, with an unspecified interval whilst the ships are at sea, this interval being of no importance in the progress of the plot. This concentration (however impossible in *fact*) is made more acceptable by the audience because Iago is constituted the prime mover of events,* *e.g.* it is due to his machinations that Cassio is deprived of office ; due to him that Cassio seeks

---

* For the importance of the loss of the handkerchief by accident and not by Iago's theft, see p. 198.

Desdemona's help, and due to his constant nagging of Othello that the Moor decides to take immediate action, " this night " (IV. i. 209) instead of " within three days " (III. iii. 462). Shakespeare so manages his material that the excessive speed of the action is not only convenient to him as playwright, but essential to his villain, Iago, if the plot is to succeed at all. Note, however, that when the action seems to be moving at too breakneck a pace, Shakespeare gives a specious appearance of dragging it back by bringing Roderigo along to complain of delay—most unreasonably, when we examine the time sequence in cold blood.

To sum up Shakespeare's indebtedness to the Italian, we may say that the dramatist's fancy was caught by the outline of the story : a man of honour murders his innocent wife at the instigation of a villain. The story fascinated because it proposed two questions : What sort of a man was the Moor to be convinced upon such frail evidence ? What sort of a man was the Ensign to conceive such a devilish plot ? Shakespeare set himself to give a dramatist's answer to these questions, adopting, discarding, adapting as his sense of character and the theatre dictated. As a result we have a play that has held the stage for centuries instead of a short story that would have been forgotten with its ninety-nine companions had it not been labelled " the source of Shakespeare's *Othello*."

We should be doing a grave injustice to many of Shakespeare's contemporaries if we made acknowledgment only to Giraldi Cinthio. He may have supplied the warp, but woven into the basic threads of his story are many other strands, of which a few can be mentioned. It would have been impossible even for Shakespeare himself to have told us where he got all his references and ideas from. It is more than doubtful that he kept the careful notebooks of an

AFTER A SECOND READING

Arnold Bennett or a Somerset Maugham : " My tablets, meet it is I set it down," may or may not have been a reflection of Shakespeare's own habits.

Painstaking scholarship has revealed the sources of some of his information, and it is worth while to recall them, not for dry scholarship's sake, so much as to complete our picture of Shakespeare at work. Even Prospero had books on the magic island, and did not depend entirely on the spirits he could summon at will. Here are a few of the books of which Shakespeare almost certainly had first-hand knowledge :

In 1602 an account was published of the adventures of Sebastien, King of Portugal. This sailor king, supposed to have been slain in battle in North Africa, made good his escape and wandered through Ethiopia, and after being " taken, bought and sold twelve or thirteen times," finally made his way to Venice where he was much fêted ; and doubtless he told his hosts stories of " Hair-breadth 'scapes i' the imminent deadly breach ; of being taken by the insolent foe and sold to slavery."

Hakluyt's *Voyages* was published in 1598, and in it, and in Sir Walter Raleigh's *Description of Guiana*, Shakespeare would read of a nation of people " whose heads appear not above their shoulders," who are " reported to have their eyes in their shoulders and their mouths in the middle of their breasts."

The Anthropophagi (man-eaters), a name to stick in any word-lover's head, had already caught the fancy of the writer of the tragedy *Locrine*,* published in 1595 :

> Or where the bloody Anthropophagi
> With greedy jaws devour the wandering wights.

* The title-page of the Quarto of this play reads : " Newly set foorth, overseene and corrected by W. S." The Third Folio, with little justification, ascribes the play to Shakespeare.

If Shakespeare had felt any scruples about th
authenticity of these cannibals, doubtless Ben Jonso
could have reassured him with a quotation from
Pliny's *Natural History*.

In a translation of the same *Natural History*,
published in 1602, Shakespeare may have read o
" The Sea Pontus " which " ever floweth out int
Propontus, but never retireth back again."

Gossip, too, would offer material to the playwright
In 1598 the Earl of Essex had deeply offended Si
Francis Vere (an officer well-proved in the field
when he promoted over Vere's head the Lord
Mountjoy, reputed as a " bookish soldier."

It would no doubt be possible to multiply instances
and load reference on reference. The task is endless,
for every man he met, every quarrelling group at the
street corners, soldiers, sailors, poets, courtiers, and
scholars, all these, in their lives as well as in their
writings and their conversation, served, when he
would have them serve, as Shakespeare's source-
books.

2. The Structure of the Play

Of all Shakespeare's tragedies *Othello* conforms
most closely to the classical rules. According to the
Greeks, a play must observe the *three unities* of place,
time, and action : the events portrayed must take
place on the same spot, the time-duration of these
events in real life be limited to twenty-four hours, and
the action, *i.e.* the plot, be restricted to one central
theme.

If we treat the events of Act I. as an exposition
which could equally well, though less excitingly, have
been conveyed by report at the beginning of Act II.,
we find that as far as time is concerned Shakespeare
has exceeded his limit by about twelve hours only,
whilst strictly conforming to the unity of place.

Moreover, *Othello* has no sub-plot; the affairs of Roderigo and Cassio, including the liaison with Bianca, are all bound up with the main story. Compare with this the two distinct plots of *King Lear*.

But attention to the unities was not the only concern of the classical dramatist. Once the frame within which he had to limit himself had been defined, he had to turn his attention to the "composition" of his picture, or, to change the metaphor, to the problem of the play's architecture. Aristotle's dictum that a play must have a beginning, a middle, and an end is not as foolishly obvious as it may sound. Between these parts there must be proportion. The beginning, or *exposition*, must acquaint the audience with essential facts, laying stress upon the central problem or conflict that is going to occupy the main action of the play. But too much time must not be spent upon this or the audience will be bored; they are waiting for "something to happen," and even in the exposition this demand for action must be satisfied and curiosity must be aroused. The middle of the play must alternately satisfy this curiosity and excite it afresh. The conflict hinted at in the exposition develops into action and works its way to the point of balance where the hero's fate is decided (in tragedy decided *against* the hero) but not yet consummated. This point is called the climax or the *crisis*. From this point onwards we prepare for the end. Disaster is inevitable; the interest is maintained by suspense. The question now is, "*How* will it happen?" not, "*What* will happen?"

When the blow falls (the *catastrophe*) the end has come. But so that we do not send our audience away merely terrified or stunned, the play is protracted a little longer to allow the spectators to sense the nobility of the dead (or defeated) hero and the hope for humanity that is present not in spite of, but because of the hero's suffering.

THE SHAPE OF OTHELLO

Cr. = Crisis
R. = Recognition
Ca. = Catastrophe

Act	Staging	Scene	Event
ACT ONE	TRAVERSE	Sc.i Sc.ii	IAGO explains his hatred
			First appearance of OTHELLO
	FULL STAGE Senate House	Scene iii	Senate decides in Othello's favour
			"She deceived her Father----"
ACT TWO	FULL STAGE Sea Front	Scene i ii	OTHELLO arrives in Cyprus
			IAGO develops plot against CASSIO
	FULL STAGE Castle Interior	Scene iii	CASSIO dismissed
			IAGO advises CASSIO to seek Desdemona's help
ACT THREE	TRAV.	Sc.i ii	CASSIO arranges to meet Desdemona
	FULL STAGE Castle Interior	Scene iii	IAGO opens question of unfaithfulness
			DESDEMONA loses handkerchief
			OTHELLO'S oath of vengeance
			"Now art thou my Lieutenant."
		Sc.iv	OTHELLO demands handkerchief
ACT FOUR	FULL STAGE As ACT III	Scene i	OTHELLO'S trance
			"How shall I murder him, Iago?"
	TRAVERSE F.S. Bedr.	Scene ii Sc.iii	OTHELLO upbraids DESDEMONA
			DESDEMONA and EMILIA
ACT FIVE	TRAV.	Sc.i	Attempt on CASSIO'S life
	FULL STAGE Bedroom	Scene ii	Murder of DESDEMONA
			EMILIA reveals the truth
			Death of OTHELLO

Cr.

R. Ca.

AFTER A SECOND READING

In order that the hero's defeat may convey this final message it is necessary that he should, before his dissolution, recognize the justice of his own fate. He must learn the lesson of his own destruction. This *recognition* preceding the catastrophe is important in classical drama, and it is discoverable, though often veiled, in all tragedy. In *Othello* it is as clearly marked as in *Œdipus Rex*.

The plan on page 196 showing the shape of the play is largely self-explanatory. The main line represents the dramatic tension of the play as a whole; the broken line, which falls away after the crisis, represents the fortunes of the hero. The balanced proportions and visually satisfactory line of the drawing are not the result of an artist's caprice; the space given to the scenes and acts (for the sake of clarity the arbitrary scene divisions have been retained) have been graphed out according to the number of pages in a standard text of the play. Acts I. and II., for instance, are of equal length; Act III. is the longest of all the acts and serves as a keystone to the arch; Acts IV. and V. are together a little shorter than the first two acts, but what they lose in length they gain in dramatic tension.

It will be seen that the dramatic tension rises steadily to the crisis, and it should also be noted that nearly half the play has run before Iago opens the question of Desdemona's unfaithfulness. The crisis itself is prolonged—" the plateau of *Othello* " it has been called. This plateau, however, represents the fortunes of the hero only; the dramatic tension rises steeply throughout the crisis, and the line showing the tension creates its own plateau in Act IV. This prolonged crisis is due to the difficulty of placing the exact moment at which Othello is irrevocably doomed to the murder of Desdemona and Cassio. " To seek for the *exact* turning-point in the tragedy is almost like discussing whether a man who murders his wife by small doses of arsenic becomes a murderer on the first day or on the last. The climax stretches from Iago's first whisper, 'Did Michael Cassio when you woo'd my lady . . .?' to the decisive 'How shall I murder him, Iago?'" The present plan does not accept such a delimitation of the crisis, but places its beginning at the loss of the handkerchief. Failing any other means of decision, it seems most helpful to find a point at which some clearly demonstrable *action* plays its part in determining the tragedy. Once the handkerchief has fallen into Iago's hands, Othello is doomed. It is the mention of it as being in Cassio's possession that first deeply stirs Othello (III. iii. 427–40) and brings him to the point of the oath ; its absence when he demands it, and the sight of it in Bianca's hands, finally confirm the Moor's suspicions. Certainly he is distraught from the moment of Iago's first whisper, but he is not convinced, his doom not inevitable.

A further reason for placing the beginning of the crisis—if not the exact point of the crisis—at the moment of the handkerchief's loss is that this accidental loss (not, as in Cinthio's version, its theft by Iago) seems to suggest that at this point Fate steps in and takes a hand. That the hero should be merely the victim of another man's villainy is not enough ; accident, "Fate's little irony," must take its share. The irony is, indeed, most marked. Desdemona, in wifely concern, tries to comfort Othello by placing the handkerchief on his brow. He thrusts it away himself (too " perplexed " even to notice it is his own love-gift), practically straight into Iago's hands. Additional irony ; Emilia, in fond desire to please her " wayward " husband, innocently helps in the destruction of her mistress and, indirectly, in her own undoing.

Returning for a moment to the consideration of shape, it should be noticed that the loss of the handkerchief occurs almost midway in the play, a very little nearer to the end than the beginning.

So far we have concerned ourselves with the main outline of the play, the shape of the building as a whole. But the dramatist must be craftsman as well as architect ; he must busy himself with the management of each scene, each incident and turn of the plot. His central task here is to retain the interest of his audience so that he may call upon their emotions at will. His success will depend upon his skill in the intermingling of suspense, surprise, and irony. The proportions of these three elements of drama vary according to the type of play. Farce owes most of its success to the element of surprise ; comedy to a discreet mixture of suspense and pleasant surprise ; tragedy depends largely upon suspense and irony. In brief, the task of the playwright is largely one of deciding how much an audience is to be told, how much it is to be allowed to guess, and how much is to be hidden from it until an appropriate moment arrives for revelation. The pity and terror which it is the immediate purpose of tragedy to inspire are largely the result of an audience's being in possession of important information that is withheld from the hero. By this means we recognize tragic irony.* Shakespeare is at great pains throughout *Othello* to keep his audience fully acquainted with Iago's villainy ; the spectators are made unwilling, but fascinated, " accessories before the fact." Each of the other characters in turn is repeatedly the victim of this irony : Cassio, unwillingly persuaded to drink ; Desdemona, importunate in her persuasions on Cassio's behalf ; Emilia, handing over the fateful handkerchief. Surprise and a new suspense come with the beginning of Iago's failures : Cassio not killed ; Roderigo living long enough to denounce

* " When a course of action intended to produce a result *x*, produces the reverse of *x*."—F. L. Lucas, *Tragedy* (Hogarth Press).

his murderer. Then Iago himself becomes Irony's victim, betrayed to justice by his own wife. But this trick Shakespeare keeps carefully up his sleeve. " I'm hiding nothing from you," he seems to say each time he furnishes Iago with a soliloquy; till in the last scene he brings out the trump card, balancing the surprise by the expected agony of Othello. But the suspense still holds. Othello, reintegrated in his new self-knowledge, quietly starts his last speech, " Soft you; a word or two before you go. . . ." The lines fall like a summer twilight, level rays from a clear sky, until—

> I took by the throat the circumcised dog
> And smote him—thus !

The Poet Laureate of the Immortals has ended his sport with the audience.

In the architecture of the play as a whole—the near-observance of the unities, the interference of accident, the hero's realization of the truth and self-immolation—Shakespeare chose a framework closely similar to that established by the Greek masters; and in the detailed working of his material, his understanding of the balance of surprise and suspense, of forthright action and ironic blunder, he showed himself their equal as a craftsman.

3. THE VERSE

The grandeur of Shakespeare's verse-rhythm lies in his variations on the basic pulse of the regular iambic pentameter.* The verse of the tragedies and other later plays bears the same relation to the strictly orthodox line as do the extemporizations of a first-class dance band trumpet-player to the regular beat

---

* *Iambic pentameter*, a line of five feet, each foot an iamb (‿ ‒)

and simple melody line of the original tune. In his early days Shakespeare had learnt how to write orthodox blank verse :

> Was ever woman in this humour woo'd ?
> Was ever woman in this humour won ?
> I'll have her, but I will not keep her long.
> What ? I that kill'd her husband and her father,
> To take her in her heart's extremest hate ? *

From the discipline of such writing he learnt a freedom that he rarely abused :

> He's speaking now,
> Or murmuring, " Where's my serpent of old Nile ? "
> For so he calls me : now I feed myself
> With most delicious poison.   Think on me,
> That am with Phœbus' amorous pinches black
> And wrinkled deep in time.†

Here are a few of the methods which Shakespeare used to bring variety and elasticity to the blank verse line.

1. *The run-on line (enjambment)* :

> Behold, I have a weapon ;   1
> A better never did itself sustain   2
> Upon a soldier's thigh.   I have seen the day 3
> That with this little arm, and this good sword, 4
> I have made my way through more impediments 5
> Than twenty times your stop.   6

At the end of lines 2, 3, and 5 there is no logical pause, only a " hang-back " dictated by the rhythm. But notice that this is balanced by pauses or half-pauses at the end of lines 1 and 4.   The run-on line offers the

---

* *Richard III.*, written before 1594.
† *Antony and Cleopatra*, written about 1608.

poet opportunities of subtle and varied phrasing, and is particularly effective for the expression of speed and urgency.

2. *Variety in placing the logical pause*—If the pause dictated by the sense of the lines is no longer to fall pat at the end of each, another place must be found for it. To avoid a new monotony the position of this logical pause can be varied. In the following passage the single lines represent the division into metrical feet, the double lines indicate pauses and half-pauses :

Farewell|the tran|quil mind, ‖farewell|content ;|
        (After 3rd foot.)
Farewell|the plum|ed troop ‖and the|big wars|
        (After 3rd foot.)
That make|ambi|tion vir|tue ! ‖ O,|farewell,|
       (Middle of 4th foot.)
Farewell|the neigh|ing steed, ‖and the|shrill trump,|
        (After 3rd foot.)
The spi|rit-stir|ring drum,‖the ear-pier|cing fife,|
        (After 3rd foot.)
The roy|al ban|ner, ‖and|all qual|ity,|
       (Middle of 3rd foot.)
Pride, pomp,|and cir|cumstance|of glor|ious war.|
       (No mid-line pause.)

3. *Variety in the metrical feet*—The obvious substitutes for the iambic foot are the spondee ($--$) and the trochee ($-\smile$), the latter, an inversion of the normal iambic foot, being most effective at the opening of a line.

Pride, pomp|and cir|cumstance|of glo|rious war
      (The first foot is a spondee.)

Never|pray more,|aban|don all|remorse|
    (The first foot is a trochee, the second a spondee.)

Shakespeare, in his maturer work, also makes frequent use of the three-syllable foot to replace the normal iambic beat. Very often it is almost impossible to distinguish whether we have a three-syllable foot or whether the speaker is intended to combine adjacent vowels into one sound, omit an unaccented e or i (*e.g.* matching thy inf(e)rence). The student's ear must be his guide.*

Here are two examples :

" Vēry ŏ|bēd(i)ent ;|prŏcēed|yŏu īn|yŏur tēars|
                                    (*dactyl* ‒ ◡ ◡).

Tŏ knōt|ănd gēn|dĕr īn. Tūrn|thў cŏmplēx|iŏn thēre|
                                    (*anapæst* ◡ ◡ ‒).

4. *Redundant syllables*—Elasticity is also given to the general run of the lines by an occasional " extra " syllable that is additional to the strict number of feet, *e.g.* :

And stood|within|the blank|of his|displea|sure
For my|free speech. | You must|awhile|be pa|tient.

5. *Occasional Alexandrines*, *i.e.* lines with six feet. These are not as frequent in *Othello* as in, say, *Antony and Cleopatra*. The occasional use of these longer, heavier lines serves a useful emotional purpose :

To say|my wife|is fair,|feeds well,|loves com|pany.|

Here the hexameter slows up the speech and helps to convey Othello's labouring thought.

* *Elision : e.g.* in the " farewell " speech given above, line 5, " the ear-piercing " would probably be spoken as " th' ear-piercing." On the other hand, it must be remembered that at this time the ending " ion " was usually given two distinct sounds ; see the example of the anapæst above.

6. *Short Lines*—The occurrence of lines that fall short of the usual five feet is not to be taken as an indication that Shakespeare had been careless or " gravelled for lack of matter." Like the extra long lines they serve a definite purpose that can be more readily appreciated when the speeches are read aloud or acted :

>   . . . O cursed slave !
> Whip me, you devils,
> From the possession of this heavenly sight !
> Blow me about in winds, roast me in sulphur . . .

The short line serves as a sort of spring-board to the leaping agony of the next four lines. Similarly, Othello's last line of all, " And smote him, thus . . ." accentuates the suddenness of his self-murder.

This vivisection of Shakespeare's verse and the careful tapping out of long and short into a morse-code travesty of poetry may at first appal the sensitive enthusiast. Let him remember that Leonardo da Vinci and Michael Angelo studied anatomy as carefully as a surgeon, without losing their artist's joy in the human form. No-one pretends that Shakespeare assembled his verse as a printer's compositor sets type, fitting in a letter here and a blank there ; but it is permissible to inquire why Shakespeare can apparently take such liberties with the blank verse line, and yet retain its unity, when so many others have tried the same medium and either reduced the pentameter to chaos or made it march with the mechanic precision of a military parade.

7. *Stress*—There is more in skilled verse than the careful arrangement of syllabic feet, just as music is more than a sequence of bars in triple or common time. Superimposed on this syllabic rhythm there comes, from the nature of the English language, a wider rhythm given by *stress*. Detailed scansion

is dictated by accenting of certain syllables in a word :

beautiful, design, tranquil. Wherever these words occur, the accented syllable or syllables remain the same.* Stress is determined by the sentence construction and the meaning :

> When icicles hang by the wall . . .
> When shall we three meet again . . .

Usually we find only three or four stresses to a blank verse line :

> It is the cause, yet I'll not shed her blood,
> Nor scar that whiter skin of hers than snow,
> And smooth as monumental alabaster.

Where five stresses occur the line has great weight and dignity :

> Pride, pomp and circumstance of glorious war.

Even in this line " circumstance " has less weight than the other four stressed words. The true placing of the stresses, to give expression to Shakespeare's skilled manipulation of them, is a measure of the reader's or the actor's understanding of his task.

It should be noted that the text used in this book has been prepared for the reader by omitting all e's in the final " ed " unless these are sounded as separate syllables.

4. LANGUAGE

Something has already been said † on the choice of words in the fashioning of poetry and on the use of

* Of course we have our freakish words like *con′duct* (noun) and *conduct′* (verb).

† See Introduction, p. ix.

simile and metaphor. The student of Shakespeare will find that the beauty of his poetry consists not only in the association-value of individual words and phrases, but in the sound of the words and the particular sequences in which they are arranged. The discarding of rhyme gives even greater opportunity of exploiting other tricks of the poet's trade.

1. *Alliteration and Assonance*—The obvious alliteration of initial letters (Heaven keep that monster from Othello's mind) is only one of the methods of using a sequence of similar consonants. The sound may occur in the middle or at the end of a word, and it may be disguised from the eye by being contained in a compound of dissimilar letters :

> the flinty and steel couch of war
> and very sea-mark of my utmost sail

The sequence of similar-sounding vowels (assonance) can do even more than alliteration in giving mood and colour to a line, since only vowel sounds have *tone*. The pattern may be confined to a single line or spread over several :

> Olympus high and duck again as low
>
> Whose icy current and compulsive course
>
> Ne'er feels retiring ebb, but keeps due on
>
> To the Propontic, and the Hellespont.

2. *Use of Parallel Words or Phrases*, such as en-shelter'd and embay'd ; capable and wide revenge ; exsufflicate and blown ; scattering and unsure observance ; ne'er look back, ne'er ebb. Notice that

the separate words in each pair do not, upon close examination, mean *quite* the same thing. It is not, as Saintsbury points out, "a mere draft on the Teutonic and Romance columns of a conveniently arranged Dictionary of Synonyms." "Enshelter'd" carries with it something of the race for safety, "embay'd" speaks only of the calm of the harbour itself. We have, as it were, the juxtaposition of two shades of the same colour to add richness to the texture.

3. *Play on Words*—*Othello* has little of the sparkling wit of *Romeo and Juliet* or of the lively word-play of certain passages of *Hamlet*. The little there is, apart from the very short passages between the Clown and the Musicians and Cassio, comes from Iago, and is almost confined to the short scene between him and Desdemona. Here there is self-conscious play on words for amusement's sake ; but Shakespeare does not restrict his word-juggling to light passages, *e.g.* :

My soul hath her content so absolute

Thou know'st we work by wit and not by witchcraft. . . . And thou, by that small hurt, hast cashier'd Cassio.

4. *Use of The Grand Style*—Few characters in Shakespeare's plays have more lines of concentrated rhetoric than Othello. In his most impassioned moments we find all the accepted figures of speech which characterize the grand manner.

(*a*) Similes and metaphors from the classics : Her name that was as fresh as Dian's visage. . . . The Propontic and the Hellespont. . . . The immortal Jove's great clamour. . . .

(*b*) Apostrophe : Yield up, O love, thy crown and hearted throne !

(*c*) Hyperbole : She with Cassio has the act of shame
A thousand times committed.
O that the slave had forty thousand lives !

(*d*) Personification : The bawdy wind that kisses all it meets.

But any examination of Shakespeare's worth as a poet is incomplete without mention of those passages whose crystal simplicity baffles all analysis. If there are moments in the play when he " lifts a mortal to the skies," there are others, even more memorable, when he " draws an angel down " : " He looks gentler than he did "; " Dear general, I did never give you cause " ; " What should such a fool do with so good a woman ? "

MODERN PRESENTATION OF THE PLAY

THERE is no surer way of coming to a real understanding of one of Shakespeare's plays than that of putting it on the stage. The planning of sets and scene sequences creates a familiarity with the shape of the play and the relative importance of the different scenes ; the actors, by conscientious study of their parts, gain a clear and lasting insight into the characterization and the meaning of the lines. Similarly, no one should attempt to put the play on to the stage unless he is prepared to spend a great deal of time on the study of the text.

The essentials of any production are simplicity of setting and speed of action. The suggestions which follow offer some solution of how these can be attained even on a small amateur stage.

The first problem that has to be faced is that of maintaining the continuity of the action. This is of particular importance in *Othello*, because the audience must not be given time to meditate upon the inconsistencies. The producer will probably have to make some slight concession to modern theatre habits and allow for one interval. Where, then, is this break to be placed? There is an obvious pause after Act I., but this is too early in the performance to be of much practical use. A short pause might be handy, since it gives time for the change of set, but since the audience's curiosity is only half-whetted, a long break would be bad policy.

The end of Act II. offers another logical pause after the dismissal of Cassio, but we are still only at the beginning of the main action, and if we are allowing only one interval this is still too early. Once we have begun Act III. we are embarked upon swift-moving action that carries us up to and through the crisis, and this crisis continues until the first scene of Act IV. Scene iv. of Act III. gives us a useful critical point at which to make a break: Othello has demanded the handkerchief, and is almost assured of its loss. He has been given the first apparent proof of Iago's honesty. Moreover, the Othello of Act IV. is, as we have seen, a changed Othello. If we make the break between Acts III. and IV. we leave the audience in some suspense (as we should); we give time for the poison to work upon Othello, and we start again upon a scene where Othello has " fallen into a dazed, lethargic state, and must be stimulated into action " by Iago. This necessary recapitulation of the case against Desdemona and Cassio offers a useful jumping-off point for the actors. A purely practical argument in favour of making the break here is that the second half of the performance will now take slightly less time than the first half. A study of the technique of the modern three-act play will show that the break before the third act is usually marked by an unresolved dramatic situation such as we find here. *After* this point in *Othello* a break is impossible. The only other possible point at which an interval could be placed seems, to the present writer, to be between Scenes iii. and iv. of Act III.

The next problem is that of arranging for continuous playing before and after this interval. Some kind of semi-permanent setting must be invented that can be changed in the shortest possible time and that gives, without awkward realism, some indication of where the scene is supposed to be. The accepted method is to choose certain scenes that can be played on a forestage in front of traverse curtains (*i.e.* curtains that conceal about three-quarters of the stage) whilst the setting of the main stage is being changed.

The plan on page 211 suggests an arrangement for these alternating scenes. The following notes will show that the decision is not purely arbitrary.

A break can be avoided between *Acts I.* and *II.* if the end of I. iii. (l. 301 on), after the exit of all but Roderigo and Iago, is played in front of the traverse. After Othello's exit a certain amount of pomp can cover the exit of the Duke and Senators. The traverse curtains are closed ; Iago and Roderigo have been kept well down-stage, and as Iago turns to go Roderigo calls him back. This scene plays for four or five minutes, giving ample time for a practised stage-management to change the main set.

The change from *Scene i.* to *Scene iii. Act II.* is more difficult. The short " Herald " scene does not allow sufficient time for set-changing. The best practical solution seems to be to continue playing on the forestage to line 47 of Scene iii., take back the traverse, and allow Iago to continue his soliloquy on the full stage whilst awaiting Cassio and the others. An alternative would be to play the Iago–Roderigo scene of II. i. on the traverse ; but this is a repetition of our earlier method, and the wise producer varies his theatre-tricks. The method suggested here gives us about three minutes for the change, and slick,

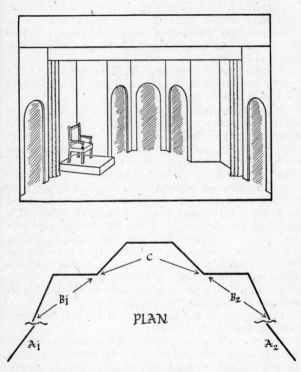

SUGGESTED SETTING FOR ACT I. SCENE III.

With slight changes, the same plan can be used for the Castle Interior and Bedroom.

well-rehearsed management should easily effect this.

Act III. i. and *ii.* are obvious fore-stage scenes, and give ample time for the slight changes of furniture (no change of set is necessary) before Scene iii. The main stage then remains set until the *end of IV. i.*

For the fore-stage scene of *IV. ii.* a chair and a table can be brought on during the black-out. These should be left on for the next scene.

IV. iii. raises a problem for the too literal-minded, since Desdemona apparently prepares for bed in the room where she takes leave of her guests. It seems a pity to waste the beauty of this scene on a fore-stage with a mere traverse backing ; the helplessness of Desdemona can be usefully emphasized by giving the scene a full-stage setting. IV. ii. gives ample time for the main stage to be reset for the final scene, and if the table and chair, or stool, of Scene ii. is retained, down-stage, for Scene iii., the full stage can be opened and the *light concentrated down-stage* on Desdemona and Emilia. We shall then have a sense of space, and the unlit, dim background of the bed-room will help the note of foreboding.

For *V. i.* the furniture is removed during the black-out and the traverse curtains are closed.

V. ii. opens on the full bedroom set, the light now concentrated on the bed.

It is possible to carry out all the necessary changes with a set of flats and screens such as are shown on p. 213. Flats A1 and A2 are fixed as permanent entrances and exits on the fore-stage. The other units are screens which stand with little extra bracing, so that they can quickly be moved to fresh positions. All screens are covered on both sides (with canvas or plain bolton sheeting) and fitted with hinges so that they fold in both directions. The middle part of unit C can be fixed permanently at the back of the

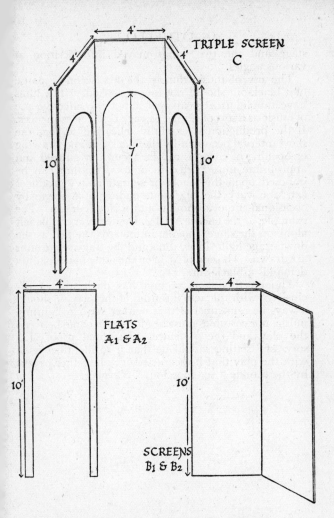

TRIPLE SCREEN
C

FLATS
A₁ & A₂

SCREENS
B₁ & B₂

UNITS FOR SEMI-PERMANENT SETTING.

stage and the two wings moved into position at various angles.

The use of music during the few seconds' pause of a black-out should not be overlooked. The films have taught us a great deal about the effective use of music as a sort of bridge passage between sequences. If the production is carefully rehearsed so that the short interval occupied by the black-out and drawing or opening of curtains can be accurately gauged and appropriate music fitted in, a total rhythm can be imposed upon the whole presentation. A producer can also vary the black-out ending of a scene by occasional use of dimming and a slow curtain. For example, at the end of Act IV. Desdemona can be left alone on the stage, moving in towards the bed as the down-stage light slowly dims and the traverse curtains are drawn. The end of V. i., on the other hand, plainly demands a black-out.

Though this short section has dealt almost exclusively with the actual setting of the play, it should always be remembered that neither setting, lighting, music, nor costumes must be allowed to come between the play and the audience. The final proof of a successful setting should be that it so identifies itself with the play that it escapes notice altogether except by the frankly " set-conscious " playgoer.

QUESTIONS AFTER A SECOND READING

ACT I

1. What reasons does Iago give to Roderigo for his (Iago's) hatred of Othello? Do you think Iago genuinely hates Cassio?

2. What methods does Shakespeare use in Act I. of revealing the characters of Iago and Othello?

3. Give an account of what happens in Act I from the point of view of (*a*) Brabantio, (*b*) Desdemona. Remember that there is some of the action of which each is unaware.

4. Give a short character sketch of Roderigo. Is there any indication that he was in Iago's power before the opening of the play?

5. Write an account in modern English of Othello's wooing of Desdemona.

6. Give the context of the following, and explain the meaning or reference of words in italics:

(*a*) Do, with like *timorous* accent and dire yell
As when, *by night and negligence,* the fire
Is spied in populous cities.

(*b*) It is a business *of some heat,* the galleys
Have sent a dozen *sequent* messengers
This very night.

(*c*)   No, when light-wing'd toys
And feather'd Cupid foils with wanton dullness
My *speculative and active instruments*.

Let housewives make a *skillet* of my helm.

OTHELLO

7. Explain and write short notes on : the toged Senator ; the Anthropophagi ; the Sagittary ; the Ottomites ; boisterous ; as bitter as the coloquintida.

ACT II

1. How does Shakespeare give us an impression of change of place at the opening of Act II., and of the time that has elapsed since the end of the previous scene ?

2. What new aspects of Iago's character are revealed in Act II. Scenes i. and iii. ?

3. " Now follows a long ramble of Jack-pudden farce betwixt Iago and Desdemona . . . jingle and trash below the patience of any country kitchenmaid with her sweetheart." (Thomas Rymer, *A Short View of Tragedy*, 1693.) Can you justify Shakespeare's inclusion of this scene at the beginning of Act II. ?

4. Dramatic irony is dependent upon the audience's being in possession of knowledge withheld from the character who is the victim of the irony. From Act II. give examples of dramatic irony relative to Cassio.

5. Write a summary in modern English of Iago's soliloquies at the end of Scene i. and Scene iii.

6. Give a short account of Act II. Scene iii. from the point of view of Cassio.

7. Give the context of the following and explain the words in italics :

(a) I do follow in the chase, not like a hound that hunts, but one that *fills up the cry.*

(b) My blood begins my safer guides to rule, And passion, having my best judgement *collied* Assays to lead the way.

(c) A subtle and a *slipper* knave ; a finder out of occasions ; that has an eye can *stamp and ocunterfeit* advantage, though true advantage never present themselves.

216

(d) 'Tis ever more the prologue to his sleep :
    He'll watch the *horologe* a *double set*
    If drink rock not his cradle.

8. Explain and write short notes on : Swag-bellied Hollander ; the guards of the ever-fixed pole ; ingener ; set down the pegs ; cast (military term) ; pottle-deep ; twiggen bottle ; spend your rich opinion ; discourse fustian.

ACT III

1. Examine Iago's method of first rousing Othello's suspicion. Why is he so successful ?

2.   Divinity of hell !
   When devils will the blackest sins put on,
   They do suggest at first with heavenly shows.

                                (Iago, II. iii.)

Examine to what extent Iago makes use of truth and half-truths, and to what extent in Act III. he uses deliberate lying in order to further his ends.

3. Give an example of dramatic irony in Act III. Scene iii. of which Desdemona is the victim.

4. " Mr. —— spoke the lines, ' Excellent wretch ! Perdition catch my soul, etc.' as though he were saying, ' *When* I cease to love you the end of the world will have come,' instead of speaking them as though they were the agonized expression of his spirit when he hates her. The line should be broken by a desperate gesture." Do you agree with Mr. Desmond Mac-Carthy ? Whether you do or not, support your argument from the text.

5. Re-read Scene iii. carefully. How far has Iago succeeded in rousing Othello's jealousy before the loss of the handkerchief is discovered ? *Or*, Do you agree with Othello's later description of himself as " a man not easily jealous " ?

OTHELLO

6. Give an account of Act III. from the point of view of Othello.

7. Give the context of the following passages and rewrite them in modern English prose :

(a) I prithee, name the time, but let it not
Exceed three days : in faith, he's penitent ;
And yet his trespass, in our common reason—
Save that, they say, the wars must make examples
Out of their best—is not almost a fault
To incur a private check.

(b) Utter my thoughts ? Why, say they are vile and false ;
As where's that palace whereinto foul things
Sometimes intrude not ? Who has a breast so pure,
But some uncleanly apprehensions
Keep leets and law-days and in session sit
With meditations lawful ?

(c) Poor and content is rich and rich enough,
But riches fineless is as poor as winter
To him that ever fears he shall be poor.

(d)   . . . Like to the Pontic sea,
Whose icy current and compulsive course
Ne'er feels retiring ebb, but keeps due on
To the Propontic and the Hellespont ;
Even so my bloody thoughts, with violent pace,
Shall ne'er look back, ne'er ebb to humble love,
Till that a capable and wide revenge
Swallow them up.

8. Explain and write short notes on : conceit ; watch him tame ; haggard ; jesses ; mandragora ; crusadoes ; sufficient.

ACT IV

1. Give examples from Act IV. of how Iago takes advantage of unexpected opportunities for furthering his plans.

2. How far do you consider the introduction of Bianca to be essential to the development of the plot ?

3. "Othello [at the opening of Act IV.] seems now to have fallen into a dazed, lethargic state and must be stimulated into action." Find instances in Othello's speeches to prove (or disprove) this, and show how Iago, even before the scene with Cassio, keeps Othello's mind at murder-pitch.

4. What signs are there, even after Othello is determined upon Cassio's death, that he might have taken pity on Desdemona ? How does Iago counter this ?

5. Of what importance in the action is the arrival of the envoys from Venice ? How does this affect (a) Othello, (b) Roderigo ?

6. Give a short account of Act IV. Scenes ii. and iii. from Emilia's point of view. Note that she probably remains within earshot in Scene ii.

7. What fresh light does Scene ii. throw upon the character of Desdemona ?

8. Examine the contrast in character between Emilia and Desdemona as shown in Scenes ii. and iii. Why is Scene iii. important in the structure of the play?

9. "In Act IV. Scene ii. we come very near to losing all patience and sympathy with Othello." Why ? And how does Shakespeare succeed in retaining him as an heroic figure ?

10. Give the context of and explain the following :

> (a)   . . . knaves be such abroad
> Who having, by their own importunate suit,
> Or by the voluntary dotage of some mistress,
> Convinced or supplied them, cannot choose
> But they must blab.

 (*b*) Or shall I say you are all in all in spleen
And nothing of a man ?

 (*c*) Is this the noble Moor . . .
 . . . whose solid virtue
The shot of accident nor dart of chance
Could neither graze nor pierce ?

 (*d*) But, alas, to make me
A fixed figure for the time of scorn
To point his slow unmoving finger at . . .

 (*e*) Why, the wrong is but a wrong i' the world, and
having the world for your labour, 'tis a wrong in your own
world, and you might quickly make it right.

11. Explain and write short notes on : hypocrisy
against the devil ; fitchew ; joint-ring ; unprovide
my mind ; crocodile's tears ; mystery ; cogging
addition.

ACT V

1. Not until Act V. do Iago's plans begin to go
wrong. Trace the failure of his various schemes up
to Emilia's denouncement of him. What attempts
does he make on each occasion to readjust matters
in his own favour ?

2. Why does Iago murder Roderigo ?

3. Which do you consider the most dramatic
moment of Act V.? Show how Shakespeare prepares
us for it.

4. What use does Shakespeare make of surprise in
Act V.?

5. Do you think Emilia has been completely innocent of Iago's plot ? Give reasons from the text for
your opinion.

6. Rewrite in modern English Othello's last
speech.

7. In Cinthio's original story the Moor dies without knowing the truth. Why does Shakespeare change
this ? Why does he make Iago kill Emilia ?

8. What reasons can you find for Shakespeare's keeping Cassio alive at the end of the play ? Can you find similar instances in other tragedies ?

9. Tell the story of Act V. from Cassio's point of view.

10. Give the context of and explain :

(a)   O Spartan dog,
More fell than anguish, hunger or the sea !
Look on the tragic loading of this bed ;
This is thy work : the object poisons sight,
Let it be hid.

(b) If I quench thee, thou flaming minister,
I can again thy former light restore
Should I repent me : but once put out thine,
Thou cunning'st pattern of excelling nature,
I know not where is that Promethean heat
That can thy light relume.

(c) Gentlemen all, I do suspect this trash
To bear a part in this.

(d) Thy match was fatal to him, and pure grief
Shore his old thread in twain.

11. Explain and write short notes on : med'cinable gum ; butt ; sea-mark ; quat ; malignant.

QUESTIONS ON LATER READINGS

CHARACTERS

OTHELLO

1. Enlarge on and discuss one or more of the following comments on Othello's character :

(i) " There is no love, not that of Romeo in his youth, more steeped in imagination than Othello's . . . Emotion excites his imagination but confuses his intellect " (Bradley).

(ii) " Iago's victim is blameless . . . human weakness is no longer allowed to share the responsibility with heaven " (J. Dover Wilson).

(iii) " The real cause of the tragedy is that Othello idealizes Desdemona but does not *know* her."

(iv) " What we [actors] need is a super-objective which is in harmony with the intentions of the playwright, and at the same time arouses a response in the soul of the actors. That means that we must search for it not only in the play but in the actors themselves " (Stanislavsky). Stanislavsky suggests that for Othello this " super-objective " is the idealization of Desdemona. Can you justify this from the text ?

(v) A. C. Bradley, when discussing Shakespeare's heroes, says, " Othello is the greatest poet of them all." If you agree, find evidence to support this from Othello's speeches and compare him with any two other heroes in Shakespeare's plays.

QUESTIONS ON LATER READINGS

2. Find about half a dozen examples of what you consider to be the most significant in self-revelation of the lines spoken by Othello.

3. " Strip Othello of the poetic trappings in which Shakespeare has wrapped him and the man becomes a sordid figure of supreme contempt." Discuss.

IAGO

1. " An honest man acts upon a plan and forecasts his designs ; but a knave depends upon temporary and local opportunities, and never knows his own purpose, but at the time of execution " (Dr. Johnson). How far does this description of a villain apply to Iago ?

2. Prepare a speech for defending counsel at Iago's trial (assuming modern procedure) in which he is trying to get a verdict of " Guilty, but insane." And/or assemble the arguments of prosecuting counsel against this.

3. The cleverest of criminals usually makes one mistake or miscalculation. What was Iago's fatal mistake ? Do you think he could have foreseen this ?

4. " His creed is that absolute egoism is the only rational and proper attitude, and that conscience or honour or any kind of regard for others is an absurdity " (A. C. Bradley). Give instances from the text of (a) Iago's egoism ; (b) his callous indifference to the suffering of other characters ; (c) deliberate breach of faith.

5. " The part would hardly be tolerated . . . but for its indefatigable industry and inexhaustible resource " (Hazlitt). Give instances of Iago's " industry " and " resource."

6. Make a list of the chief happenings of the play ; underline those for which Iago is *directly* responsible ; then discuss the following comment by A. C. Bradley : " The skill of Iago was extraordinary, but so was his good fortune."

7. "Iago is an extreme instance of diseased intellectual activity, with an almost perfect indifference to moral good or evil, or rather with a decided preference of the latter because it falls more readily in with his favourite propensity. He is quite or nearly as indifferent to his own fate as to that of others ; he runs all risks for a trifling and doubtful advantage ; and is himself the dupe and victim of his ruling passion—an insatiable craving after action of the most difficult and dangerous kind " (Hazlitt). Give instances from the text to justify or refute Hazlitt's phrases : diseased intellectual activity ; indifference to moral good or evil ; indifferent to his own fate ; insatiable craving after action of the most difficult and dangerous kind.

8. Re-read carefully all Iago's soliloquies. Do you think Iago really knows himself and reveals himself fully in these speeches ? What other characteristics would you add to those which Iago ascribes to himself ?

9. Re-read question 4 under " Othello." What " super-objective " would you choose for Iago ? Suggest desires and motives which are almost certainly present in every man, upon which an actor might build in order to create the part of Iago.

DESDEMONA

1. From the speeches of Desdemona choose half a dozen lines which you consider to be most revealing of her character. Use these as the basis of a short character study.

2. In the course of the play *Romeo and Juliet* the young girl Juliet develops into a woman. Is there any similar change in the character of Desdemona before the end of the play ?

3. How far is the tragedy due to Desdemona's character ? Do you agree with the statement that

QUESTIONS ON LATER READINGS

" a Beatrice, a Portia, or a Juliet would have averted disaster " ?

4. " The soft simplicity of Desdemona, confident of merit, and conscious of innocence, her artless perseverance in her suit, and her slowness to suspect that she can be suspected . . . " (Dr. Johnson). Justify from the text these various attributes given to Desdemona.

EMILIA

1. " Stupid, vulgar, good-hearted, and loyal." Do you think this is a good description of Emilia ?

2. How far is Emilia's behaviour in the final scene a complete surprise, and how far has Shakespeare prepared us for it ?

3. Tell the story of Act V. from the point of view of Emilia, laying particular emphasis on her realization of her husband's treachery ; in particular show what is passing through her mind between Othello's line, " Thy husband knew it all," and her own speech, " Good gentlemen, let me have leave to speak."

CASSIO

1. " A half-articulate, sensitive, baffled loyalty is the essence of the part " (Desmond MacCarthy). Discuss.

2. What justification could an actor find in the text for playing the part as a lively, cultured man-about-town of the period ?

3. " That Cassio loves her, I do well believe it." Can you find any references in the text either in support of or in flat contradiction of this ?

4. How far is the character of Bianca, and Cassio's intrigue with her, essential to the plot ?

RODERIGO

1. Write a brief account of Roderigo's part in the play. How far do you consider him an innocent

victim of Iago, and how far a joint-villain in the plot?

2. There is no character corresponding to Roderigo in the original Italian story. What reasons can you give for Shakespeare's inventing the character?

THE MAN WHO WROTE *OTHELLO*

1. Give a brief account of Shakespeare's life, indicating the different types of play with which he occupied himself at different periods.

2. Imagine yourself a young man-about-town of 1604, taken by a friend to the Mermaid Tavern, where you are introduced to Shakespeare. Give an extract from your diary, recording your impressions of the poet.

3. Give a brief account of any three of the following contemporaries of Shakespeare: Ben Johnson, Sir Walter Raleigh, the Earl of Essex, Sir Francis Bacon, John Donne, Inigo Jones, Michael Drayton.

4. "The notion that when a great man speaks bitterly or looks melancholy he must be troubled by a disappointment in love seems to me sentimental trifling" (Bernard Shaw). Give some account of contemporary conditions during Shakespeare's "tragic period" which would seem to support Shaw's contention that Shakespeare's work was conditioned more by the circumstances of his time than by personal emotional experience.

THE TEXT OF THE PLAY

1. Summarize the history of the publication of Shakespeare's plays, with special reference to the text of *Othello*.

2. What arguments can you find in support of the idea that the First Quarto was printed from an actor's script that had been used in rehearsal?

QUESTIONS ON LATER READINGS

PRESENTATION OF THE PLAY

1. What references and indications can you find in this and other plays by Shakespeare to conditions in the Elizabethan theatre and to the art of acting?

2. A modern producer (for a stage with limited facilities) who wishes to put on *Othello*, maintaining the continuity of Shakespearean conditions, would probably make use of a traverse curtain to divide his stage, and play short scenes in front of this whilst making slight changes on the main set. Work out which scenes could be played before the traverse and which would need the full stage, with minimum changes of scenery. Compare your own scheme with the plan on p. 196.

3. Compare the final scene of (*a*) *Hamlet*, (*b*) *Romeo and Juliet*, and (*c*) *King Lear* with the last scene in *Othello*, commenting on how Shakespeare had to adapt these endings to the conditions of his stage.

4. "Shakespeare painted his own settings in verse." Give examples from *Othello*.

5. "Une œuvre de théâtre ne s'explique pas, elle se joue" (Louis Jouvet). Discuss this in the light of apparent inconsistencies in *Othello*.

6. "What scenery should aim at is the expression of a beauty consonant with the underlying emotion which runs through the poetry of a scene, act, or play" (Desmond MacCarthy). Make sketches of a suggested setting (or settings) for *Othello*, with some indication as to lighting, colour, etc., and justify your designs from the text of the play.

SHAKESPEARE'S WORKSHOP

I. SOURCES AND STRUCTURE OF THE PLAY

1. Give a brief account of the original source of the story of *Othello*, pointing out the alterations and additions made by Shakespeare.

2. Imagine that you have called at Shakespeare's lodgings ; he is out, and whilst you are waiting for him you examine the books lying about his room. Give an account of what you would be likely to find there.

3. What evidence can you find in *Othello* of contemporary superstitions and belief in witchcraft ?

4. " A play must have a beginning, a middle and an end." Group the events and scenes of *Othello* into these three main divisions.

5. Compare the exposition of *Henry V.* with that of *Othello*. Which do you consider the more satisfactory, and why ?

6. What is meant by the " three unities " ? Shakespeare could have confined the whole action to " a seaport in Cyprus," giving only a report of events at present in Act. I. Write a short scene in modern English which would serve as an exposition to such an arrangement of the play.

7. " The third act of *Othello* is his masterpiece . . . of the knowledge of character with the expression of passion, of consummate art in the keeping up of appearances with the profound workings of nature, and the convulsive movements of uncontrollable agony, of the power of inflicting torture and suffering it " (Hazlitt). Discuss, giving detailed references to the text.

8. " The leading personages of *Othello* are, in character, variations of a single passion, suspicious jealousy, and their position in the play is exactly determined by their relation to this passion " (R. G. Moulton, *Shakespeare as a Dramatic Artist*). Examine the characters of Othello, Iago, Cassio, and Desdemona in the light of this statement.

9. " The tragedy of Othello is his (Iago's) tragedy too. . . . It shows us . . . a thoroughly bad, *cold* man who is at last tempted to let loose the forces within him, and is at once destroyed " (A. C. Bradley).

QUESTIONS ON LATER READINGS

Show how Iago is betrayed by allowing his passions to over-rule his cynical philosophy.

2. VERSIFICATION

1. Give three examples each of : (i) lines which are regular iambic pentameters ; (ii) lines beginning with (a) a spondee (‿ ‿) ; (b) a trochee (‿ ◡) ; (iii) lines containing tri-syllabic feet ; (iv) lines in which the logical pause falls in the middle of a foot.

2. Mark the scansion in the following lines :

(a) For when the outward action doth demonstrate
The native act and figure of my heart
In complement extern, 'tis not long after
But I will wear my heart upon my sleeve
For daws to peck at.

(b) A sybil that had number'd in the world
The sun to course two hundred compasses,
In her prophetic fury sew'd the work.

(c)   Let's to the seaside, ho !
As well to see the vessel that's come in
As to throw out our eyes for brave Othello,
Even till we make the main and the aerial blue
An indistinct regard.

3. Mark the pauses and stresses in the following text :

(a)   Something, sure, of state,
Either from Venice, or some unhatch'd practice
Made demonstrable here in Cyprus to him,
Hath puddled his clear spirit ; and in such cases
Men's natures wrangle with inferior things,
Though great ones are their object.

(b) Be not afraid, though you do see me weapon'd ;
Here is my journey's end, here is my butt
And very sea-mark of my utmost sail.
Do you go back dismay'd ?   'Tis a lost fear ;
Man but a rush against Othello's breast,
And he retires.   Where should Othello go ?
Now, how dost thou look now ?   O ill-starr'd wench !
Pale as thy smock !

4. Can you suggest reasons for Shakespeare's use of prose for the scenes between Iago and Roderigo?

5. How would you maintain the rhythm of run-on lines if reading the play aloud or acting it?

3. LANGUAGE

1. Define the following terms and give three examples of each from the text of *Othello* : alliteration, assonance, hyperbole, apostrophe, play upon words.

2. Choose two passages in the grand style that you consider the finest, explain any allusions, and try to illustrate from the passages Shakespeare's command of poetic technique. In contrast with these, choose two of the simplest passages that most appeal to you.

3. "It appears to me that Shakespeare held the Grand Style in the hollow of his hand, letting it loose or withholding it as good seemed to him." Can you justify this statement with examples from the text of *Othello*?

4.   (a)   . . . O thou weed,
Who art so lovely fair and smell'st so sweet
That the sense aches at thee,
Would thou hadst ne'er been born.   (Folio.)

   (b) O thou black weed, why art so lovely fair?
Thou smell's so sweet that the sense aches at thee;
Would thou hadst ne'er been born!   (First Quarto.)

State which of these versions your prefer and justify your choice.

CHIEF EVENTS OF SHAKESPEARE'S LIFE

1564   26th April, William Shakespeare baptized at Stratford-on-Avon parish church

1582   Marries Ann Hathaway

1583   Daughter Susanna born

1584   Birth of twin children, Judith and Hamnet (Hamnet died 1596)

1592   First mention of Shakespeare in London. Attacked in a pamphlet by Robert Greene. The publisher's apology, which followed, shows Shakespeare to be well established as an actor and playwright and in favour with certain gentlemen of the court

1593, 1594 Publication of *Venus and Adonis* and *Lucrece*, dedicated to Earl of Southampton.

1594   Shakespeare mentioned as an actor in Lord Chamberlain's Company

1596   John Shakespeare, granted coat-of-arms

1597   Shakespeare buys New Place, Stratford

1598   Francis Meres publishes *Treasury of Wit*, which extols Shakespeare as greatest dramatist of the time

1599   Globe Theatre built. Shakespeare a shareholder

1601   Death of Shakespeare's father

1602   Shakespeare buys arable land near Stratford

1603   James I. licenses Shakespeare's company as The King's Servants or The King's Company of Players

1605   Shakespeare buys a moiety of the Stratford tithes

1609   Becomes shareholder of Blackfriars' Theatre

1610   Buys pastoral land near Stratford

1611   Settles at Stratford

1616   Death of Shakespeare (23rd April) ; buried in parish church, Stratford-on-Avon

APPROXIMATE DATES OF THE PLAYS

1590–91	2 Henry VI 3 Henry VI	
1591–92	1 Henry VI	
1592–93	Richard III Comedy of Errors Venus and Adonis	
1593–94	Titus Andronicus Taming of the Shrew Rape of Lucrece	
1594–95	Two Gentlemen of Verona Love's Labour's Lost Romeo and Juliet	First Period
1595–96	Richard II Midsummer Night's Dream	
1596–97	King John Merchant of Venice	
1597–98	1 Henry IV 2 Henry IV	
1598–99	Much Ado About Nothing Henry V	
1599–1600	Julius Cæsar As You Like It Twelfth Night	
1600–1	Hamlet Merry Wives of Windsor	
1601–2	Troilus and Cressida	
1602–3	All's Well that Ends Well	
1604–5	Measure for Measure Othello	Second Period
1605–6	King Lear Macbeth	
1606–7	Antony and Cleopatra	
1607–8	Coriolanus Timon of Athens	
1608–9	Pericles	
1609–10	Cymbeline	
1610–11	Winter's Tale	Third Period
1611–12	Tempest	
1612–13	Henry VIII	

PRINTED IN GREAT BRITAIN AT
THE PRESS OF THE PUBLISHERS